D0823577

Along
came
a
Stork

Along came a Stork

MARISA MACKLE

POOLBEG

Published 2012
by Poolbeg Press Ltd
123 Grange Hill, Baldoyle
Dublin 13, Ireland
E-mail: poolbeg@poolbeg.com
www.poolbeg.com

1

A catalogue record for this book is available from the British Library.

ISBN 978-1-84223-498-3

Typeset by Patricia Hope in Sabon

Printed and bound by CPI Group (UK) Ltd, Croydon, CR0 4YY

www.poolbeg.com

About the Author

Marisa Mackle is the number-one bestselling author of *Mr Right for the Night*, *Man Hunt*, *Mile High Guy* and many more. She also writes children's books and teaches creative writing. Her work has been translated into over a dozen languages. She lives in Dublin with her baby son Gary and her cat Jagger.

www.marisamackle.ie

Acknowledgements

Thank you to Paula Campbell for welcoming me to Poolbeg. Thanks to my editor, Gaye Shortland, for all her hard work. Thanks to God and St Jude. Thanks to my family and friends and my readers, who encourage me to keep writing.

This book is dedicated to the memory of both my grandmothers.

1

New Year's Day

1st Jan

Dear Brand-New Diary,
I am so hung-over it's not even funny. I woke up this morning screaming when I saw a big black spider on my pillow. I thought he was dead because he was lying in a pool of blood. But then I realised that it was just one of my false eyelashes, which must have fallen off at some stage during the night, and that the pool of blood was actually the remnants of the large goldfish-bowl-sized glass of red wine that I'd brought to bed with me. Yes, Diary, how sad am I that I actually thought it would be a good idea to bring my glass of wine up from the residents' bar? But since I'd paid a crazy hotel price for it with my hard-earned money, I'd decided I was going to drink it come hell or high water. I hate to see anything wasted, what with the recession and all.

I stayed in a very fancy hotel last night. It was an old period house in its own grounds. Five-star with all the trimmings and – wait for it – Jo Malone products in the bathroom! Me and the girls, Vicky and Selina, stayed in a triple room. At least it was supposed to be me and the girls.

And at the beginning of the night that's what it was but 'we' soon became 'me'.

Yes, just little old me on my ownio. It ended up being more of a girl's-night out (singular) than a girls'-night out (plural) because the others met a couple of men (seriously not my type at all) in a bar in town early on in the evening and disappeared off with them into the night, not to be seen again for the duration of our, eh, 'fun' weekend away. I thought it was quite mean of them not to say goodbye really. I was in a strange place and had to get a taxi back to the hotel all by myself, and because it was New Year and every other person in the town was also looking for a cab at the same time, I ended up in a queue outside a dodgy chipper in the rain waiting for one. I began to wonder why I'd forked out on such an expensive hotel when I'd ended up, not snuggled up in a lovely comfy warm bed rubbing Jo Malone products onto my skin as a treat, but on an unfamiliar street with some teenager vomiting all over my cute strappy silver sandals. Yes, it was really gross but let's not even go there right now as I'm trying to block that particular memory from my mind.

Anyway I was about to report my friends to the police as missing persons when I got up this morning and noticed that the other beds in my room were still not slept in but then I got a text from Vicky going 'Hope u got back 2 hotel ok. X'.

Hope I got back okay? Was she bloody serious? Well, it's a bit late to be worrying about me now, Missus, I thought to myself. She'd a bit of a cheek really. I mean anything at all could have happened to me in a strange town. I could have been murdered in the taxi on the way back to the hotel and she'd have been none the wiser until this morning. So much for the sisterhood, huh? But do you know what really gets my goat? Vicky is one of those girls who is always shouting her head off about stuff like girl power and women sticking together, but after a few vodkas if there's so much as a sniff of an available man, all that girlie-support lark goes straight out the window.

Anyway, Diary, I am just home now. Just in the door less than an hour ago actually, looking like something the cat dragged in backwards. My eyes look like two bullet-holes in my sunken face, thanks to the smudged mascara, and supposedly waterproof liquid eyeliner that I'd borrowed from Vicky as I'd forgotten to pack my own.

The first thing I did when I got upstairs was to run myself a steamy hot bubble bath using the Jo Malone products I'd swiped from the hotel bathroom. Well, I reckoned I totally deserved the lot as the other girls hadn't even bothered staying in the room at all and probably hadn't noticed them. But, alas, now I've blisters on both my heels after standing in the taxi rank for so long last night. Oh God, it was freezing standing outside that chipper. Minus two degrees or something. My legs had never been so cold in all my life. They were numb until that idiot got sick on them and kind of warmed them up. Oh stop! Block it out, Diana. Block. It. Out.

The taxi home cost a fortune too. They really do screw you for having to work on a Bank Holiday, don't they? I should have driven, but then again I'd probably have been over the limit even today after all the booze we consumed last night, and the police always go a bit mad on special occasions such as New Year's Day trying to breathalyse people. Still, the taxi almost cost as much as the hotel which is kind of killing me because I'm smashed broke at the moment. I don't know why I'm always penniless. I'm single, I live at home, and I don't have too many commitments or loans except for my car loan. But I just never have any money to call my own.

Anyway, it was better to take a taxi rather than face taking two buses home across the city on New Year's Day when there are hardly any services running. It probably would have taken me about six hours to get home – same time as a flight from New York to Dublin.

Diary, dearest, I know it's not so good me introducing myself to you when I feel like someone is bashing my head in with a sledgehammer and my mouth feels like the bottom of a sewer, but normally I'm way more upbeat and together than this. I'd kind of forgotten how bad hangovers feel. It's funny how you forget, isn't it? The way you go 'Never Again' and then say the same thing a week later when you've done the same stupid thing all over again. One of my many New Year's resolutions for this year is not to drink. Well, not as much as I usually do. Well, between two and three glasses, maybe. If you don't drink more than three glasses you're laughing. Hmm, DEFINITELY no more than five glasses. And lots of water in between. I'm going to stick to that. No, really. I know I'll have you to answer to the following day so I'm going to keep that in mind next time someone suggests a Jameson or ten for the road.

I'm twenty-nine now. It's not good for me to be behaving like an eighteen-year-old who's just left home and is going nuts away from the parents. And I'm known too. Yes, I mean this is a bit embarrassing and I don't want to come across as big-headed, but as my Diary I can tell you anything so let me fill you in. I recently started writing a dating column in a magazine, which is really quite popular, and I get letters and emails in from people all over the country. I've a little fan club of my own going on. People can register as a member of my website and read my tips on how to get a man, how to win a man back and how to get that ring on your finger. Hilarious really, considering my own wedding finger is completely ring-free. But it's very popular all the same.

My photo always accompanies the column so now I'm a tiny bit recognisable too. I'm not telling you all this to be blowing my own trumpet but just so you understand that it is definitely not a good idea for people to see me staggering around some strange street not remembering where I am or what my name is. Because they will probably remember. And tell all of their friends. And it could get back to the magazine – and my boss, nice and all as she is, might take a very dim view of it all.

So, this is going to be my year hopefully. Yes. I really believe that this is the year that my career suddenly takes off and I become the success story I've always secretly dreamed of being. I know I say every year that this might be the year but this time I really, really mean it. No more messing around. It's now or never. This is the year Diana hits the big time and finally meets a nice man. Nice is nice. I don't care if nice is boring. I'll settle for nice. All the cars and fancy suits in the world don't do it for me. He can look like Brad Pitt but, if he's not a nice man, I'm not interested. Don't think I'm settling for less. You have no idea how hard it is to meet somebody who is simply a nice person!

Jesus, my head! My hangover's getting worse, not better. Right, that's about it for now. Sorry but I have to lie down. I thought I was fine but I'm obviously not. Please excuse me, I'm going back to bed.

D

2

2nd Jan

Dear Diary,
Hi again, it's me. I feel much better today. Like a spanking brand-new person. I'll start off with a compliment by saying you're so lovely and pristine clean and you even smell nice. I hate even writing on you because it almost feels like some sort of vandalism, but it has to be done.

My sister Jayne gave you to me. She doesn't give me much because money is always tight with her even though she still lives at home as well with Mum and Dad and is manager of the spa of a top 5-star hotel. She hardly ever spends any money and blames the recession for everything. Nobody in Ireland has embraced the credit crunch more than my sister, who uses it as an excuse never to put her hand in her pocket these days. Would you believe, she doesn't even let Mum and me use the facilities of the spa because she says it would be abusing her position of authority and she might get into trouble with the hotel. But she does our nails and stuff at home when we beg her which is handy 'cos Mum and I are always broke. She charges us a fiver each for manicures and pedicures and ten euro for a full body-spray tan. Yes, I know you're probably really shocked that she actually demands payment from her own flesh and blood, but at least we don't have to fork out full price somewhere else. Anyway, I find it really embarrassing standing in a salon wearing paper knickers while somebody blasts my boobs with fake-tan spray while asking me in a chatty voice whether I'm going on holidays this year or not.

So although Jayne's a scabby so-and-so and only gave me a diary for Christmas, because of her we don't ever have to go to the beauty salon, except for leg and bikini waxes. I mean we wouldn't ask Jayne to do that. And she wouldn't offer.

But things are looking up. You see, because my column is popular with all the single ladies out there (I write the sort of personal stuff most laydeez would rather not admit to but secretly love reading!), I've been getting lots of other offers like radio interviews and TV appearances and stuff. My editor is really pleased with me because every time I'm on air I plug the magazine so it's great publicity for her too.

I write a lot about being mercilessly dumped and being two-timed and being hit on by sleazy married men (isn't there an octopus in every office?). Love rats are kind of my forte and, you know, the good thing is that I don't have to do much research because I have probably met more rats in my lifetime than the Pied Piper of Hamelin, the latest being Roger the Rat who dumped me for a girl a decade younger than me who has just finished school. He dumped me because he said I was putting pressure on him to commit. Obviously because the new girl is barely out of her school uniform and the ink is still dry on her Leaving Certificate exams, she isn't talking about babies and settling down right away, which in his eyes obviously makes her infinitely more attractive than me. Not that I am broody or anything. I mean, that's where Roger got it all wrong. Of course, he probably got the wrong idea when I asked him to come into Mothercare with me to have a look at the cute little baby clothes. It wasn't like I was dropping hints or anything but it's just that, ever since my brother's wife had a baby girl, I just love baby stuff and I can't pass a baby shop without wanting to run in and buy something for my little niece.

Looking back, I can kind of understand why Roger freaked a bit, but the way he ran out of the shop was a bit pathetic. It was like somebody had taken out a match and set fire to his balls. He dumped me soon after that. Well, he didn't actually have the decency to tell me to my face. Instead he did it the cowardly way: not answering his phone or emails or fax messages or texts or letters or answering his front door. Oh yes, I tried everything until I finally got the message that our relationship was probably over, and the only person in town who didn't seem to know it yet was me.

But I'm better off without him. Oh God, yes. Like, did he think he was some great prize or something? The nerve of him making out that I was this crazy woman with a biological clock the size of Big Ben! That was so not the case. I didn't even have a doll when I was a little girl for goodness' sake. I was more into kicking a ball around the place and robbing my brother's toy soldiers. I never dreamed of having a big brood. I mean, I adore kids in small doses and think they're really cute, but at the moment I'm far too busy progressing with my career to even contemplate giving it all up for a life of domestic bliss. I, of all people, KNOW that becoming a mum is the end of life as you know it. God, I was even an au-pair in Normandy back in the day and I never got a minute to myself. Even going to the loo in peace was a rarity because there was always some little fist banging on the door demanding that I come out and watch Barney speaking French. I actually don't know how mothers stay sane at home all day listening to that big purple eejit dancing on the telly. It's a long time now since I minded children but to this day I still can't stand the sight of Barney's silly goofy oversized head. Or the Teletubbies' annoying babbling. So you understand, I'm just not the maternal type. Love kids, just as long as I don't have to wipe their bums or noses.

Anyway, now that Roger is trying to relive his youth by hanging out of a teen, I'm back living at home with my parents and older sister Jayne, and when I'm not out and about pretending to be loving the single life as research for my column, I'm holed up in my room reading all these self-help books in an effort to get on with my life and not become a bitter person. I have even recently taken to putting little positive post-it notes around the house, like on the fridge and the wall opposite the toilet saying 'What's for you won't pass you,' and all that. Dad's going mad because when he went to the bathroom the other day one of them stuck on to his jumper and he was walking around Supervalu doing his shopping and he said people were staring at him and laughing and he couldn't understand why. I'm sure he was exaggerating though. I mean the post-it notes are so small that nobody could have possibly seen the 'I am the most important person in my life' message stuck to his back. Not unless they were right up close behind him.

But, to be honest, I don't think there is such a thing as a quick fix for a broken heart. It's not like you can go out and buy glue to put it all back together. Only time, and lots of it, can help the Cupidly wounded. I know that for a fact. Like I look back on men I used to pine over and think I couldn't live without, and now I honestly with hindsight can't think of one reason why I fancied them in the first place. The whole 'grieving' process roughly takes about two years which is a bit annoying but I put it down to the fact that my star sign is Cancer and I'm a crab. Crabs find it extremely hard to let go. They'll cling onto their past with every pincer.

So I know with Roger it's going to take time. But not forever. I'm going to deal with the break-up in a mature dignified way and I'm not going to indulge in irrational behaviour such as rushing to the hairdresser's to cut off all my hair, or dramatically losing weight in an effort to lure him away from his teenage love. I don't want closure. Feck closure. Too many people waste so much of their lives looking for closure instead of just throwing their hands in the air and going, 'Hey, it just didn't work out.' Look, life shouldn't be about getting closure. If you get fired, you might not be given the right reason for why you're losing your job, but you don't spend the rest of your life asking yourself why oh why oh why and asking your old boss to meet up in the hope of gaining closure. No, the thing is, you move on quickly and find yourself another job fast, and vow to be more punctual and work harder and not turn up to work hung-over with a ladder in your tights ever again. I'm going to take that same professional attitude when it comes to relationships. I mean, it's mad, isn't it? There I am with a dating column and often on TV being introduced as a dating guru, putting myself out there as some kind of expert with people phoning in looking for advice, and I myself don't have a clue! Jesus, I haven't ever been able to hold down a relationship for more than a few months! What does that say about me? After all, I am the common denominator in all my failed liaisons. So maybe, just maybe, the problem is mine.

Until tomorrow.

Diana xx

3

4th Jan

Dear Diary,

Actually do you mind if I call you something else 'cos writing 'Dear Diary' makes me feel like I'm about thirteen instead of a woman fast approaching thirty? I thought Molly might be a nice name for you. Molly rhymes with jolly and I like happy-sounding names especially since we're in the middle of a recession at the moment and everybody's going around with gloomy faces, convinced that if they smile they're going to be out of a job. In fact, if I ever have a daughter I'm going to name her Molly so she can bring joy to other people when they ask what her name is.

I find it really therapeutic writing to you today. After all, it hasn't been a great day so far. It's been pretty dismal actually and I can't help feeling low. I was on Facebook earlier and Roger had changed his status to 'In a relationship' and he'd stuck up about a hundred photos of himself with his silly child bride hanging out of him with such a grateful look on her face. I know I shouldn't have done it but I read some of their public messages to each other, about how much they love each other, and can't keep their paws off each other, and all the romantic holidays they're planning to take together and as I kept reading, getting more and more depressed and downhearted as I did so, I couldn't help but wonder if each and every one of those messages had somehow been written for my benefit.

What should I do? Should I immediately delete him as a friend? Or would that just make me as ridiculously immature as he is? God, Facebook completely does my head in sometimes. I think we were all better off not being in contact with all these people in cyberspace. Like I think I have about two thousand Facebook friends but if I was sick how many of them would I contact in my hour of need? How many would lend me a fiver to get me out of a financial rut? Exactly.

Mind you, there was some good news today. Well, potentially good news. I have been invited to try out for a new dating show on TV. The producer, who called me just before five today, taking me completely by surprise, said that I had immediately sprung to mind when considering presenters for the show. He said that he specifically wanted somebody young, free and single to do a kind of Irish version of Blind Date. "Does that mean if I got it I'd be the Irish Cilla Black?" I asked.

"Something like that," he said laughing. "Only it wouldn't just be about pairing people off. We'd be discussing all types of things like marriage and divorce and dating after divorce, and how to get over a broken heart."

Jesus, I thought, I wish I knew how to do that!

He sounded really good-looking over the phone if that makes any sense. Like he sounded kind of sexy with a deep, confident tone of voice. I can't wait to meet him. I mean, even if I don't get the gig – and I probably won't 'cos every single young one coming out of school these days and every model in Ireland wants to be on the telly – we could go on a date, which would be a nice consolation prize. Then again, he could be bald. Or married. With bad breath. Or all of those. So I shouldn't really get my hopes up.

I'll keep you posted.

D xx

4

8th Jan

Dear Molly,
I'm in shock! Yes, total and utter shock!!! I'm so stunned I can barely write this as my hand is shaking. I got the TV gig. I sailed through the first interview because I wasn't at all nervous. The reason I wasn't nervous was because I thought there wasn't a single chance of somebody like me beating off all the models in Ireland who were sick of promoting scratch cards on Grafton Street for a living. There are probably more ex-TV presenters in Ireland than civil servants at the moment. I was mad in the head going up against them. Or so I thought. Turns out they didn't want some model with no experience, but a real woman with experience of matters of the heart, and the very next morning they invited me back for a second interview. Me. Little old me who just a year ago was fired from a temping job for ordering a tuna instead of a cheese sandwich for my old boss. I know you're thinking how could anybody be let go for something so trivial, but apparently my boss was allergic to tuna and the sandwich in question gave him three days of diarrhoea. It wasn't my fault.

I didn't know anything about his allergies. He should have warned me.

Anyway it was almost a relief to be let go. Of course they said the official reason for my departure was due to cutbacks and not because the boss was on the loo for half the week. That was just so that I wouldn't sue them for unfair dismissal. I'm not stupid. You can be damn sure the boss wouldn't have liked to have to go to court and discuss his diarrhoea in front of some judge.

They gave me a month's pay in advance so I was laughing. I'd only worked there a couple of months but I was dying to leave that horrible little insurance firm. It was so boring working in an open-plan office of six people where I was the most junior and considered incapable of doing anything except franking the mail, putting callers on hold and giving the staff the runs. Why couldn't they all have got their own lunches anyway, the lazy things? Considering the grotty office where I worked was never heated because of the supposed recession, it was a wonder my old boss didn't make his own sandwich and lead by example. Huh!

But once I'd got over the humiliation of being escorted out of the office for the final time in front of everybody with my little fake Gucci briefcase under my arm (*sooooooooo* embarrassing!), I decided the time was right for trying to get into the media. I had to go for it. Time wasn't on my side any more. Just short of thirty isn't exactly what anyone in the media is ever looking for. I knew that applying for a TV presenting job was almost a non-runner. All those show reels that prospective people send in go right in the bin no matter how good they are. No, really, they do. I know this for a fact because my friend Vicky's sister works in administration in a TV station and she says that's exactly what happens.

I also knew that trying to get a staff journalism job was

next or near to impossible, which was a bit of a problem because journalism was something I really wanted to do. I mean, that's what I have my diploma in. I did a diploma after my degree in Social Science in UCD. Straight after I graduated I started bombarding women's magazines with dating ideas for their features section. And even though most of my emails remained frustratingly unanswered, I persisted until I eventually saw my name in print. But I never in a million years thought I'd ever be on the box. Up there with the likes of Jay Leno, Oprah, Ellen. Oh seriously, who do I think I'm kidding?

Anyway the final interview was yesterday with the producer, Dan (and yes, although I wasn't sure about the shaven head at first, he is very HOT and I didn't spot a wedding band either!). And it had all boiled down to just five people after they had received over four hundred applications. The other four people that had made it to the final interviews were professional dating coaches and 'experts' whatever that means. Personally I think these, eh, dating experts are just chancers, really. I've never heard of a degree course where you come out with a degree in dating, have you? Seriously, would that be a BA or a BComm?

So they told us they'd let us know today and I went home thinking I hadn't much of a chance because another guy who was sitting outside the waiting room with me was going on and on about the fact that he'd had zillions of experience and he'd even been on TV in America. I think he was either doing it to big himself up or else stick a pin in my proverbial balloon or both. But it worked because I told my mum when I got home that I didn't think I'd got the gig and I was feeling pretty downhearted about it all, about having got my hopes up. Then I went to my room to consider other career options.

And then this morning, to my complete amazement, I got a call from Dan himself and I got terribly excited because I know from experience that they never phone with bad news – bad news invariably comes via letter or email – and I struggled to remain calm as he offered me the gig although I wanted to scream with joy. After all, we're in the middle of a recession and jobs in entertainment are thin on the ground at the moment to put it mildly. I had to keep pinching myself to make sure I wasn't hallucinating.

Afterwards I just sat on my bed shaking, and as my heartbeat returned to normal I just kept thinking 'I'm going to be on TV' – 'I'm going to have my own show' – 'I'm going to be a household name' – 'People are going to know me on the street'. It was slowly sinking in that life as I knew it was about to change forever.

D x

5

9th Jan

Molly,
I'm going to seriously have to lose five pounds. Oh, who am I kidding? Ten pounds must go. Very quickly. I can't be on TV looking like a big fat lump and, as everyone knows, the camera simply piles on the pounds. Especially on those widescreen TVs that everyone seems to have now. I've got to be disciplined. The booze and biscuits must be binned. I must start chanting all these mantras like 'A moment on the lips, a lifetime on the hips' etc. This is a once-in-a-lifetime chance to make a name for myself and it's now or never. If I blow this, I'm finished. I mean once you've been on TV, and it doesn't work out, what do you do then? What do TV people do exactly when they're not on telly anymore? What happens when you're famous for being an ex-star, but not rich, and have to get the bus everywhere? You can't exactly send your CV around shops and places when you've been fecked off the TV, can you? It'd be too mortifying. Like if you went into a shoe shop and somebody from your ex-favourite TV soap was trying to find your exact shoe size you'd think it was really weird, wouldn't you?

I know I couldn't ever go back to temping and being a

slave for stuffy office workers. I'd hate it. From now on I don't want to work anywhere where I can't use my brain. I've done it all, worn the vest. I've worked as a dental assistant in a very grand city-centre cosmetics clinic, and a sales assistant in a small gift shop, neither of which worked out, and before that I taught English as a foreign language, and that wasn't my cup of tea either. Prior to that, I had a stint working as a Dublin tour guide on an open-top bus, going around the city shouting into a microphone. That was okay but as it's always raining in Ireland, and cold, I was permanently catching the flu. In the end I had to give it up for health reasons.

So as you see, I've tried my hand at various things and nothing has quite gone to plan. And now I'm twenty-nine and it's time to cop on or I'll still be living at home at thirty-nine like a sad case.

I told my family last night that I'd got the gig. Dad duly opened a bottle of champagne and Mum gave me a half-hearted kiss and then immediately told me that the next-door neighbour's daughter, Kate, had got engaged to a doctor. And that my brother Tony in Boston had got promoted. Like what had that got to do with my brilliant job? I was really annoyed about her lack of interest. Anyone can get engaged or promoted but how many people get their own TV show? I texted my brother but he never texted me back. And the only thing that my sister Jayne was interested in was whether I could get her salon a mention on TV. I told her it was a dating show, not a beauty show, and she just shrugged and actually had the cheek to say "Well, suit yourself then." I don't know why, but I'd really thought my family would be a lot more pleased for me. I might as well have told them I'd just won an egg and spoon race at the local school sports day for all the interest they showed. Our two spaniels, Gina and Ruby, were the only ones to show some excitement and that was only at the popping of the champagne cork. Now I wish I hadn't said anything and had just left it as a surprise.

Maybe they want to make sure I stay grounded and don't get a swelled head but c'mon, it's a small Irish TV show that'll be broadcast in the afternoons when most people are at work, so it's not like I'm going to become the most famous person in Ireland and have my own stalkers and stuff. Dad asked me how much money I was going to be making and when I said that I'd be on twenty-seven grand for the first six-month probation period he just shook his head and said I was being exploited. How could I convince him that this was a once-in-a-lifetime opportunity that thousands of young people in this country would actually do for free? Why all the negativity? Does he not watch the news and realise how many Irish people are signing on the live register right now? I was really disappointed by their reaction to be honest. When Jayne was made salon manager last year my parents were so supportive that you'd have thought she'd just gone and won herself a general election!

After I had the champagne, instead of feeling elated, my tummy felt a bit funny. With all the excitement earlier of finding out I had the TV gig, I hadn't eaten anything, and I didn't feel hungry anyway. But now, even as I'm writing this, I have an ache in my tummy that won't go away. Maybe it's stress. After all, the last few days have been pretty anxious. I'd no less than four interviews altogether before I finally landed the much-coveted gig. And I had to do lots of practice takes in front of the camera to prove that I could do the job and not crumble under pressure. The people on TV always make it look so easy but it's so not. And your face literally aches from smiling.

Oh, God, what's wrong with me? I've just thrown up. I wouldn't mind but this time I'm not even hung-over!

D xx

6

19th Jan

Oh Molly, I love my new job. I really adore it. The first time live on air was pretty sickening and I have to admit I did throw up in the toilets on the morning of my first ever appearance. But apparently that kind of anxiety is normal for newcomers. It's like stage fright even though you can't see the audience.

Everything went very well once I got over my initial nerves. In fact I got a real a buzz out of it. It took me ages to come down from the high afterwards, until I realised that this was my job now so there was no need to overexcite myself into a frenzy every time I went in to do my job.

Also, you should see Dan, my producer. He is seriously gorgeous. I find myself in our production meetings trying my best not to stare at him. We work pretty closely together. Sometimes for hours on end. I'm finding out quickly that being a TV presenter doesn't mean sitting in Hair and Make-up all day while somebody makes me look pretty. God, no. It's not like that at all. First of all, the powers-that-be more or less expect you to come up with most of your own ideas, and then you have to ring around people and try your best to persuade them to appear on the show. Much grovelling happens. Then you have to fill an entire hour talking about dating and divorce, celebrities and sex and relationships, all with a big smile plastered on your face. And then people phone in and ask you questions and you have to pretend to take it very seriously and know all the answers because basically you've put yourself out there as a dating 'expert'. In addition to all of that, you have to go out to shopping centres and stand on busy streets in the rain and do vox pops which can be a nightmare sometimes because as soon as people see you approaching them with a mike they go kind of crazy and run away shouting 'No comment!' You may as well be chasing them with a loaded gun the way they rush off in fear. It's bizarre but sometimes it seems that the only people who want to be on TV are young annoying boys who try to make their friends laugh by jumping up and down behind you on the street when you're presenting to camera. The little feckers!

But, listen, I just want to tell you that despite all the hard work, the low pay and the constant pressure, it really is the best job ever. No two days are ever the same and the constant adrenalin keeps you going. Mind you, it's not without its drawbacks. Like when I come home I'm so exhausted I practically crawl into bed, and my life's not my own any more. Then again I didn't particularly like my life before this so I don't miss it. And you kind of have to develop a really hard neck when it comes to publicity and reviews. I got so completely slated by two of the newspaper TV reviews that I actually had to disappear off to the toilets in work and sob for a little bit. Afterwards Dan told me to take no notice of either the good or bad reviews because criticism is just something that comes with the territory. He said TV critics are often just failed TV pundits. But even though I nodded and tried to rise above it all, I still felt like I'd been the victim of a personal assault. Jesus, what had I ever done to those two TV critics? I mean, had I met them before in real life and insulted them somehow without knowing it? Had I had a dalliance with one of their partners? There seemed to be no reasonable explanation for their vitriol.

But there are other nicer experiences. Like sometimes when I pop out to the shops, old dears come up to me and tap me on the arm telling me they love the show. Things like that really make my day, Molly. They're sweet and really give me the strength to keep going. But I can't rest on my laurels. Not when people are losing their jobs all around me. It's super-scary. The country is on its financial knees! Even Jayne was moaning the other day (yes, I know you're thinking 'nothing new there') that the usual rich bitches who normally flood her salon are resorting to shaving their own legs and cutting their own toenails, now that their husbands' jobs are in jeopardy. She even told me this afternoon that two of the part-time therapists have been laid off due to lack of business. Now that's really petrifying. A year ago Jayne had a waiting list as long as your arm of lunching ladies willing to be plucked and massaged within an inch of their lives. Now they're all disappearing.

There's not a great atmosphere in the TV station either. There's always tension in the air with people wondering who'll be next for the chopping board. Nobody here is permanently employed, everyone's on contract. Ten people were let go the week before I arrived and because of that the atmosphere is tense and awkward. I know I shouldn't feel guilty, because I didn't take their jobs away. But apparently it was awful and the en masse departure sent shock waves through the station. The redundant staff only got about ten minutes' notice to clear their desks, and more shockingly, were informed of their imminent departure via email. Can you believe it?

Those positions were in administration though, and therefore completely unrelated to my position as a presenter, but sometimes the way people glare over their desks at me when I walk past makes me wonder if they somehow blame me for their colleagues' departure. It's not easy being the new person anywhere, but especially not in such economically challenging times. But then again, why should I feel guilty? I work long hours for a paltry wage and I've zero security in my job. If I don't pull in the viewers you can be damn sure it'll be my head offered on a plate. No pressure then, huh?

The other thing is, I'm totally whacked all the time. Seriously, I wake up exhausted and flop into bed at night totally drained. I've developed dark bags under my eyes which I never had before, and a couple of fine lines are suddenly criss-crossing my forehead. I'd always sworn I'd never succumb to Botox but I think I'm going to have to renegade. Apparently absolutely every person you see on TV has had it done. The trick is not to get too much poison injected into the bloodstream. You need to look politely surprised when the people you're interviewing reveal their innermost secrets on TV. Namely people plugging their autobiographies. Nobody else would be bothered to be honest.

I can't wait for this weekend to come so I can actually have a night on the tiles. I feel I haven't been out in so long. At least I get my hair blow-dried for free in work which is great. My Friday morning blow-dry should last until Saturday. Such a pity that my expertly applied make-up never lasts more than a few hours!

Anyway, myself, Selina and Vicky are heading to Krystle

for the night. I haven't met up with them since our disastrous New Year's Eve celebrations and I've warned them that if they leave me on my tod again, the friendship's over for good. I'll keep you posted, Molly.

Too tired to write any more. My stomach's at me again. I don't know what's wrong but if things don't improve by tomorrow I'll really have to see a doctor. Maybe he can give me something to settle the tummy once and for all.

D x

7

23rd Jan

Oh Molly!
I had five cigarettes last night. Please don't be shocked. That's really nothing for me on an average night out. Normally I have way more. And I had just three vodkas and Coke the whole night long. So I was good all round. But then I threw up six times during the evening and now I feel like I'm at death's door. Apart from me throwing up on the pavement on Harcourt Street at 3.00 a.m. in front of God knows who (let's hope the paparazzi had gone home at that stage), I had a great night. We started out with a couple of drinks in The Ice Bar of the Four Seasons. Then we went to Krystle where we got a nice seat in the VIP bar. There was a time I couldn't get a foot in the door of any of the trendy clubs in Dublin but now I get the red-carpet treatment everywhere because I'm on TV. It's such a perk of the job. No more queuing in the rain, I get the best seat in the house, strawberries and champagne, and I love it. Krystle is by far my favourite club at the moment. It's always wall-to-wall full of glamour and trendy people-about-town. You never know who you'll bump into there.

Anyway, it was a girls' night out, and lots of people I didn't even know were coming up to me and congratulating me, and I was beginning to feel like a bit of a celebrity (yes, I even got snapped on my way into the club walking behind former Miss World, Rosanna Davison) when my tummy started at me again. Like a really sharp pain. I had to go outside onto the balcony for some fresh air. Everyone out there was smoking so I joined in. But weirdly, as I puffed on my Marlboro Light I kept thinking how much I wasn't enjoying my ciggie. I couldn't understand it. I mean, I've been smoking for a decade and I've always really enjoyed my dirty habit even though I know it's terrible for my health and it makes my clothes stink. Despite all that I've never been able to go without them apart from a few half-hearted attempts to give up at the beginning of Lent that never seem to work.

In fact, my habit's so bad that normally I can't get out of bed without a cigarette. And I can't sleep unless I know I have at least three spare within reach should I wake up in the middle of the night. Now all of a sudden the very smell of nicotine just makes me want to gag. What in the heck is going on?

"Have you got a light?"

Yep, Molly, it was that old classic chat up-line so I just threw my eyes up to the open sky. I handed over the lighter to the owner of the voice without even looking.

"Keep it," I said dismissively. "I don't smoke anymore." I stubbed out the ciggie. And the really weird thing is that I meant it. I don't know why but suddenly I felt that smoking was the filthiest most disgusting thing in the world and I didn't want to be part of the Inhale Brigade any more. Only losers smoked.

"You're funny," the voice said as I was walking away towards my healthy new smoke-free life.

I turned and looked over my shoulder. And then looked

up. He was tall, the owner of the voice. I reckon he was at least six foot two so I had to crane my neck to get a good look at him. He looked tanned like he'd just flown back from sunny Spain that morning, and had short black spiky hair. He also had teeth a dentist could advertise on the waiting-room wall. Molly, you should have seen him.

I said "Thanks" and I kept walking. Not 'cos I think I'm drop-dead gorgeous and that the TV gig has suddenly gone to my head and I think I'm such a great catch. No, not at all. If anything, I'm still feeling really insecure after getting dumped on my ass by Roger. I mean, how can I hold up my head and think I'm fabulous when I was ditched on Facebook for crying out loud? So the reason I swaggered off is not because I thought I was too cool to be chatted up, but basically because after I'd handed over my green Bic lighter, my stomach had started to heave and I was worried I wouldn't make it to the bathroom on time. So I ran and thanks be to GOD there was no queue and I was able to shoot into a cubicle and shut the door behind me.

I was so sick you'd swear I'd been pigging out on chocolate and chips all day. You'd think I'd been gulping down shots of pure vodka or had just gone on the rollercoaster ten times in a row at Funderland. I couldn't understand it. I'm never sick. Even though I've hated all my previous jobs I've never had a sick day in my life no matter how nice or nasty the weather has been. And now that I've a job I really like, I sit there every day on air terrified I'm going to throw up. At first I thought I'd caught a bug but now I'm getting really worried. No bug lasts this long, does it?

When I eventually emerged from the bathroom I had to interrupt a major flirtathon going on between my friend Vicky and some random man with a bald head wearing a pink flowery shirt. I told her I'd have to leave immediately.

She said I was a funny green colour. She didn't even have to. I'd just seen myself in the mirror and I could see for myself how ghastly my reflection was. She asked if I was okay to go out by myself and I said I was. I mean, what else could I do? Force her to go home?

So I tottered down the back steps and out the door without saying goodbye to anybody else. I'd never craved my bed so much in my life. I moved down the street and, as I said before, ended up getting sick again on the pavement.

I even remember a group of obnoxious girls laughing loudly at me as they passed by, obviously presuming I'd overloaded on the booze. I knew I had to stop throwing up or no sane taxi driver would take me home. Eventually one stopped and I quickly hopped in the back, hoping he wouldn't be able to get the smell of sick from my hair. I asked him to let down the window because I was feeling a bit faint and he duly did that. Thankfully I managed not to puke until I was safely home, although I had the handbag open wide the whole journey home just in case. And then I got sick again on the front doorstep.

As I crouched down on all fours puking my insides out on to the concrete below, unable to stop the tears streaming down my cheeks, I could suddenly hear voices approaching from out of nowhere. Jesus, Molly, I got an awful fright. I thought I was about to be attacked. Like my heart was racing and I was thinking who on earth could that be in the garden at 3.00 a.m.? Turns out it was my sister. And she had some tall – and from what I could see through my tears – very well-dressed man with her. Obviously a secret date that she had been hiding from us. And I heard the absolute horror in her voice as she shrieked, "Diana, what on earth is going on!"

D x

LATER

I'm very much in the bad books right now. Jayne is absolutely furious that I disgraced her last night. Apparently she's had her eye on that guy she was with for absolutely ages, and he's supposed to be this really good catch and now she's not talking to me because she thought I was being drunk and disorderly when she found me crouched on all fours on the doorstep. Which is so unfair.

This morning when I went downstairs to get myself a glass of water I heard her bitching about me to Mum. They didn't hear me come into the kitchen at first, and when they did Mum said something like she was very disappointed in me. Normally there'd be a big row over something like that but I actually felt too weak to argue back with them.

I practically crawled back up the stairs again to my room feeling like I was at death's door. I don't want to alarm anyone, Molly, but what's wrong with me? I woke up this morning, dehydrated and miserable with the pain searing across my stomach like I was being stabbed.

I think I am seriously ill and it's worrying me. If I take any time off from the show, I might never get back in again. If they find a replacement for me, they could then decide that the replacement is much better than me. That could spell bye-bye Diana Kay forever. It's a chance I can't afford to take. I've never in my life been afraid of the doctor but now the idea that I might be dying terrifies me. What if it's more serious than just a bug? Could it be swine flu? Or worse? Suppose it's the end of the road? Suddenly I want to live. I don't think it's my time yet. Oh. God. Help. Me.

Diana x

8

29th Jan

Dear Molly,
I

9

30th Jan

Sweet Mother of Divine Jesus . . . I just don't know how to write it down. If I write it down it will make it seem more real. At the moment it's just a nightmare I'm hoping to wake from . . .

10

31st Jan

Molly, I'm pregnant.
There I've written it.
Hasn't sunk in.
At all.

11

3rd Feb

God, Molly, sorry for leaving you in the dark for so long. You must be wondering how on earth I got myself into this situation. I'm in shock and in turmoil. My head's spinning still and my, eh, news definitely hasn't sunk in even though I've had a few more days to come to terms with the facts.

Nobody knows except for the doctor of course. And you. Who else can I tell? My parents? How can I? They think I'm single, which I am. In fact I've never felt more single in my life. All this will destroy them. The timing couldn't possibly be worse. What will I tell them in work? So many people went for this job and I was the chosen one. Now I feel I've let everybody down. I can't even imagine going into Dan's office and breaking the news. What can I say? That I'm looking for maternity leave when I've only just joined the station as Ireland's so-called dating queen?

Do I tell Roger? How can I call him when he's accusing me of stalking him? What if his silly teenage girlfriend answers the phone? What then? Do I leave a message with her telling her to tell Roger, if she doesn't mind, that he's expecting a baby?

But you know, at least there's something positive about all of this. I know it sounds ridiculous but at least I'm grateful not to be dying and not to be seriously ill. I know it might seem silly but I had actually convinced myself that I was dying after I collapsed in work and was dramatically rushed to the hospital. I'd just come off air and was touching up my make-up in the bathroom when suddenly I was doubled up with stomach cramps. The walls of the room seemed to cave in all of a sudden and the room went black. I fell backwards and hit my head off the tiles and woke up in the hospital after my boss called an ambulance and rushed me in through Casualty.

Molly, it was the most terrifying experience of my life so far. When I woke up with a thumping headache as a result of my fall, the doctor asked me a million and one questions and then I was brought in for an emergency ultrasound. They smeared some sticky goo all over my tummy and then he rubbed this cold metal yoke all over it while looking at a screen the whole time. All kinds of thoughts were racing through my head. Like, what was he looking for? Ovarian cysts? A tumour? Several tumours? Was this the end of the road for me? Was it all over before it had even begun? I started to imagine my funeral. Would many turn up? Would everyone be sad? Would Roger have the neck to show up and pretend to be upset? I'd a feeling that he would. It was all very morbid.

I was sent home eventually and told that the results of the ultrasound scan would be promptly sent to my GP. Fair enough. I tried to be patient and block it from my thoughts. But I didn't sleep very well that night and then his secretary rang the next day and left a message. As soon as I came off air I got the voicemail. I was to come into the surgery urgently. Urgently? The word rang terrifyingly loud in my ears. Oh God, it was bad news. It had to be. Medical secretaries are not in the habit of telling patients to come into the surgery 'urgently' if there are no complications. I knew I sure as hell wasn't being called in to have a little chat about the weather.

Within seconds my whole world seemed to collapse around me. As soon as I got home I asked Mum to drive me to the doctor's because I was incapable of driving myself. I was shaking and she was crying all the way in.

Mum was convinced I was dying too. We thought it was the end of the road for Diana Kay. Mum sat outside in the waiting room saying prayers for me as the doctor calmly told me over his fancy mahogany desk that I was expecting a baby.

I was so shocked when he told me I was in the early stages of pregnancy that I actually thought he was joking. I even laughed. Yes, I laughed although it was quite the unfunniest thing I'd ever heard in my life. But then I realised that a doctor doesn't make jokes at the patient's expense. Or at least he shouldn't.

Our doctor is in his early seventies and has been the family doctor for years and years, even attending to me when I was a baby. He's always been very fond of my mother and when I finally accepted that I was indeed pregnant and it wasn't some kind of cruel hoax, he asked me if I wanted to go into the waiting room and tell Mum the good news. I was aghast. Molly, could you imagine? I'm sure my mother thinks that all I've ever done is hold a boy's hand. I am as good as gold in my parents' eyes. I mean, my sister Jayne has been on holidays abroad with several blokes and you can bet your life she wasn't staying in twin-bedded rooms – but me? Well, I'm almost nun-like. Almost, but not quite. Because obviously I'm pregnant now.

When I came out of the GP's surgery, dazed and confused,

and saw the worried look on my mother's white face I nearly burst into tears. I wanted to throw my arms around her, squeeze her and tell her that everything was okay, that I wasn't going to die or anything. But instead I found myself dumbstruck.

The GP started talking to her about the weather or something. I can't even remember because it's a bit of a blur now. I mean, I was trying to digest really quickly the fact that I was going to have a baby all on my own. So when we got into the car Mum asked me if everything was okay. I said, yes, everything was okay but that it had been discovered that I'd a couple of cysts on my ovaries.

It was true. A couple of harmless cysts had also been found but none of that seemed to compare with the enormity of the unplanned pregnancy.

Mum said that she'd also had ovarian cysts and that was why she'd had to have a hysterectomy. She said I'd probably have to have a hysterectomy too. She went on for a bit about the hysterectomy and about other women she knew who had cysts and all kinds of gynaecological problems. And just I sat wordlessly in the passenger seat of the car, only half-listening because I was wondering where on earth I should go from here.

"But at least it's not serious," she said, finally drawing her rather long monologue to a hasty conclusion as she parked outside the front door of our home. "Thank God for that anyway."

Not serious?

Oh God, Molly, I didn't know whether to laugh or cry.

Diana x

12

21st Feb

Hiya, sorry I haven't been in touch in a while. I've just been trying to sort my head out and it's all a bit crazy. I'm just over eleven weeks pregnant. I can't believe that I hadn't even considered pregnancy being a possibility before now. After all, between stomach cramps and throwing up, feeling nauseous and all of a sudden not being able to bear the smell of cigarette smoke, you'd think a little voice in my head would have spoken up beforehand. But no, it genuinely didn't enter my head that I could be preggers. I think, with all the excitement of getting my own TV show and everything, it didn't occur to me to question why my period was so late. My clock is all over the shop usually anyway 'cos I go on these crazy starvation diets every now and again where I basically don't eat for three or four days in a row and drink nothing but Diet Coke. I'm kind of addicted to fasting but obviously all that has to stop now that I'm carrying a child.

I keep patting my stomach and wondering if maybe the doctor hasn't made a big mistake. After all, he is pretty old and technically should have retired years ago. Maybe his glasses need strengthening or something. But then in the mornings, when I have my head firmly down the toilet bowl and I feel like I'm just short of throwing my guts up I begin to think, you know something, he's probably right.

As for cravings? Well, I have an inexplicably crazy yearning for grapefruit juice. It's bizarre because before this I think I probably tasted grapefruit juice just once or twice in my life and I didn't even particularly like it. Now I drink gallons and gallons of the stuff. I bring a least four large cartons of it into work and hide it in the staff canteen.

Nobody in work has noticed anything yet. Thank God. In fact the TV show is doing so well that I'm getting nothing but praise from my superiors, and viewers are texting and emailing in their support in their droves. Apparently single women all over the country really love the fact that I'm giving them a voice and that I empathise with their search for a man in Ireland. It seems that all the men in this country are gay, married or dysfunctional. The female viewers think I'm truly one of them, going off on all these mad dates and relaying my experiences on camera afterwards. I'm trying so hard not to think about what will happen when they inevitably find out that I'm a fake.

When do I come clean about my condition? And confess that I'm not dating anybody at all? Laughably nothing could be further from the truth. All my dates at the moment are with the toilet bowl. They say morning sickness lasts about three months so I've another month to go. Don't know how I can stick it any longer though. I have an empty bucket and a towel always at the ready beside the bed, so I can empty out my insides before I go to sleep at night. Honest to God, why don't people warn you how awful being pregnant is? It really is true about the joke which says if men and women were to alternate giving birth there would never be more than three in a family: the woman would have the first baby, the man would have the second, the woman would have the third and that would be that. They haven't a clue what it's like and I reckon most of them want to be spared the gory details. The worst is the nausea though. It never goes away. I'm still amazed I haven't thrown up live on TV yet! It feels like it's just a matter of time before that happens!

My doctor says I need to book myself into a hospital straight away. At my last appointment he offered me a list of gynaecologists that he said he highly recommended. I asked how much that would be and nearly fell off the chair when he said four grand. Four grand? I almost had an on-the-spot seizure. Where on earth would I come up with that kind of money? I've been broke all my life and still owe two and a half grand on my credit cards as it stands.

That's the worrying thing about being on TV. People think you're rolling in money and that's so not the case. I told him outright that I wanted to go public and he just stared at me like I'd suddenly grown a second head. "You wouldn't go into a public ward," he said, aghast. I told him that I most certainly would. That I had to. I'd no other choice, being a single mother with no support.

But he shook his head, not taking into account my financial woes or my single situation, and simply said I'd hate it. That I'd be shoved into a ward with ten other women with their partners coming and going all day and night and making lots of noise, and talking loudly on their mobile phones and that it would be unbearable.

"Treat yourself to a bit of comfort in a private room," he insisted, handing me the list of his colleagues' names and the numbers of their secretaries.

He calculated my due date, though I was a bit vague

about the date of my last period, and said my baby would be born around thc 9th of September. Then he weighed me and took my blood pressure. I thanked him for everything, left the surgery, and when I was safely out of sight and earshot, burst into tears.

D x

13

14th March

Hi, Molly,
Three and a half months gone now and my tummy hasn't even popped yet. I just kind of look fatter and my face is quite round and puffy. I'm sure in work people must think I've been munching on the pastry pies big time. If only. I can't keep anything down even if I felt like gorging! I'm still waiting for my weight gain to be commented on in one of those internet forums where people come on and slag off well-known faces. Like, how do those anonymous haters even get the time to write vindictive stuff about people they don't know? Why would you even bother? I try so hard not to read the negative stuff, but it's impossible not to Google your own name out of sheer curiosity. Everyone does it. And never believe anyone in the public eye who says they don't. They're lying!

Oddly enough I don't feel pregnant apart, of course, from the mad cravings and the constant throwing up. I can't pass McDonald's without wanting to puke and the smell of petrol upsets my stomach big time. Still going through the grapefruit juice like there's no tomorrow and I'm totally digging the fresh doughnuts with jam you can buy in a bag in Tesco. If you go down in the evening after work they reduce them in my local store. I bring them home, put two in the microwave and heat them until the jam gets hot and oozes out over the rest of the sugar-laden bun. Yum!

For somebody who's been on every crazy diet known to man during my lifetime, I now love having this alleged pass to allowed naughtiness. The downside to it, however, is that I have been forced to tell my stylist at work (I know, sounds so grand, doesn't it?), that I've gone up a dress size so there's no point in getting clothes for me in a size ten any more. Now before you think I've got some kind of massive clothes budget or anything, let me set the record straight: the clothes that I wear on screen are all borrowed clothes. I don't get to keep them, God, no. They are sent in to the show's stylist and production team by designers and shops in exchange for publicity.

It's a win-win situation for both the show and the designers. You see, sometimes people ring in during a show to ask what dress I'm wearing and where it's from. Then I'm able to say the name of the shop on air. It's the kind of publicity you couldn't pay for. Although sometimes I wonder if it's the shops themselves who phone in with these silly requests. I wouldn't be surprised at all. The retail business is suffering like never before. It's so competitive. Women out there are making do with last year's buys, or going to swap shops, or fishing out the needle and thread and repairing their worn clothing. It's not like the way it used to be with the glamorous ladies of Dublin hitting the city centre, credit card at the ready. One thing's for sure: the glamour gals certainly are not buying an outfit for every time they go out, like used to be the case in Ireland during the so-called economic boom.

I have put all my skinny clothes up in the attic now. I can't even fit a leg into the skinny jeans I bought in Lara last year. Hopefully I'll fit into them again after I have the baby. Then again, that's such a mammoth thought. That I'm going to have a baby. Me? Sometimes I forget and then it hits me. Lord above, sure I can barely look after myself, never mind being responsible for another person. How am I going to lose weight once he or she is here? There'll be no cavorting in the gym anyway. It'll be hard enough trying to feed us both once I'm out of a job. I mean surely it's only a matter of time before I get my marching orders. Who wants a dating expert who's up the duff?

Di x

14

24th March

Molly, today our programme focussed on dating for single mothers. It was enough to sink me into a deep depression. I spoke to mothers who were stunning, intelligent, funny and manless. They said it was impossible to meet nice men in Ireland. I began to panic. I mean, if I couldn't hold onto a man when I had no ties and no commitments, how the hell am I going to fare once the baby comes along?

I asked them how they found dating as mothers. They were all fairly unanimous in their answers: young babies and dating just don't mix. By the time you've your baby washed, fed, changed and put down to sleep, all the bottles put in the steriliser, the bins put out and the baby clothes hung out to dry, the very idea of going on a date is laughable. All you want to do is have a relaxing bubble bath and then flop into bed.

At least doing this TV show has given me a much needed wake-up call. My life as I know it is about to change forever and it's completely terrifying. Things that I take for granted now, such as going to the hairdresser and relaxing with a gossipy magazine over a mug of coffee, are soon to be things of my past. And what will I do for money?

Babies cost so much money and you can't justify splashing out on a trendy new nail polish when you're running out of milk powder. I'd no idea how much childcare cost until today. How much do baby-sitters cost an hour? According to the panel of women I interviewed today, the average baby-sitter charges ten euro an hour. Ten euro? That's almost what I make myself! So if you do happen to go out from say, eight to one, that's fifty quid. Fifty quid for the baby-sitter? Not to mention the thirty-odd quid for taxis in and out of town, and an extra taxi (approx 10 euro) for the baby-sitter to go home? In addition, if you're drinking you'll hardly spend less than forty squid on booze. That's a hundred and thirty squid on a night without even getting fed? That's a hundred and thirty squid without even getting your hair blow-dried or buying something to wear for your night out? And we're bang in the middle of a recession. My foreseeable future is fecked! I'd better start getting used to spending Friday nights chez Mum & Dad. That's if they don't kick me out when they hear the news.

I'm dreading that bit actually. The 'talk'. That's the worst part of all of this. Telling my mum. I feel I've let her down. She and Dad had such high hopes for me and Jayne. They always let Tony do his own thing but with us girls they were extra protective. No man was ever good enough for their two precious princesses. Now Mum's dying for one of us to get married so that she can pick out the wedding dress and help write out the invitations. She says it's not the same when a son gets married. Tony didn't want a fuss made at all and Mum really felt insulted when he and his American wife got married in a no-frills registry office instead of a church. Ever since, she's depending on myself and Jayne to give her a big day out. And now, with no such nuptials in sight, one of us is about to become a single mother.

Mum still asks me embarrassing, awkward questions like "Any men?" It's awful. How can I tell her that there's no man and there's unlikely to be one for a very long time. I mean you can't go on dates when you're pregnant, can you? It would be just far too bizarre. Anyway I'm in emotional turmoil at the moment. The last thing I need is for yet another man to come along and wreck my head.

We went shopping the other day. Mum and myself. I was looking forward to getting a few new things, something different from my 'work clothes' – those blinging made-for-camera garments chosen to make me as glamorous as possible on TV. Not that I get to keep any of those clothes, as I told you, but I wouldn't be able to wear them anyway even if I did. Things that sparkle and shine look great on screen but in real life look a bit naff. The type of attire that looks fantastic on camera wouldn't look so hot when you're down in the local supermarket pushing a trolley around. Nobody in their right mind likes to sparkle and shine off-air unless they're in a nightclub or something.

So Mum and I set out for Kildare Village Shopping outlets last Saturday morning. She wanted to stock up on kitchenware and Molton & Brown bathroom products, and I wanted to buy something that wouldn't attract the magpies' attentions every time I left the house. Something smart and respectable, and a little larger than my current clothes, which are all getting way too tight around the tummy area.

So when my mum was off pottering around the pots and pans I ventured off on my own into one of the clothes shops. I tried on a pretty lemon dress but was worried that it might look a little tent-ish on me. It came in just under the bust and then flowed out a little, disguising my growing bump perfectly. I thought it'd be a nice comfy dress to wear when I was off duty. It was causal enough to wear over leggings or jeans also, which I reckoned would be a bonus in our ever-unpredictable Irish weather.

But then Mum arrived into the shop, her arms laden with bags, to see if I wanted to grab some food in the Italian restaurant. Her legs were killing her and she wanted to sit down. I said I'd love lunch but first of all could she give me her honest opinion about the dress as I was still a tiny bit iffy about it.

I tried it on and I knew by the look of horror on her face as soon as I'd done my twirl that the verdict wouldn't be favourable.

"Diana, dearest. You couldn't possibly go out wearing that!" she said in a loud, overbearing voice. "You look at least three months pregnant!"

I gulped. "I know," I said. "I do. Don't I?"

Di xx

15

29th March

Okay, Molly, I've done it. I've finally done it. I've booked myself into a public maternity hospital and my first appointment is in three weeks' time. I'm dreading it though. I'm going to wear my glasses at every visit in the hope that nobody recognises me. You'd swear I was Angelina Jolie or somebody the way I'm going on, but I'm so afraid a fan of the show might spot me and then my secret would be out in the public domain. And consequently I could be out on my ear.

I'm going to have to chance it. I'll bring in several magazines, keep my head down and hope for the best. As I can't discuss my pregnancy with anybody because it's all a big secret and deep down I'm probably still in a bit of denial about the whole thing, mostly I rely on internet forums to see what people do. There are always debates going on about choosing between public and private maternity hospitals. In Dublin they do semi-private in some hospitals which means that you will share a ward with three or four other semi-private women and pay a small amount if you're already covered by health insurance, which I'm not. I started up my health insurance again as soon as I got the TV job but unfortunately as I only registered a few weeks ago (and the price of it almost killed me – the cost of a fortnight in the sun!) I'm not covered for maternity care. What a bummer!

You can, of course, if you're either wealthy or married to a wealthy man (which I'm obviously not), check into a luxurious maternity hospital for the couple of days and be pampered like a queen and have nice food, all for an exorbitant fee. I can't avail of it, not on my wages naturally, but I can always dream about how nice that would be.

Mind you, according to some people, you can pay the price of a new car to be seen by a certain consultant but there's no guarantee they'll actually turn up themselves at the delivery on the day. Why not? Well, for a number of reasons. They may be on holidays, or may be sick themselves, or indeed two of their expectant patients may present themselves at the same time on the same day, which does often happen.

Babies rarely arrive on their due date, as I'm beginning to find out from various mums-to-be forums. I've become obsessed with pregnancy websites, Molly. Seriously, they are in danger of taking over my life which is definitely not a good thing. I need to be interested in dating and stuff for my show, not scans, maternity wards, breast pumps and pain relief. I should put all that childbirth stuff aside until it's nearer the time. I'm supposed to be giving the country advice about Irish men, not babies.

Oh, but I'm not loving my countrymen at the moment and it's so hard to be positive and smiley and tell the women of Ireland that there are lots of nice men out there when I damn well wasn't even able to get one myself. Not one that would stick around anyway, once he'd gone and impregnated me.

In the name of Jaysus, how did I end up with the one man

in Ireland who had as much interest in being a daddy as he had in becoming a missionary nun? How did I get to be so unlucky? There must be lots and lots of men out there with strong paternal instincts just dying to have cute little offspring. How come I didn't make babies with one of them instead? How could I have been so bloody stupid? I'm going to pay for my mistake for the rest of my life. I'll never be able to move on. Not entirely anyway. Because every time I look in my child's face I'll see his father in it. A constant reminder of the man who callously traded me in like a pair of old slippers once he was finished with me. I'm so annoyed at myself for being such a bad judge of character I can't even begin to describe it!

Anyway, now that I'm booked in, at least that means I've accepted that I'm going to have a baby. Sort of. Now maybe it's time to tell my bosses the truth. And give them time to figure out what is the most humane way to fire an unwanted employee. God help me, Molly.

Diana

16

1st April

April Fool's Day. And that's exactly how I feel. I'm a fool. I couldn't go through with it, Molly. I chickened out. I was honestly all set to tell everybody, but then we were all in the boardroom sitting around the table, coming up with ideas for the show, and the producer was saying that the pressure was really on us now because advertising revenue was heavily falling and that more cutbacks would have to be made, so that we had to really up our game to keep our current viewers and win some more.

The producer specifically said to me that I should be doing more media stuff like press and radio interviews to really raise my profile and that of the show. Maybe I could go out more and be pictured with various celebrities? That was his suggestion. And what could I do? Turn around in the middle of it all and tell them, "Actually, haha, I'm almost four months pregnant, lads!?"

The timing wasn't right. No. In fact it couldn't have been more wrong. Everyone in the station is terrified of losing their jobs. I'm on probation. And as it's usually last in, first out, in these types of situations, it kind of goes without saying that I would be the first person escorted out the door.

As it is, it can't have gone unnoticed that I'm filling out a bit. There's nowhere to hide on TV. I'm insisting on smock tops at the moment. I tried to convince my stylist that smock tops were very much still in vogue when we were going through my wardrobe the other day. I also said that's what I was most comfortable wearing on TV. To be honest, I'd love to stick to black as it's the most slimming colour but the stylist nearly collapsed with horror when I asked if I could wear black now and again. It's a big no-no on screen, you see. It drains you. Makes you look like the living dead. I wanted to scream out loud that I'm expecting a baby and I can't wear cute little pink baby-doll dresses anymore but I forced myself to stay silent. It's killing me keeping all this a secret but I'm between a rock and an awfully hard place. If I can keep going until my probation ends, if I can just cover up for the next two months until I'm home and dry, if I can just . . .

Why did this have to happen to me? Why did Roger dump me? He never really gave me a proper reason except to say that things had got "intense" between us. He said he needed space to sort his head out. Well, that was a joke if ever I heard one. Space in which to find somebody else, more like. That's obviously what he meant.

It's like he had a complete personality change overnight. I mean, he'd been the one to tell me he looked forward to being a dad one day. He'd been the first to tell me he loved me. He told ME he loved me before I told HIM. I still have that very same text saved on my phone. Sad but true. I deleted all his other texts but when it came to the 'I love you' one I just couldn't bring myself to do it.

Now he's gone. As if it had meant nothing at all. And I'm

left with just an old meaningless 'I love you' text on my phone and a part of him growing inside of me. A baby he doesn't bloody want!

Oh, fuck you, Roger Matherson. You absolute bastard for doing this to me!!!

Di

17

2nd April

Dear Molly,
The trouble with good old-fashioned diary-writing is that there's no delete button or else I'd just scrap that last diary entry. Unfortunately I can't find any Tippex either. My latest rant, to my shame, makes me seem bitter and twisted and a total man-hater and that's the last thing I want to become. I wrote that last night and everything always seems that little bit more hopeless at night when it's dark and I'm alone in my room stuck with my thoughts. And I'm scared. I'm terrified of being a single mum and coping by myself with no support. And I suppose it's unfair of me for having a go at Roger since he doesn't even know I'm pregnant. I haven't even given him a chance to react. For all I know he might be thrilled to be a dad and want to become as involved as I am and support me all the way. I have to give him the benefit of the doubt. After all, he didn't know I was pregnant when he dumped me. And it's not his fault that he suddenly fell out of love with me after he'd slept with me. Maybe I was, like, crap in bed or something and he was too polite to say it to me. I have to

give him the chance to prove himself to be a devoted dad. But I'm finding it impossible to even come to terms with the whole idea of being a mother myself, never mind confiding my fears in anybody else.

Maybe I should tell my mum. Perhaps I should just tell somebody instead of shouldering all this worry all by myself. Thank God I've got you, Molly, to write to, but I need somebody who's going to talk back and give me the answers I so desperately need. It'd probably be a load off my mind if I told Mum. I mean, I'm going to have to tell her one day, aren't I? So I might as well get it over with. I was thinking of telling Mum and Dad together. Sitting them both down and then telling them face to face. But then again I find the idea of that so overwhelming that I don't know if I could actually get the words out.

I'm not afraid of my parents. Definitely not. I know they're not going to hit me, or shout at me, or chuck me out onto the street. But can I face seeing the disappointment in their faces? Can I face my sister Jayne's disapproval? She is sure to be furious about all of this.

I feel I've let everybody down. It was just the other day that Mum told me Dad was so proud of me with the TV show and everything. Apparently people come up to him in the golf club on a regular basis telling him they saw me on TV. Mum says I'm a credit to them both.

But, Molly, isn't it best that I tell the daddy first? Isn't Roger entitled to be the first to know? What are the rules? I wish somebody could give me a perfect answer. Doesn't the biological father have a right to know before I tell anybody else? Will he even care or will he be absolutely furious with me and try and wriggle his way out of his parental duties? Anyway, as soon as I tell Mum and Dad, they're going to want to know who the father of my child is, and what kind of support he's going to offer me and the baby. That's a given. Of course, I don't believe that they'll expect Roger to produce an engagement ring on the spot and immediately march me up the aisle, but they'll expect him to help out in some way. So will I, of course. After all, I didn't make this baby all by myself.

Diana x

18

3rd April

Dear Molly,
I finally told somebody. Yes, I told Vicky. We were having lunch in Milano's and straight after dessert I came right out with it. Her jaw nearly hit the floor. Her face was so funny it made me laugh. She seriously thought I was joking. Like as if I would make something like that up. As if I would think something like that was hilarious!

Then, once she got over the initial shock and found her voice again after it had momentarily disappeared, she gave me a great big hug and said she was truly delighted for me. It was just the boost I needed. I desperately wanted for somebody, ANYbody just to say, "Diana, it's not the end of the world and everything's going to be okay."

A huge weight has been lifted off my shoulders. Really, the relief is enormous. It's no longer my big guarded secret that I'm carrying around like a burden weighing me down all day.

"Is that why you're not drinking then?" she asked me then as the penny suddenly dropped. "Aha, now everything's making much more sense. You absolute rascal!"

You see, Molly, I haven't had a sniff of alcohol since I found out I was pregnant. I'd felt so guilty after getting completely bollixed on New Year's Eve. Even now I still can't believe I was doing shots of Jaegermeister while I was pregnant, not to mention all the flipping Marlboros I smoked that night.

But the good thing is that I've since quit the fags. And there's no going back. Seriously, even the thought of being anywhere near a cigarette right now makes me want to gag to be honest. Funnily enough I haven't had any nicotine cravings whatsoever. It's great! Giving up alcohol though has been a lot more difficult. Especially now that I'm alone and lonely and scared and would just love to forget my woes with a bottle of chilled sparkling wine and a bumper bag of Doritos. In private I'm a far cry from the public bubbly blonde girl everyone sees on TV. On TV I have a permanent smile painted from ear to ear. Inside, however, I'm crumbling and I regularly soak my pillows at night trying to get to sleep.

Vicky says I have to tell Roger immediately. She says I need to give him the benefit of the doubt and that I shouldn't be so quick to condemn him. She even went so far as to say he'll probably be thrilled that he's about to become a dad. I'm not so sure that I share her well-intentioned optimism myself. He's not with me. He dumped me because he obviously got tired of me, or thought he could do better. Those are the harsh facts. So I actually can't imagine him being over the moon at the fact that we are going to be joint parents and that, because of that fact, we'll be tied to each other forever and ever. Still, I've decided to give him the chance to make his own mind up. I'm going to send him a text now before I change my mind, asking him to meet me. ASAP.

Diana

19

7th April

Oh Molly, it didn't go down well at all. Not at all. Actually that's the understatement of the century. It was a complete disaster. I think Roger was hung-over when we met for coffee in Samsara yesterday afternoon. He was unshaven and bleary-eyed and he looked like shite. Mind you, I probably did too. I had minimum make-up on my face and had my hair scraped back into a simple ponytail. I was also wearing my disguise – thick glasses.

I barely recognised him as he looked dishevelled, pale and unwashed. He looked like he'd slept in last night's clothes – a Guinness T-shirt, faded denims and sneakers that had seen better days. I couldn't believe he'd made so little effort.

"Hi," he said lazily, pulling up a seat and then waving at a waiter across the room in an attempt to catch his attention.

I didn't know whether to shake his hand or kiss his cheek as an acknowledgement. In the end I did neither. Nothing seemed appropriate. He wasn't offering either hand or cheek anyway.

"How are you?"

"I'm fine, thanks. A bit wrecked, but I'll survive. They're trying to make us do more hours in work for less pay. It's fucking ridiculous."

Roger works as a gym manager. That's why he usually looks so fit. Not today though. I believe the city's gyms are in trouble. People are cancelling in their droves. With the recession there'll be a lot more people pounding the pavements instead in a bid to keep in shape.

I waited for him to at least ask me how I was, or how my new job on TV was going but he didn't. So I got straight to the point.

"I'm sure you're wondering what this is all about," I said soberly, not wanting to prolong the agony. "So I may as well come straight out with it. I'm expecting a baby, Roger. I'm four months pregnant."

The waiter was ready with a pen and notepad.

"Can you just give us a few minutes?" I heard Roger say to him in a strangled whisper. He looked like somebody had just shoved a loaded gun down his throat. He then turned to me, obviously shell-shocked. "You're what!?"

"Ssshh, there's no point letting the whole bar know. I'm pregnant," I said with a dead-pan face. "And you're the father."

He gulped. "How can you be sure?"

I was stunned by his implied accusation. What did he think I was? The city bike? I told him I hadn't been with anyone else all the time I was with him. I'd always been faithful. I hadn't been with anybody since we'd broken up either. He didn't even ask me how I was feeling, Molly. He was just so angry. Angry and shocked. Like his whole world had been shattered. He asked me what I wanted to do.

I swallowed hard. What did I want to do? What was he talking about?

"What do you mean?"

"Are you going to keep it?"

"Would you prefer if I didn't?"

I was greeted by a stony silence. He kept tugging at his fingers.

"Have you thought very carefully about the implications of all of this?" he said.

"I'm not getting rid of our baby," I answered very definitely, looking him straight in the eye, "if that's what you're hinting at."

"What do you want me to do?"

"Well, I hope you'll be a father and step up to the mark."

"Mmm."

"What's that supposed to mean?"

"I don't want you to get your hopes up, Diana. I know how clingy you can be."

I looked at him quizzically. Clingy? What was he on about?

"Look, if I don't run for the hills, it's out of a sense of duty, right? Nothing more. I don't want you to think this means anything – like that we'll be getting back together or anything. Understood?"

"Fine."

How insulting!

"I've moved on. I'm with somebody else now. Somebody very special. I don't want to hurt her."

Like he hurt me.

Oh, Molly, it just went on and on and on. He kept speaking to me like a robot, telling me he didn't want to get my hopes up. We were just going around in painful circles.

"This isn't about me. Or you," I said eventually, struggling to keep any emotion out of my voice. "It's about the baby. That's what matters from now on."

The waiter was back. My coffee had now gone cold. I ordered another one, but Roger said he wouldn't have anything else. He had to go. It was his girlfriend's birthday. They were going out for lunch. So I cancelled my order. I needed to go home and be by myself.

"You need time to think about this," I said.

"You need to think about it too," he glowered.

"I've done nothing else but think about this for the last few weeks. There's no decision to be made as far as I'm concerned. You've got to decide whether you want to be involved."

"I want a paternity test."

"I was with nobody else."

"I need proof. You can't just present me with this kind of news and expect me to be jumping up and down with joy. I've moved on with my life."

"I know," I told him. "So you keep saying."

I had moved on too, or at least I thought I had.

Until I got the baby news.

"You can't just throw this at me. I want a paternity test."

"So you said. You'll get one, when the baby is born. It's not possible to have one before then."

What did he want us to do? Apply to go on The Jeremy Kyle Show?

"Well, fine then. We'll take a paternity test when the baby is born and find out for sure."

I asked him what I was supposed to do until then. He looked genuinely confused and asked for clarification. At this stage I was trembling but secretly praying that I wasn't betraying any emotion. I needed to be strong at this point and not crumble in front of him.

"There's things to be done. Like hospital visits."

"You can't expect me to go with you to the hospital! We're not a couple. We are no longer in a relationship. Not that we ever had much of a relationship in the first place. It was just a couple of one-night stands as far as I'm concerned."

I was stung. A couple of one-night stands? Was I hearing things? My head was reeling, my self-confidence in tatters. I could feel blood flushing my cheeks as I struggled to maintain composure. Why didn't he just dig the knife in further and completely finish me off there and then? I felt like taking out my mobile phone and showing him the text where he'd said 'I love you.' He'd obviously forgotten he'd ever sent it to me.

I fought so hard not to cry. I desperately didn't want him to see me in tears. To think I had been deeply in love with this unfeeling man at one point! I had idolised him and obsessed over how I could make him happy. I'd cooked him dinners and even cleaned his flat for him on several occasions. I'd spent a full week's wages on a digital camera for his birthday. I'd thought he was The One and that we'd probably get married and live happily ever after. He'd told me that he'd loved me and now he didn't remember. I decided not to prolong my despair by showing him his own text. If it had meant nothing at the time, it was hardly going to make a difference now. I'd only end up alienating him even further. How short a memory he must have. A couple of one-night stands, huh?

I couldn't believe how callous he was being. This was a far cry from the charming gym manager I'd met on my first day at the fitness centre over a year ago. Roger had given me a personal tour and I'd been unable to tear my eyes away from his amazing physique. But it wasn't just his abs that had attracted me. He'd had a glint in his eye and a cheeky, friendly smile. It had been love at first sight. For me anyway. Things had moved at breakneck speed. After a mere few dates, Roger was talking about growing old together with me. I'd hardly imagined all those conversations, had I?

"Anyway, I'm not ready to be a dad." He shrugged as if it

were just a simple matter of an opt-out clause. Like as if somebody decided not to go for a walk because it was raining or something.

I couldn't believe this was the father of my child sitting in front of me and he was refusing to accept the fact that a child, HIS child, was on the way. How dare he just sit there thinking he could insult me! He was deliberately degrading me by demanding a paternity test.

The last thing I'd been expecting were accusations of cheating. I wouldn't have dreamed of even looking at another man when I was with Roger. He was my one and only. It hadn't even occurred to me that we might one day split up. I'd thought he was my soul mate. I'd seen qualities in him that obviously weren't there. I had misjudged him so much it was scary.

Then again, he'd totally given me mixed signals. He'd spoken fondly about his four godchildren and his nieces and nephews. He'd said he'd like to be a dad one day.

One day. Not today or tomorrow. I guess that was the catch.

Diana x

20

10th April

Mum and I went shopping again today, Molly. We drove all the way back down to the Kildare Village outlets. Mum's kind of obsessed with buying bargains like discounted stuff and so we always go back to Kildare for the sheer choice. When we got there she thought she might look at some clothes in the Ralph Lauren shop. She particularly wanted some golf-type attire. She's not so great at golf but likes to look the part nonetheless. So we went inside the shop and she started trying on these pink striped polo shirts. At one stage I had to go off to the Ladies' and throw my guts up, and when I came back again she'd found a nice little size-ten mauve-coloured maxi dress that she thought would look nice on me. I took one look at the clingy cotton fabric and immediately saw that it was a no-no. I picked out another, looser, sky-blue dress and held it up to me. Mum wrinkled her nose, conveying her disapproval. "It's too short," she said. "For a woman of your age."

I tried it on regardless because I wanted to buy something. Anything. I'm the type of person who has to buy something when I'm shopping or else I feel depressed if I go home empty-handed. So I tried it on and surprisingly it fitted. And it hid my tummy perfectly as it came in just under the bust and then kind of fell down. I thought it looked nice. And the colour complemented my eyes.

"It's awful," Mum said bluntly. "You look very big in it. You're putting on weight, dearest. I'm only saying it to you because you're my daughter and I'm the only one who's going to be honest with you. Look at your sister and how disciplined she is about keeping her figure."

But she's not pregnant, I wanted to yell.

I coloured and ran back into the safety of the cubicle to change. I hated hiding this important news from her. I didn't want to keep it from her. She had every right to know that five months from now I was going to make her a grandmother for the second time. Tony had a daughter but since he lived in Boston Mum had only met the kid twice. She was always lamenting the fact that she didn't get to see her grandchild as much as she wanted to.

But no matter how hard I tried I just couldn't face having THAT conversation. I didn't want to see the disappointment in her face. Herself and Dad are such a conservative couple. I didn't want to let them down but yet I knew I was going to have to.

"I don't want to buy anything here," I said when I finally emerged from the changing room and hung the dress defiantly back on the rail. "Let's go for something to eat."

Thankfully Mum thought it was a good idea. We went to the Italian restaurant and I ordered lasagne while she opted for the tagliatelle. She asked if I wanted a glass of wine with my lunch but I shook my head resolutely. The thought of alcohol made me want to gag. And I still haven't quite come to terms with the guilt I feel over getting so pissed on New Year's Eve. After all, they say that everything a mother-to-be consumes is passed on to the embryo. I just shudder even thinking about it.

"I've temporarily given up alcohol," I told her truthfully. "There's too many calories in wine and I'm trying to be healthy."

After lunch (no desserts, although I did kind of have my eye on the tempting tiramisu), Mum dragged me around to the Wolford shop on the corner. She was looking through a rack of bodysuits on a rail and showed me one gorgeous white one with chiffon sleeves that was heavily discounted. Well, pregnant women, I needn't tell you, have no need for bodysuits but of course I didn't let on to her. Instead I muttered something about having to save my money for a deposit on a house. "I can't live at home forever, you know?" I laughed, and she let it drop, saying nothing. I think privately she'd like myself and Jayne to stay at home for as long as possible as she likes having people to fuss over. But the reality is that I can't stay at home once I have the baby. It's just not an option. The house isn't big enough for all of us and I need my independence.

However, once the TV station find out I'm up the duff, I'm in serious danger of losing my job and then there won't be a chance in hell of me renting a nice place. Or indeed any place at all. Worrying about it all keeps me awake at night. How could my life, that was going so right, have ended up going so wrong? And in such a short space of time too?

Mum ended up buying two pairs of Wolford tights and then asked me if I wanted to pop my head into Coast. I said I didn't.

"But you love Coast," she insisted.

This is true. I usually do love their dresses and I also love the fact that they always have cute matching bags and little cardigans with bows at the back to go with most of their dresses but they don't do maternity wear as far as I know. Pity, that.

I told Mum I was kind of tired and wanted to go home. She seemed genuinely amazed.

"But you haven't bought anything yet!"

"I know. But with the recession and everything I feel guilty buying things, even at discount prices."

But then as we were passing Le Petit Bateau, I insisted that we drop in for a look.

"Whatever for?" Mum wanted to know. "Do you know somebody expecting a baby? I won't let you buy any more for Tony's little girl – you've bought tons already. It's just wasteful."

I told her that it was always handy to have a few baby clothes spare because people were always having babies. Just like having a drawer full of birthday cards, Mass cards, and Get Well Soon cards, it was a good idea to have a few baby clothes (in pink and in blue of course) just in case.

She seemed to go along with this notion and we spent ages looking around the shop at the cute little outfits. I ended up buying three drop-dead gorgeous velour Babygros in white. Even Mum was swooning over them. This was such a good and clever idea I thought as we drove home towards Dublin. If I continue to buy baby clothes and talk about babies a lot when I'm in her company, then she'll probably just guess that I'm having a baby and I won't even have to tell her outright. I wish I'd thought of doing something like this a bit sooner.

When we got home Jayne was in the kitchen watching Xposé with her hair wrapped in a large bath towel. She was sipping a large mug of coffee.

"Ooh! Shopping bags! Show us what you bought," she said, jumping up and opening the bags anyway. "Tights?"

"They're Mum's," I said.

"What did you buy?" she asked, giving me an eagle-eyed stare.

"Oh, just a few baby things."

She continued to eye me suspiciously. She thought I was lying. I know she did. She thought I was lying and that I'd hidden my purchases from her. It wouldn't be the first time. I often have to hide my best clothes from Jayne as she has a horrible habit of borrowing my stuff without asking. I even have a padlock on my wardrobe door to prevent my sister from nicking my stuff when my back is turned. Mind you, I've been guilty myself of borrowing a couple of her things without asking. Like that time I wore her brand-new white Paul Costello coat to Ladies Day at the Leopardstown races. Well, it was the only thing I could find that would go with the hat that I'd paid a fortune for. And I couldn't justify shelling out a huge amount of money for something I was only going to wear the once, now could I? Anyway Jayne was off in Liverpool on a hen weekend and I felt perfectly safe, knowing that if I wore it and took great care of it and put it back in her wardrobe before she came back from the airport, she'd be none the wiser. And she wasn't. The borrowed coat was much admired, so much so that I was even chosen out of hundreds of ladies to go forward for the best-dressed competition. I didn't win top prize but to my delight I won runner-up, was presented with a beautiful bouquet of flowers and got my photograph taken.

Jayne came back from Liverpool and the coat was back hanging in her wardrobe as good as the day she bought it. She even commented on my flowers and I told a little white lie and said that I'd received them from a secret admirer. She looked a bit surprised (I know, the cheek of her!), but seemed to buy my explanation all the same. All was well and I thought I'd got off scot-free until disaster struck a fortnight later. Jayne was in the hairdresser's having a nice relaxing time getting her highlights done and flicking through Image magazine when she spotted me beaming out at her from the society pages. All hell subsequently broke loose. Quick as you'd know it, she was yelling a message into my phone, competing with the noise of the hair-dryers. And even though it was hard to hear what she was saying, I was left in no doubt that she was not a bit pleased. Actually that's an understatement. She was flipping furious! In fact she was so mad that when she came home waving the magazine in my face, with smoke coming out both her ears, she made me buy the coat off her. You'd swear I'd somehow contaminated it!

Then to make matters worse she absolutely insisted that I buy it from her at full price, i.e. the price she'd paid for it in House of Fraser. I thought it was pretty mean of her to demand so much money from me, especially as she'd bought the coat in London at sterling prices. So not only did she sell me a second-hand coat for an exorbitant sum of cash, she even made a profit out of it.

Now that white coat is the only white thing I own and believe you me, Molly, I will never in my lifetime buy another white coat or anything white again. I've since spent more money dry-cleaning the damn thing than I paid Jayne for it in the first place. Every time you sit down, it gets marked. Every time you wear make-up it smears all over the collar and you end up keeping a constant fifty yards distance away from anybody with a drink or cigarette in their hand.

"Baby things?" Jayne's shrill voice interrupted my train of thought. "Who do we know that's expecting a visit from the stork?"

I turned away from her quickly so she couldn't see my reddening face. "A girl called Sarah. I don't think you know her. It's a girl from work. She's a sound technician."

"Oh," said Jayne, rapidly losing interest as she realised I didn't have any scandal for her. "And did you not buy anything else for yourself? I'm surprised you even went shopping now that you can wear free clothes every day at work. Sometimes I'm sorry I didn't become a TV presenter myself instead of a beautician."

Molly, I had to bite my tongue to stop myself from retorting. It's actually hilarious the way Jayne dismisses my TV gig as something absolutely anyone at all could do. What's she like? It's not something you just apply to do after you get your Leaving Cert and it's certainly not as easy as it looks. I mean, the other day I was out on the street in the pouring rain with my microphone, asking women about separation and divorce. Nobody, but NObody would give me a quote on camera, and the only people that would were foreign women and I didn't understand a word of what they were saying.

When I got back and explained to the producer that we couldn't find enough people to talk, instead of letting us off and filling up the programme with more chat and celebrity gossip about divorced Hollywood stars, he almost had a hissy fit and made myself and the cameraman drive out to Blanchardstown shopping centre to get more sound bites. I think I don't fancy Dan any more after that. Bloody slave driver.

"They're cute," said Jayne, taking the tiny velour Babygros from the bag and cooing over them. "It's hard to believe that somebody could be so small. I hope I have a girl one day when I'm married," she said dreamily. "It would be more fun to dress a little girl than a little boy, wouldn't it? Mind you, these things cost quite a bit," she added, checking the price tags. "This Sarah girl must be a really good friend. How come you've never mentioned her before?"

"Oh, you know . . ." I trailed off. "I'm not giving all of them to Sarah. I'll keep some of them for myself."

I gulped. Oh God, if that wasn't a hint, what was? Jayne would know now for sure. She'd figure it out and say something to Mum and they'd put their heads together and put two and two together. Or that's what I thought. However, Jayne just laughed condescendingly.

"For yourself? You're mad in the head, so you are. Why are you buying baby stuff? How can you be planning to get married? You're not even seeing anybody!"

Di xx

21

17th April

Dear Molly,
Every time I see a baby now on the TV, I point out how cute he or she is. I couldn't possibly be more obvious.

"Look," I say loudly. "A baby!"

But still, they ignore me. My family carry on doing whatever they're doing as if I'm simply not there. It's quite incredible how they haven't suspected anything yet. Even, the other day Mum and I were in Tesco and when I steered the trolley down the baby-stuff aisle, Mum just said nothing. I actually had to stop just in front of the Pampers range to make her say something.

"We don't need anything here," she just said absently.

"Do we not?"

"Ah Diana, I'm in a hurry, come on, stop your messing," she snapped impatiently.

When we eventually packed the groceries into the car I started talking about nappies again. I asked her if it had been difficult in her day to cope without disposable nappies when you had to wash all the nappies by hand. She said it was a lot of hard work and then she phoned my dad on the mobile to ask him if there was any milk in the house as she'd forgotten to pick it up in the shopping centre. Dad couldn't understand why she'd forgotten the milk as that had been the main reason for us going to the supermarket in the first place. And then Mum said the reason she'd forgotten the milk was because I, Diana, had been distracting her by talking about nappies. And I sat in the passenger seat, rigidly, with my heart in my mouth. This is it, I thought. Dad's very smart and nothing ever gets past him. He's going to know I'm pregnant, no doubt about it. He's going to be at the front door with a shotgun demanding to know who the father of my child is. I braced myself for the showdown.

But when we got home Dad and Jayne were watching some wildlife programme on TV and nobody said a word to me about anything. It wasn't like they were pretending to ignore my pregnancy or anything – they quite obviously just hadn't guessed.

Then we had salmon for supper and I said, "Can pregnant women eat fish?" And Dad said he had no idea and Jayne said she didn't know either and Mum said it was probably best if they didn't eat fish in case they took an allergic reaction to it. And still nobody guessed. Molly, at this stage I want to bang all their heads together out of sheer bloody frustration.

Diana x

22

20th April

Dear Molly,
I've been to the hospital. I went to the wrong place at first. I queued for quite a bit but when I got to the top the administration woman asked me for my hospital number and then said I had to go to another place which was for public patients. All conducted in a very loud voice.

So then I had to queue all over again. A much longer queue this time. There were lots of people in the waiting room. Lots of couples. And a few single women. Like me. Well, I don't know if they were single or not, but they hadn't any men with them. Just like me.

There actually were a lot of men there. Which was annoying really. Because there weren't a lot of seats and there was a bit of a squash. And I stood for quite a while glaring at a man in a tracksuit reading The Sun. He was sitting directly under a sign which clearly stated that seats were supposed to be given up for patients. Idiot! There was quite a bit of a boring wait and then I went for my initial assessment with a midwife in a little cubicle.

She asked me if this was my first child. I said it was. And then it all suddenly became a bit real. I was having an actual child and it wasn't a dream anymore. I was in a maternity hospital and there is no way I would have been there if I wasn't expecting a baby.

She proceeded to reel off a lot of questions about blood pressure and smear tests and then she asked me if I'd be breastfeeding. The question came out of the blue, taking me completely by surprise. Was I going to breastfeed? Well, I hadn't thought about it at all. Would I? I mean, if I was going to keep my job as a TV presenter, it wouldn't do to be whipping out the boob mid-air, would it? Then again, once the cat was out of the bag or the baby out of the womb to be more precise, they were hardly going to keep me on as their dating guru, were they? It was all over for me, I supposed, tears welling up in my eyes. I was vaguely aware of the midwife banging on about breastfeeding and statistics and the fact that Ireland had a very low rate of breastfeeding women compared to say, Norway, where ninety-nine per cent or something of the female population breastfed their babies, but then she stopped suddenly with a look of alarm on her face when she noticed the tears rolling down my cheeks.

She asked me what was wrong and I told her I was a single mother. And then I sniffed dramatically and reached for a tissue from my bag. I blew my nose loudly.

She said that being a single mother was very common these days and there was lots of support available for women like me. She asked again if I would be breastfeeding. I said I would be, just to get her off my case, and I don't know if I imagined this or not but it seemed to me like she punched the air with joy. Then she asked me if I would like the phone number of a social worker. I said I would. I don't know why. I had no intention of going to see a social worker. The nurse scribbled down a phone number on a piece of paper and handed it to me. "Good girl," she said as though she were talking to an infant. I thanked her, wiped away my tears, made my next appointment at the reception desk, and then wandered down the hospital corridor past women in dressing gowns who were so huge they looked like they could be expecting baby hippopotamuses.

That's going to be me in a few months, I told myself, feeling shell-shocked all of a sudden, and then with my brightly coloured plastic maternity folder tucked safely under my arm, I stumbled out into the daylight and the rain.

Diana

23

22nd April

Molly, I can't wait to tell people I'm pregnant. I'm bursting to make an announcement at this stage. I'd much rather people thought I was pregnant than that I was simply fat. I think that in work, however, they're beginning to suspect something. Especially since last night I was at this corporate buffet thing with some of my colleagues and I filled my plate five times and didn't have anything alcoholic to drink. Now if that's not a sign I don't know what is. Women on the TV rarely eat but usually like to sip the free champagne that's always in abundance at these corporate things. It's one of the perks of the job – the pay might not be great but we get everything for free, including booze.

Okay, some of my colleagues might moan that we have to give our borrowed clothes back, but so what? I mean, once you've worn them on air you're not going to turn up to, say, a wedding, in something that thousands of viewers have already spotted you in. Honestly, some people are never happy. The egos at the station are something else too. Like some of my colleagues think they're Ireland's answer to

Oprah Winfrey and constantly complain loudly about being in the papers. Then when they're not in the papers they become paranoid that nobody is talking about them and they start turning up at every envelope-opening for about two weeks until the gossip columnists start writing about them again.

Nevertheless I've made a handful of friends in the station. Not that many though because TV presenters, especially established female TV presenters, are always wary of somebody new coming along. It's very territorial in Tellyland and nobody particularly wants to share the limelight. I'm glad I have my old school pals Selina and Vicky to keep my feet on the ground. They couldn't give a hoot about celebrity gossip really. Mind you, Selina does keep asking if I've met Colin Farrell yet, which is a bit weird. Like, why would he be on my show? To get dating advice? To come on and talk to the afternoon viewers about being a father to two children by two different women? Like, hello? As if he'd waste his time.

Anyway we don't have the luxury of having major celebrities ever appear on our show because we don't have a budget for celebrity-appearance fees. Simple as. Even ordering a taxi for a guest speaker to come on and waffle about a subject for forty minutes is a major conundrum. And there's everybody thinking TV work is so glamorous. It's so not. And it's getting worse. With the current economic crisis and everything and advertising revenue plummeting in the last few months, they've even removed the water coolers from the corridors. We have to buy our own liquids now. And rumour has it that we're going to be asked to do our own make-up before going on air in the not too distant future. God forbid.

At the weekly meeting today the powers-that-be said we need to spice the show up a bit. Maybe talk about sex a bit more. Add in some more controversy. Cook up a storm etc. Of course, we can't talk about orgies and the like because the show goes out in the afternoons and needs to be kept family-friendly, but we are allowed to talk about sex aids and affairs and stuff as long as we give a little verbal 'parental guidance' warning just before the show is aired. Dan says we could try and make the show a bit more personal too. Like, you know, the way Ellen DeGeneres often talks about herself? So that you actually feel you know her?

I was about to say in a jokey kind of way that I couldn't talk about sex because I don't have any experience of it. Well, not any more. But then instead of arguing with the heads that the show shouldn't be about us but the viewers, I ended up agreeing that it was a great idea to make it more personal.

Then we discussed what the topics could be for that week. One of the researchers, a rather peevish-looking individual by the name of Eileen, who always wears black and is so skinny she'd give Mrs Beckham a jog for her loot, piped up and said we should do another programme about single parenting as it always proves to be a popular subject. Dan thought that was a great idea. He said he reckoned that lots of people watching daytime TV would be single parents themselves, and then he laughed kind of nastily, and said, "Sure what else would they be doing?" I was fairly affronted. Definitely don't fancy him any more with that kind of condescending attitude.

We agreed to focus on all things to do with single parenting the following week, covering pregnancy and dating and money issues.

"We've got to find some more single parents to come on the show," said Eileen in a loud, overbearing voice. Her voice really isn't in proportion with her weight. Weird.

"What about you, Diana, do you know anyone?"

Did I know anyone? Other than myself? Oh my God, I felt myself going absolutely puce. I could feel my face burning and Eileen was just staring at me the whole time, her beady eyes boring into me. I don't like that girl at all and I have the distinct feeling she doesn't like me either. I've always thought that she was a bit miffed that they brought somebody like me, a complete outsider and a nobody in her eyes, in to present the show when she, the talented skinny Wonder Girl, was under their noses the whole time. Often she'll sit in on the brainstorming sessions and completely ignore me, or else put down any of my suggestions. I also always catch her looking up adoringly at Dan and I'm convinced she'd do anything to jump his bones.

Anyway, there was everyone staring at me and I was racking my brains trying to think of any other single parents that I might know. In fact I know quite a few single parents but whether they would be prepared to sit on national TV and air their dirty laundry to the entire country was quite a different matter altogether. Believe it or not, it's actually easier to get a celebrity to come on the show and spill the beans on their lives than it is to get an ordinary civilian to talk. That's because there's nothing in it for the man on the street to talk about his or her private life, but the celebrity gets to keep up his profile and plug his new book/art exhibition/film/charity gig or whatever.

"I can't think of anyone off the top of my head, but I'll rack my brains overnight," I told Eileen and Dan and the two other researchers in the room who were chewing the ends of their pens thoughtfully. "Do you know anyone?" I fired back at Eileen.

She bit her lip and gave Dan this coy, sycophantic look. "A girl I went to school with is a single mum," she said. "I'll give her a ring but she'd probably be too embarrassed to come on TV, the poor thing."

I felt my hackles rising. "What do you mean exactly by 'the poor thing'?" I shot back at her.

Molly, you could have cut the air with a knife. It was terrible. Everybody looked at me in amazement at my sudden outburst. But I really was angry. With her smug little self-satisfied expression, Eileen had managed to rile me in a way I would not have thought possible.

She looked quite taken aback but still made an attempt to defend herself. "Well, you know, it's not the kind of thing you'd want to shout from the rooftops. I know it's more acceptable and everything to be a single mother these days but it's still not quite the done thing, is it?"

"Not 'the done thing'?" I wanted to explode. "Not 'the done thing'? Do you think women go out there and try to become single mothers ON PURPOSE? Do you really believe that's what they want? That it's something they dream about? There are no single mums in fairytales, you know. Most people become single mothers through no fault of their own. In fact, they usually become single mothers because some selfish prick has left them high and dry!"

There was a collective gasp from around the table. Nobody spoke for quite a while. Suddenly I felt as though a fist was clutching my heart. I began to panic. Shit. I should have kept my big trap shut.

Then Dan cleared his throat, breaking the awkward silence. "Do you know something? I think this would make for a great live TV debate."

I gulped. "What do you mean? Would you want me to curse on air about deadbeat dads?" There's no way I was going to do that. It was completely out of the question. I would come across as bitter and angry. Also, my family would definitely disown me and then I'd be a pregnant, homeless woman. Anyway, was I missing something? We were supposedly a family-friendly show, not Jerry Springer.

Dan shook his head calmly. "I don't mean that. What I

mean is that whether you agree with it or not, there's still a stigma of sorts out there. We've come a long way from the Magdalene laundries where fallen women had to give up their babies and work for the nuns for the rest of their lives as some kind of penance, but then we have people like Eileen here feeling sorry for her single friend and glad she's not her."

Out of the corner of my eye I could see Eileen shift uncomfortably in her seat. You could see this so wasn't going the way she'd intended it to. Good.

"I'm not being disparaging about her," she insisted straight away, obviously terrified of falling out of favour with her beloved Dan. It's actually really embarrassing the way she fawns over him sometimes. "But it's tough for my poor friend," she continued, pretending to be sympathetic. "It really is. She used to be such a party animal and now she's stuck at home all the time because she doesn't have the money to go out. She can't get a job anywhere, because she can't afford full-time childcare. And most men run a mile when they hear she has a kid. They can't handle women that already have baggage."

"It would make a very interesting debate, you're right, Dan," said Francie, one of the other researchers. "We could have Diana passionately defending single mums and then we could bring on somebody else to argue with her and –"

"But nobody in their right mind would come on and damn single parents on live TV," I pointed out.

"Eileen would," said Dan optimistically. "Wouldn't you, Eileen?"

Everyone turned their attention towards Eileen who looked suitably horrified. I tried my best not to smile. Let her work her way out of this one, I thought smugly.

"But I'm just the researcher," she objected huffily, for once prepared to act as though she wasn't running the show. She ran her hand nervously through her unruly mousey curls. "It would be a bit weird if I was involved in the live debate."

Oh, Molly, you should have seen her face as she backtracked furiously. Her plan was backfiring at tremendous speed. Even I was intrigued as to where all this would lead.

"But the viewers at home won't know that," said Dan who clearly didn't want to shelve his great idea now that he was on a roll. "And besides, you've expressed an interest in going in front of the camera in the past."

Eileen looked mortified. Hmm. That just confirmed my suspicions that she had always harboured a desire to be in front of the camera rather than behind it. I also knew she wouldn't be one bit pleased now that her secret had been made public.

"Okay then," she agreed reluctantly. "I'll do it but I'm not going to damn all single mums and land myself in a load of hot water just so ratings will go through the roof. I'm just going to say how tough it is for them, and be like, sympathetic. Else I'll be inundated with sack-loads of hate mail from single parents."

Dan turned towards me. "Are you up for that?"

I nodded my support. What else could I do? He's the producer. You don't argue with the producer. We decided that our big debate would take place on Friday afternoon. That way the weekend TV critics could include it in the Sunday papers and it would give viewers food for thought for the weekend. Then we all went home. I felt drained. Dreaming of my bed and a nice hot-water bottle to snuggle into.

Oh Molly, I'm exhausted. I don't know about this TV thing anymore. It takes up so much energy and I don't have much spare energy just now. Maybe I should try and get work in a post office or something. I can handle selling stamps. I can. I know I can. I think I just want a simple life from now on. Or in my circumstances, as simple as it can possibly be.

Diana

24

27th April

Molly. I think this is it. I think it's all over for me. They know. The TV producers know. The whole country knows. Mum and Dad know. My siblings know. Everyone knows I'm pregnant. I'll tell you more tomorrow. I'm too upset to write just at the moment.

D x

25

28th April

Dear Molly,
I feel better now. Or as good as I think I can be all things considering . . . I still think my TV career is over though. Finito. Flushed down the toilet and away out to Dublin Bay. The TV debate thingy that our producer had such high hopes for was a complete and utter disaster. Jesus, you couldn't make it up if you tried!

I'll fill you in anyway. It had all started off quite pleasantly. We had two single mums on the panel (we couldn't find a single dad to come on unfortunately), and then there was Eileen and myself of course. We had a general chat about how hard it is to be a single mum on your own with no emotional support and the two girls were very honest and refreshingly outspoken about their different situations. Then we had an older woman on the show, a lovely gentle lady called Peggy who had got pregnant in her teens. All by herself of course, as women in Catholic Ireland seemed to do in those days. Her family had cruelly disowned her and she'd given up her baby boy for adoption and had never seen him again. She issued an appeal to find him live on air and I found myself shedding a quiet tear because I just couldn't believe how unfair it all was. I mean, the father of her baby had gone on to marry another woman and have five children. He became a successful businessman and lived a 'respectable' life while she had been sent to the Magdalene laundries in Dublin and then had to go to England and work as a cleaner in a boarding school for the rest of her life, always wondering what became of her precious child. It was so, so sad and I became so wrapped up in her story that it was like I completely forgot I was live on air.

I gave her a hug and said that I couldn't even begin to imagine what she had gone through and that it would kill me if I had to give up my own child. She asked me if I was pregnant and I said that I was. There was something about the way she had looked in my eye and asked me the question straight out. She knew. And I couldn't deny it. And she asked me if I was in a relationship and I said that I wasn't, and that I was finding it very tough. And all the time I was aware of the shocked expression on Eileen's face at these startling revelations. But I just didn't care. I was feeling so emotional at this other woman's story that I hadn't any sympathy left for myself any more. I just kept thinking how lucky I was that nobody was going to take my precious baby from me once it was born. But then when she asked me if I knew who the father of my child was, I was suddenly jolted back to reality, and I realised that not only were we not having a cosy get-together somewhere private and quiet but that we were live on air and the other panellists had now been stunned into silence. Also, I had a rather nasty vision of Roger watching this at home and getting onto his solicitor as the camera rolled. I knew I couldn't name him. I knew everyone would be wondering who the cad of a father was who had left me high and dry to cope with my pregnancy alone, so when the old lady repeated the question, I said I wasn't sure who the father was. "He could be anyone," I heard myself saying as the lie tripped easily off my tongue and then I gazed into the camera with a half-smile on my face until we went to a hurried ad break.

Of course, Eileen must have been raging afterwards because she was all set for this big steaming debate and she never did get to live out her TV dream. She'd dressed up in a short tight red lycra dress which personally I thought was very inappropriate for a daytime show about single mothers and parenting. And after my big revelation she never got to have her say, because, well, there was nothing she could have possibly added to the discussion at that stage. For the rest of the show we chatted about pregnancy and weird cravings and I told everyone I was addicted to grapefruit juice. And one of the other girls said that when she'd been pregnant she'd had these mad cravings for cubes of ice and would bite into them all day long. And the sweet elderly lady said in her day she'd had these crazy cravings for buttered toast. And Eileen had to sit there all that time in silence, totally surplus to requirement. I'm sure our regular viewers were wondering what on earth she was doing sitting there looking ridiculous. I could tell she was absolutely seething. I'm sure she thought I'd had the whole thing planned, simply to discredit her. But nothing could have been further from the truth.

I'd felt so overcome with emotion after speaking to that dear old woman that I just ran with my gut feelings and once I'd started I couldn't stop. And even though I knew I'd more than likely be sacked and thus face financial ruin, the words came tumbling out one after another, and then suddenly it was all over and the floor manager was making furious signs indicating to me to wrap things up. So I said goodbye to my viewers, knowing it would probably be the last time they'd ever see me. And then, after I stumbled unsteadily off the set thanking my guests at the same time, I ran into the staff kitchen and drank a pint of water all in one go. I was so hot and flustered I felt I was going to faint.

When I emerged from the kitchen I heard my name being called from down the corridor. It was Dan's unmistakeable booming voice. And I didn't turn around because I didn't want to receive a public firing in front of all the staff members at the station. I preferred to quit myself, and for it to be my own choice so I ran and ran and kept running all the way to the car park, ignoring his shouting. I got into my car. Fastened my seatbelt. Put my foot on the pedal. And drove all the way home, ignoring my phone which kept ringing and ringing and ringing. I arrived home, sweating profusely, ran upstairs to my bedroom and blindly threw a few bits of my belongings into a little carrier bag, stuffed the bag into the tiny boot of my car and then turned off my phone which was still ringing like crazy and started to drive. And I drove towards the M50 and then took the turning for Liffey Valley. But I didn't stop there. I kept driving and driving. I was heading for the West of Ireland. To a remote place where nobody would know who I was. Or where I was. I needed to get away. Escape. To figure out what I was going to do with the rest of my life. I couldn't face my mother's disappointed face or my sister's disapproving one. I couldn't bear the thought of answering my phone and having to put up with journalists asking me for a quick comment on my surprise TV outburst. I couldn't face getting a bollicking off my boss (knowing of course that he'd be livid and egged on by the not-so-lovely Eileen). Let him give my wretched show to Eileen now, I thought wearily. Considering she's so dying to step into my shoes.

I kept driving. It started to rain but that didn't matter. In less than four hours I was in Connemara. I am hoping everything will feel so much better over here. Maybe I can make sense of my life now I am away from all the pressure of the city.

I'll go for long uninterrupted walks, feel the light West of Ireland mist fall against my unmade-up face and have time to gather my thoughts with no cameras in my face. I am now unemployed, broke and nearly five months pregnant. But at least I feel free. Finally.

D x

26

29th April

Dear Molly,
I have fifty-nine missed calls on my phone. Fifty-nine! Oh. My. God. How can that be? I've had my phone switched off of course. I'm flummoxed by the amount of missed calls. Who would have known I was that popular? Only joking.

I needn't tell you that I didn't bother checking my voice mails. Fifty of those calls are probably from Dan telling me I'm fired. I don't need to be told fifty times that I'm now facing the dole queue. I already know. That's why I'm here. To get my head around things. To come to terms with the fact that I'm basically unemployable now. Who would want me? Really, who would want to hire me with my track record? Somebody who would go completely off the rails on live TV and carelessly throw away their career? I've been exposed as a cheat and a liar. I kept my pregnancy a secret from my bosses and also from the whole country. I pretended I knew all there was to know about dating and put myself up there on TV as some kind of dating queen who had all the answers to everything. I had lengthy chats with my production team, talking all about single parents without ever revealing to them that I was about to become one myself. They must think I'm the sneakiest individual ever.

And then, to make things worse I go on TV and tell the whole country I'm pregnant, subsequently making fools of my entire production team. And God only knows what my family think. They must be furious and mortified and even though deep down I know I should phone them and explain everything, I can't bring myself to do it because I don't even know what to say to them. I have absolutely no idea why I blurted out all that stuff on TV. But I do know that I've let myself and those closest to me down big time.

Molly, in case you're wondering where I am, I'm in Spiddal, Co Galway. Not in the village itself but about one kilometre outside it, about halfway up a small boreen in a tiny two-bed cottage where I have a heavenly unobstructed view of Galway Bay. On a clear crisp day like today I can see right across the ocean all the way over to the Clare Hills. I love this place. It's wilderness. From the top of the boreen I can feel like I'm on top of the world and see the waves crashing against the rocks in the distance. Nature thrives here in the wild. From where I'm standing there are no houses, cars or people. Just the faint smell of burning turf mixed with the smell of fresh dew.

I feel nobody can get to me up here. It's just me. Well, me and my precious bump. I'm sitting here on a rock, next to a bunch of purple heather, scribbling into my diary. I'm well wrapped up but the sun is on my face, and it feels amazing, and I take deep breaths to fill my lungs with the freshness of the air, a freshness that is so far removed from the polluted city-centre grime I left back in Dublin.

The little cottage where I'm staying belongs to my Great-Auntie, Noreen. She hasn't been well for some time, and she fell a while ago and broke her hip, God love her. She is currently staying in a nursing home up in Dublin where she's being well taken care of. When she initially went into the home she asked myself and Jayne, her two favourite grandnieces, to keep an eye on the cottage for her. But Jayne wouldn't dream of coming here for a peaceful break. She came down for one night a few months ago but found she was bored rigid. "There's no shops or anything around the place," she complained bitterly on her return. "Nothing to do."

But that's the beauty of it all. There really is nothing to do. Time stands still down here. And I've been meaning to visit, I really have. But with getting the TV show and being so busy writing my column for the magazine and throwing up all the time and feeling exhausted, I haven't managed to get down at all. Of course, now that I'm here I wonder why I didn't come sooner. Yes, it's a bit damp and dusty because nobody has been here for the duration of the winter, but the first thing I did when I arrived was light a little turf fire and open all the windows. Then I took a damp cloth and some bleach and completely scrubbed the place down. I took a short leisurely stroll up the boreen, collected some wild flowers that were growing randomly against the stone walls, and brought them back to the cottage and placed them in a vase. The cottage looks habitable again. And pristine clean. And cosy. And safe. Which is nice. I kind of wish I could stay here. Forever.

D xx

27

1st May

Hi, Molly, me again. A new me! I've just spent a lovely afternoon relaxing. I walked all the way to Spiddal Harbour and watched the fishermen working on their boats. The sun came out as if to welcome me here and glistened on the ocean, and everything looked fresh and summery and oh so promising. I gathered up some seaweed too that had been washed in by the earlier tide. I intend to make myself a genuine seaweed bath later to soak in – you know, you'd pay a fortune for that in a fancy salon like Jayne's!

I've decided to do my own beauty treatments from now on. Recession-style, now that I'm unemployed! On my way back to the cottage, as I sauntered along with the wind in my hair, I passed the most stunning grey Connemara pony I have ever seen. She had her head tilted out quizzically over the gate and I felt guilty for not having a nice lump of sugar or a juicy apple or something to give her. I patted her between the ears and vowed to myself that as soon as I'm no longer pregnant I'm going to take up horse riding again. I miss it. Really, there's nothing like cantering along a deserted beach with the wind in your hair to make you feel absolutely amazing – to feel that you can take on the whole world.

The crisp, unpolluted countryside air has done wonders for me already. I know I've only been here a few days now but already I feel like an entirely different person. I've had time to think about my options. I haven't got too many of those of course, but I do have some. I could live here. I could ask my Great-Aunt Noreen if she wouldn't mind me taking some time out here to gather my thoughts. Okay, I wouldn't have much money rolling around in my pockets but there's a little internet café in the craft village up the road where I could write my column. That's if I still have my column of course. Now that I'm pregnant it might not be appropriate any more for me to be writing about dating every month. I must go to the internet café and email my editor tomorrow to see what the story is. Or maybe I'll just carry on as normal, submitting my copy to her, and maybe she won't have the heart to ditch me. Fat chance, I reckon.

There's a little garden here at the side of the cottage. Of course it's terribly overgrown at the moment because it hasn't been tended to in a long, long time but I reckon if I managed to get the weeds down I could grow my own vegetables here. I could also book myself into a maternity hospital in Galway so I wouldn't have to go up to Dublin for my regular hospital visits. The more I think about it, the more I warm to the idea. I'll make a little organic life for myself down here. No drama here. Just peace.

Yes, that's what I'll do. I'll stay down here and find myself. I don't want to be in Dublin any more. I don't want people to recognise me and point and say, "There's yer one who used to be on the telly until she made a tit of herself and they fired her.' Why should I give the begrudgers their big day out? I'll stay here. By myself. I'm not hiding. No. It's not like that at all. I'm merely taking some time out to find myself, that's all.

Write later,

D x

28

2nd May

Molly, I woke up really early this morning. The people in the house behind this one have a cock that started yodelling at the ungodly hour of six thirty. So much for a bit of peace and quiet! At first I woke up in fright thinking it was my alarm clock and I was supposed to be somewhere. But then I realised to my intense satisfaction that I didn't have to get up. I had nowhere to go. Nobody would be looking for me. I don't have a job and I no longer live in the city. Oh, the joy of feeling free!

Of course at some stage I suppose I'll have to go back and face the turbulent music. I'll wait until all the furore dies down of course and then I'll go up and collect my stuff. A few tracksuits and a good rain mac is all I need really. I've no need for my city outfits down here. God, no. I'd look like a right fecking eejit up on the bog in my fake furs and Louboutins. No make-up or jewellery or anything for me now, thank you very much. I don't even really need moisturiser as the constant mist and drizzle they experience here is doing absolute wonders for my skin. It's as soft as a baby's.

I don't understand why more people don't choose to escape the rat race that is the city centre and come to live in the West of Ireland. There's no traffic here. Or queues. Or aggressive behaviour. Everything is very relaxed and laid back. They speak Irish in most of the shops but recognise that I'm not a Gaeilgeoir and therefore speak English to me.

I don't know what the locals think of me being down here to be honest. They must know I'm not a native of course and, because I'm on my own, and by the way I'm dressed, they probably know I'm not a tourist either. I don't go around with a bucket and spade dangling from my arms, and a camera draped around my neck. I don't stand in the main street holding a huge map of Ireland out in front of me, nor do I prop up the bar in any of the village pubs.

But they've a little library here which is great. It's just the cutest little building ever on the main street next to the public toilets, and I went in yesterday and borrowed a book. It's Marian Keyes' latest and I was thrilled to find it there. I'd completely forgotten to bring a book with me in the hurry to escape Dublin, but the West of Ireland is somewhere you just can't be without a good book to read by the turf fire in the evenings. I thought if I didn't find a good book I'd go mad. I'd half considered driving into Galway city to find an Easons bookshop. Unfortunately there's no proper bookshop in Spiddal and I refuse to buy a paper or turn on the TV to entertain myself. I simply don't want to know what's going on in the real world right now. I don't want to hear about recessions or NAMA or childcare cuts or falling house prices. I don't want to be drip-fed dreadful news about stabbings in Limerick or bad banks and the greedy developers that were loaned crazy amounts of money, or how many billions the Irish government owes. I just want to potter around Noreen's adorable, quaint little cottage, reading my book, writing to you, feeding the local stray cats and pondering on life in general.

It's less stressful down here, Molly. It's a million miles away from the constant strains of living in the capital. It's peaceful and mellow and –

Oh. My. God. What on earth is my mother doing standing outside the front door????

NIGHT-TIME

Molly, my mum has just gone to bed. I'm sure you're wondering what on earth is going on. Oh, the drama of it all! I still can't believe she drove all the way down here to find me. She says she's been frantic with worry since I left which I don't really understand because, I mean, I did text her as soon as I got here to say I was okay. I'm not a bad egg. I wouldn't deliberately scare my mother. I would never intentionally do anything to upset her. She says the whole country is looking for me. She was not joking, Molly. She said that I've been all over the news and how couldn't I have known?

And I said back to her that, yes, of course I was aware that there would be something said in the media about my sudden departure from my job, but wasn't the country in serious debt and was people losing their jobs not more important than me finding myself in the West of Ireland? I'd quit my job, big deal. People do the same thing every day. Okay, so maybe I should have departed the TV station in a more dignified manner, but the way she was describing the mass hysteria, you'd swear I'd gone on a major killing spree before I'd left the TV station!

Then she produced all the papers over the last few days and, Molly, I felt sick just looking at the amount of coverage that I'd been given. However, I think I was even more upset about the dodgy photos that accompanied the articles. People I know must have sent them anonymously into the newspapers. Cowards! And, I know this is terrible and makes me kind of vain, but I couldn't help but feel dismayed at how fat I looked in some of the photos. I mean, I'm not being funny but my face looks like Garfield in some of the pics. And my upper arms are huge. Jesus, I may be pregnant but the baby isn't growing in my arms. The Cookie Monster has finally caught up with me!

"They're saying all kinds of ridiculous things about you," said Mum, and you know, Molly, I did feel guilty then because I'd run away and left my family behind to deal with my mess. I shouldn't have. My family are the least media-savvy folk I know. "They even asked me how long you were pregnant!"

"And what did you say?" I asked, suddenly feeling nauseous. The room had started to spin around in circles. All my previous euphoric thoughts were slowly ebbing away . . .

She said she told the journalist that I was nothing of the sort. Molly, you should have heard the indignation in her voice! Apparently she even did an interview with the Evening Herald saying it was all nonsense, that I couldn't be pregnant because I wasn't even seeing anybody. And the newspaper, delighted with her quotes, sent a snapper round to the house. She showed me the newspaper cutting where she's standing outside the family home with her arms crossed defiantly. She even went and got her hair blow-dried for the photograph.

Jayne, of course, not wanting to miss out on all the excitement, got her photograph taken for The Star and gave a little interview saying how worried she was about me and that nobody knew whether I was even still in the country. She was pictured outside her salon with the salon's name clearly in the photo. Mum and herself thought it would be great publicity for the salon incidentally.

Then Mum turned to me and said, "Mind you, I'm not surprised that they all think you're pregnant, darling. You have got rather large!"

I just stared at her incredulously before bursting out "But I am pregnant, Mum! Jesus Christ, isn't it flipping obvious? The whole country knows now, everyone knows, and you and Jayne are the only people on earth who haven't accepted it yet. I knew you wouldn't understand. I knew you wouldn't be able to get your head around it all. I'm five months pregnant and I'm mortified about it and I don't know what I'm going to do about it. In four months' time I'm going to be a mother and my whole life is going to change forever. I'm sorry if I've disappointed you, Mum, but that's that."

And then Mum's face turned a ghostly shade of white and she finally shut up, found an old bottle of whiskey in Noreen's sideboard and retired to bed for the night.

Diana xx

29

3rd May

Dear Molly,
Mum left this morning, not having managed to persuade me to go back with her despite trying her very best. She said she had phoned Dad late last night to tell him that I was indeed pregnant and it hadn't been a kind of crazy hoax after all. Apparently my family genuinely thought I'd dreamed it all up in an attempt to boost ratings for my show.

I can't believe they actually think I'd be so sad as to do something like that. Do people really have that sort of impression of me? Even my own family? God, shoot me if I ever become that shallow. The show doesn't mean THAT much to me. Although I did enjoy it a lot and it was a wonderful experience, it is, or rather, was only one part of my life. Not my whole life. The TV thing is a job, that's all. I will never live for work. And certainly not now that I'm halfway towards finding myself.

Mum said that the family was prepared to support me no matter what and that I wasn't to run away again. "Feel the fear and do it anyway," she said solemnly.

"Do what?"

"I don't know," she said vaguely and then said she had to go back to Dublin. "They're all looking for you," she grumbled. "You can't stay here forever."

"Why not?" I said defiantly.

"They're looking for you at work. Dan, your producer, even called to the house."

"Probably to hand me my P45 personally," I said grimly. "How thoughtful."

"He said he needed you to contact him urgently."

I shrugged. "Nothing is ever that urgent. You realise that when you're down here in the West for a while. The tide comes in and out every day. Nothing can stop it. It stops for nobody. We can't control nature. Life goes on with or without us. None of us are irreplaceable."

"Yes, well, some of us have to be realistic. You can't stay here with no job and a baby on the way. You need to cop on. You're nearly thirty. It's time to face up to your responsibilities."

I still refused to back down. "I need time out. I was too stressed anyway back in Dublin. I couldn't cope with everything. Anyway I'm sure they've already replaced me on my TV slot –"

"Well, some girl called Eileen –"

I interrupted with a hollow laugh. "Oh, Eileen? Surprise, surprise. It didn't take her long, did it? Oh well. I suppose I more or less offered her my job on a plate the day I walked out. I was asking for it really. Anyway, I wouldn't go back even if they wanted me. I thought I'd love life on TV but it's not what I thought it would be. It seems glamorous but it's not. It's political and bitchy and it's all about ratings. And as a woman you only have a short shelf-life anyway. I'd rather get out before they boot me out."

"But you're only just in," my mother argued. "Why make it easy for them to get rid of you?"

On and on it went with neither of us getting anywhere until Mum eventually conceded defeat. Before she left she opened her handbag and handed me two crisp fifty-euro notes.

"I couldn't take those!" I shook my head, mortified. "I have a bit of money of my own saved."

"Yes, but with no money coming in, you'll find that what you have will soon run out. If you're trying to find yourself, you'll find yourself dead of starvation if you're not able to buy yourself groceries. The air may be nice and fresh down here but you can't live on it."

She had a point. I took the notes reluctantly from her, feeling bad for doing so. "Thanks, I'll pay it back."

"Just come back soon," she pleaded. "We miss you. Even the dogs miss you. Especially Gina."

I made a sad face. I missed little Gina too. I should have brought her down to Spiddal with me. She would have loved chasing the seagulls on the strand. "Okay, I'll think about it. I'll ring you in a couple of days to let you know how I'm getting on. But I need this. I need to be here. I'm afraid to go back."

"Feel the fear –"

"I know, I know. Okay then, well, drive carefully. Are you sure you wouldn't like to stay a couple of days?"

But Mum kind of shivered and shook her head. "I don't like this house," she said. "I never did."

We embraced really tightly. I felt her cling to me almost in desperation. Poor Mum. She's so protective of me even though she often has a hard time showing me affection. I think it's got something to do with the fact that her dad died in a car accident when she was little and her mother, Ita, had always been out working to provide a home. Mum had never really known the joy of having loving parents herself, so she was at a disadvantage when it came to showering her own kids with affection.

She got into her car and then she was gone. It was sort of sad watching her little green Ford Fiesta disappear down the drive. I know she meant well and her heart was in the right place. I know she thought she was doing the proper thing trying to save her eldest daughter from going off the rails. But she doesn't understand. I'm not on the brink of no return. I haven't suddenly gone and lost my marbles. I have to be here. I'm not sure exactly why but I just know that I do. It's weird.

And now it's just me again. Alone in Noreen's cottage. Well, me and Babser of course. I felt her kick earlier for the first time. I was so excited you wouldn't believe it. Up until now I've just been having tiny flutters. I think it's a she anyway. I don't know why. It's like I have a second sense or something. They say most mums just instinctively know anyway what they're having. But anyway not to jinx things I'll call the baby 'it' for the time being. So I felt 'it' kick anyway and almost died of excitement. I clutched my tummy and willed it to kick again but it wouldn't. At last it's beginning to feel real, Molly. I really am going to be a Mummy!

D x

30

4th May

Hi Molly,
It's me. Today is another perfect day. The sun is shining on Galway Bay and the sea is calm and a glorious turquoise colour. I took a walk up the boreen earlier and the air was intoxicating. It felt so good to be alive and alone with God's nature. I'm here over a week now. I'm not bored or anything. Far from it. I've actually totally embraced country living. I'm even contemplating going for a swim later on the main beach.

I haven't watched TV or read a paper or looked at the internet for days, apart from that one time I went to the internet café to send my column into the magazine the day after I got here. It's amazing how liberating it is not being a slave to technology. When I worked in TV I spent every minute of the day Googling stuff. I ended up wasting so much of my precious time reading random forums and nonsense. Like I told you, I even used to Google myself and then get all depressed when I stumbled across unfavourable reviews of the show. One day I even found some snide comments online about my appearance. People were discussing my weight and saying I'd got fat! I hope those same people feel guilty now that they know I'm pregnant and I'd a valid excuse for piling on the pounds.

I took a wander into the little craft village opposite the prom earlier. It's really cute, consisting of two rows of whitewashed bungalows and they make all kinds of stuff like bathroom candles and oils, and they make pottery and sell it there too. I thought it was all very inspiring. It made me think that I should start making my own jewellery or something and start selling it here. What an idyllic life it would be! Every day I could have my lunch in the little café/restaurant where the internet place is. They do a gorgeous carrot cake that melts in your mouth. In the afternoons I could paint landscapes. The colour of the sea and the Clare Hills seems to change on the hour. You'd never be short of inspiration living by the coast. Maybe I could also start collecting mussels and selling them in the Thursday market up in the village. Really, there's lots of things I could be doing here if I settled into village life. I could even keep hens and sell the eggs? The possibilities are simply endless.

Right, Molly, I'd better go. I've finished that Marian Keyes book and I need to bring it back to the library pronto.

D xxx

31

5th May

Dear Molly,
I'm in complete and utter shock. You are not going to believe this! I can hardly even believe it myself. It's such an amazing and bizarre coincidence. This morning, I went up to the attic to see if I could find some paintbrushes. You see, the paint on the outside walls of the cottage is beginning to peel badly and I thought it would be nice to spruce them up. I found an unopened tin of paint in a press under the sink but there were no paintbrushes to be found anywhere.

As a last resort I took the stairs up to the attic on the off-chance that I might find an unused one stored up there. The place was so dark and clouds of dust were swirling around. So much so that I was thinking I was very lucky I wasn't asthmatic or anything. When I was up there and my eyes became accustomed to the poor lighting I completely forgot about the brushes. You see, I stumbled across some photo albums full of old black and white photos. There were pictures of three young girls on the beach right here in Spiddal in those funny old-fashioned swimsuits and swimming caps with flowers on them. I recognised two of the girls vaguely – my granny and my Great-Aunt Noreen, I think, but I didn't recognise the other girl who was with them. She seemed to be a bit younger. She had the prettiest little face I had ever seen. She looked like a little fairy and bizarrely she looked quite familiar to me.

She was in all the family photos which I thought was odd. After all, my granny, Ita, only had one sister and that was Noreen. Maybe the other girl was a neighbour or a friend? But then again there was a striking resemblance between the third girl and my aunt and Granny. Puzzled, I kept sifting though the photos. Some were very faded but I could clearly make out the faces of the people in them. Those photos just screamed fun. Playing with sandcastles. Splashing each other in the sea. Standing on the rocks, hands on hips, big wide toothy smiles – there was also a mongrel dog in that photo with a ball in his mouth. There were literally hundreds of photos. Somebody in my family must have been a keen photographer. Maybe my grandfather? My mum would love these, I thought. They were wonderful keepsakes. I wondered if Auntie Noreen had forgotten about them. With her bad hip in recent years I doubted very much she would have been up in the attic. I decided I was going to bring the photos back to Dublin and show them to her. Maybe I could even get a couple of them framed as Christmas presents. And then, as I turned one of the photos over, I noticed some faint writing at the back.

It read: Noreen, Ita and Molly Jones – Summer '57

And my heart just lurched. Because that girl's name was Molly, just like you. Isn't that just such a mad coincidence? And I felt like I knew her. I couldn't take my eyes off her image. How could I possibly have known that girl? I couldn't have. The photos were so old. But the eyes seemed like they were looking into my own eyes. And I wanted to know more. My heart was beginning to beat faster. Who was this Molly? She had the same surname as my grandmother and Noreen. Could she have been a cousin? Did she still live around here? Maybe I could go and visit her and research my family tree or something? That's something I'd never had the time to do in Dublin. Maybe this was the perfect opportunity?

But then, Molly, I went on to another album where the girls were a bit older. And there was my granny and Noreen but there was no sign of Molly. There were photos of them in their school uniforms, and photos of them in Galway city, and then there were photos of them all at a big family wedding. But Molly wasn't in any more photos and a strange feeling washed over me. Something wasn't right, I thought. What had happened to Molly? Had she passed away or something terrible like that? I just had to find out.

I searched through more and more albums. But I came up with nothing. Poor Molly seemed to have just disappeared off the face of the earth. It was as if she'd just been erased from existence. I continued my search though the attic. There were bundles of old moth-eaten, damp-smelling clothes. There were armless dolls and one-eyed teddies. And then there were old books with pages torn off them. And a diary.

Now, Molly, this certainly piqued my interest. It was a diary with a little padlock on it but there was no sign of a key. It was faded pink so I knew it must have belonged to a girl but there was no name on it. Only the year: 1960. I took it down from the attic and brought it into the kitchen where I wiped it clean with water and some kitchen roll. My heart was racing as I took a kitchen knife and prised open the lock. It almost disintegrated it was so old and rusty. It was as if I knew that I was about to stumble upon something incredible.

I felt a jolt of surprise when I read inside the flap: 'Private – Molly's Diary'.

And still in shock, I somehow managed to retain my composure and, sitting at the kitchen table, read the first, delicate yellowing page.

> Dear Diary, today is my fifteenth birthday. I feel all grown up. I'm almost an adult now. You can get married at sixteen, you know.
>
> You are a present from my sisters, Ita and Noreen, and I'm going to treasure you for the rest of my life. I am so pleased I've got somebody to write to even if you're not real. Sometimes it's hard to talk to real people. They don't want to listen. People only want to talk about themselves. It's difficult being a teenager and being the youngest. Is the youngest person in every family ignored or is it just me?

My heart beating faster I read on and on.

> Dear Diary, I met this boy. He is gorgeous. He looks like a film star and his name is Tommy. He is one and a bit years older than me. He asked me to to meet him at the school dance. All my friends were jealous because he's tall, dark and handsome. I hope he becomes my boyfriend even though Dad says we're not allowed have boyfriends until we are eighteen. I don't want to annoy my father. If I

annoy him he'll drink too much and hit Mammy. And then I'll start crying like a baby again because I'll think it's all my fault.

I flicked the page.

Dear Diary, Tommy and I got together, we had our first kiss. Up at the harbour. Behind the fishing boats. So romantic, under the moonlight, just like in the films. It was even better than I thought it would be. I've been practising kissing my pillow for the last couple of years but the real thing is so much better. I wonder if he loves me.

I kept going, gripped.

Dear Diary, Tommy and I met up at the harbour once it got dark . . . He tried putting his hand up my jumper. I said he could feel outside my bra, but not inside it . . . after a while I made him stop. I didn't want to but I was scared somebody would see us. Dad is in bad form these days and if he knew I had a boyfriend he would make all our lives hell.

On and on I read.

Dear Diary, I am mad as a brush about Tommy. My sisters don't think he's good enough for me though. Ita says he's a player. She says she's heard things about him, like he went all the way with a girl who lives about a mile out the road. I asked him about it and he said it wasn't true, that he'd only do it with somebody he loved. He said he was waiting for the right person. Somebody like me.

An hour later and I was still reading.

Dear Diary, we finally did it. Tommy's parents went to Dublin for a funeral and we did it in their bed with the lights off. I was so nervous but it didn't hurt half as much as I thought it would. Tommy told me how much he loved me afterwards and promised that we'd be together forever. I think the experience has brought us so much closer. I think I am the happiest girl in the world right now!

Oh. God.

Dear Diary, I missed my period. I'm so worried. I feel sick to my stomach. I can't concentrate in the classroom and the teacher keeps giving out to me. What if, no, it's too terrible even to contemplate. I'll just have to pray very hard that I'm just late. I'm going to promise God that I'll never have sex again until I'm married. My mother would murder me if I came home and told her I was pregnant. That's if Daddy didn't murder me first. I keep thinking about Maggie O'Reilly from the class ahead of me in school and the rumours that were going around about her and everyone whispering, and then she just disappeared.

Molly, I couldn't stop reading. I couldn't find out fast enough what was going to happen. I turned the page quickly.

Dear Diary, I saw Tommy at Mass earlier on today. He was with his parents and completely ignored me. I kept looking over at him but he was buried in his Mass leaflet. He just wouldn't catch my eye. It hurt so much that he wouldn't even acknowledge me. I don't understand. What has changed? He said that he loved me so much that words couldn't even describe it. He said we'd be together forever so why wouldn't he catch my eye today? Why am I so alone and desperate?

I was crying by this time, Molly. Like the pain was my own.

Dear Diary, my tummy is so swollen now. My breasts have gone up a size too and I can't fit into my older sister's bras anymore. None of my clothes fit, including my school uniform. I'm absolutely terrified and I'm nauseous all the time. I called to Tommy's house this afternoon and asked for him. I was shaking when I spoke and his father said he wasn't there but I know that he was. I could feel his eyes on me, peering through the curtains as I walked away from the house. I know his sisters and everyone were watching me too. They were all watching.

I carry a big plastic bag around with me all the time to get sick into. What's going to happen to me? I didn't do this all by myself. I'm so tired all the time and I'm miserable and very scared. Who can save me now?

Molly! It felt like I was reading about myself. It was freaky. The words and sentences sent shiver after shiver down my spine. It was getting dark now so I took the diary up to my bedroom, turned on the light and got into bed. I hadn't eaten a thing for hours. I wasn't even hungry.

Dear Diary, the priest called up to the house today to have a chat with me at my mother's request. There was a lot of talk about avoiding shame and penance and things like that. Father Patrick has arranged for me to go to Dublin on Monday. Apparently he has made arrangements for lots of girls like me before. He even made the arrangements for Maggie, the girl ahead of me in school who nobody ever heard of again. Tommy's parents are sending him to stay with his cousins in Limerick until all the fuss dies down. I've been told not to contact him again or tell anybody, especially my sisters. It's for the best, say Mammy and the priest.

At this stage I couldn't fight the tears back any more.

Dear Diary, tomorrow the nuns are going to meet me off the train in Dublin. I'm to carry a cardboard sign with my name on it so that they'll know it's me. I've never been to Dublin but some of the girls in school have been up on shopping trips and say it's great. The travel arrangements have all been sorted. I've told my sisters I'm leaving home even though I was told not to speak to them by Father Patrick and my parents in case I corrupted them too. But I thought it would be mean for me to go without saying goodbye. They won't stop crying now. They say I won't be back, like Maggie. I'm trying to keep my chin up but deep down I'm terrified.

And then it just stopped. Suddenly. There were no more diary entries. It's as if lovely little Molly had just vanished.

Diana

32

7th May

Molly, the maddest thing ever happened to me today. There I was sitting out on the patio enjoying a bit of sun on my face when I heard the sound of a car coming up the drive. My heart gave a little lurch because I honestly wasn't expecting anyone and it's pretty secluded here – the cottage is surrounded by fir trees. For a fleeting second I was worried and then I was amazed to see a spanking new Mercedes convertible coming up the drive.

I peered through the sunlight to see who the driver was. At first it was hard to make him out behind the wheel as he was wearing sunglasses but then I realised to my horror that it was my former boss, Dan. Can you believe it? Oh God, I thought, what on earth was he doing here? How in the hell had he managed to track me down? My mother must have gone and told him where I was. But why? Why did she have to do that? I felt like I'd been turned in!

Then it suddenly dawned on me that I looked a complete and utter state. I realised I was wearing no make-up and I hadn't washed my hair in three whole days and that I really did look like a Wild Woman of the West. At least I was wearing tights though so he couldn't see my hairy legs. That was something.

Seriously though, to say I was completely stunned to see Dan is an understatement. He had a newspaper in his hand and he was waving it in the air as he got out of the car, and I immediately thought, Oh no, what have I done now? Surely there must be somebody more interesting for the journalists to be writing about. Isn't there a famous movie star in town or anything? I can't believe the press are still interested in me.

"Hi, Dan," I said sheepishly.

Why had he come? Surely he knew by now that I hadn't been abducted but had left Dublin out of choice? I hadn't done anything illegal.

"Diana, you've had us all worried sick!" he said before throwing his arms around me in a really dramatic way, like we were in a film or something.

The wild gesture took me completely by surprise. I mean, I know he works in telly and everything, but please! At this stage I was really beginning to panic. Couldn't he just accept that I had moved on with my life? Mind you, he did look kind of hot in a crisp white shirt unbuttoned at the neck and his sunglasses on top of his head, and I can't say I wasn't a tiny bit flattered that he had driven all the way across the country to try and locate me. No man had ever done anything like that before.

"I'm fine," I said, trying my best to stay cool as we sat down. "I don't want a huge fuss made or anything. I need to be by myself to deal with my pregnancy and stuff. I know I've let everybody down and I'm sorry, I really am sorry but everything just got to me."

"Have you seen this? The front page?" He held up the paper but it was all rolled up so I couldn't actually see what was on the front page. A wave of panic then washed over me. Jesus, I thought, it must be pretty bad if he's driven all this way to show it to me in person.

"I left a message on your phone," he said, squinting in the sunlight.

"I don't check my messages," I said sombrely. "Not any more. Hey, would you like a tea or coffee? I'm out of milk, I'm afraid."

"Not just yet, thanks." His face was dead-pan.

"Okay." I folded my arms over my bump. "So what have I done now? Go on, tell me. It never ends, does it?"

"What never ends?"

"The press intrusion. No wonder I had to escape town."

And then he kind of frowned at me and gave a sigh. "It's not about you," he said. "Everything isn't always about you."

He sounded a bit weary then and I felt embarrassed for jumping to conclusions and thinking that everything was all about me and that the press had nothing better to write about – and for having airs about myself and being delusional, thinking I was as big as Madonna or somebody when the likelihood was that probably nobody cared.

Dan unrolled the paper and I stared at the front page but nothing seemed to sink in. It was a big picture of an old woman and a middle-aged man and they were both smiling and then, Oh God, it sank in. That was the woman I'd interviewed on the show on my final day of working.

"It's her, isn't it?" I said, genuinely gobsmacked.

Dan nodded and said it was Peggy and that an Irish-American tourist who happened to be over from Boston on holidays saw the show and it turned out he actually worked with Peggy's son Peter and that Peter had been talking about looking for his mother for a very long time and had got in touch with the show.

"It's a really big feel-good story with a happy ending,"

said Dan. "Everybody's talking about it. We want to have both of them on air so it would be great if you could come back and interview them."

I was so shocked. He wanted me back after all that had happened? Even after I had walked out and left them all in the lurch and been on the verge of a nervous breakdown?

I said the first thing that came into my head. "Sorry, Dan, excuse me for a minute. I need to go to the bathroom."

I've discovered that peeing on the half-hour is an occupational hazard that comes with being pregnant. You just are bursting the whole time. Even during the night you're up every couple of hours, desperate for the bathroom. It's a terrible nuisance.

He nodded and I scuttled off. When I was in the bathroom, with my head buzzing with thoughts, I knew I had to come up with an answer straight away. This was a chance for me to get back into the game. I'd been handed a lifeline. It would be rude and so ungrateful to turn it down flat. I was Dan's wild card.

I took a deep breath and struggled to maintain composure. Deep down I knew this was a golden opportunity to correct my errors. But did I really want to go back on TV looking like the beached whale I had recently become? Surely I'd be the laughing-stock of the country! I just didn't know what to do.

I washed my hands, emerged from the bathroom, and offered Dan a cuppa once again.

He said he'd have a black coffee but insisted that he needed to get back on the road soon. I was left in no doubt that he was impatient to get going and didn't want to hang around wasting time chit-chatting. It also made me feel quite important that he'd driven all the way just to see me when his time was so precious. I made the coffee quickly, considering my next move.

"I'll be very honest with you, Dan," I said as I handed him the coffee, looking him straight in the eye. "I'm pregnant. I'm single. My confidence isn't exactly at an all-time high. I can't wear skimpy dresses and pretend on camera that my life is fabulous and that I'm part of the dating scene when I'm so clearly not."

Dan nodded slowly. "I know all that. That's why we want you back. You're a real woman. You are normal and you're funny and bright. The viewers love you. They identify with you. Single mothers will especially identify with you now. In fact they already have. We've been inundated with calls and emails from viewers wanting to know when you're coming back."

I was stunned, Molly, I really was. I didn't think anybody even liked me, never mind loved me! All this time I've been hiding away, mortified, thinking everyone despised me when all along people genuinely liked me.

"Are you, serious, Dan? I'm really chuffed. I can't tell you how much. So I wouldn't have to talk about dating and relationships all the time if I returned to my old position?"

He shook his head. "No. It will be a completely different format. New set and everything. Of course we'll use dating as a subject every now and again because love is always a popular subject, but we won't limit you to matters of the heart."

He had a twinkle in his eye when he said that and I felt a huge sigh of relief wash over me. I felt as if I'd been offered an unexpected Get Out of Jail card that I didn't really deserve.

Fighting back the tears, I impulsively threw my arms around him and gave him a hug. "Thanks for giving me another chance."

"No worries," he replied, squeezing me back gently even though it was difficult with my growing bump in between us. "Welcome back, hun."

And then he was gone. And I spent ages just sitting on the patio outside the cottage on a rickety old deckchair looking over to the Clare Hills which were hardly visible now as they were shrouded in mist and it felt like I was dreaming. I'm back in the game, I told myself over and over. I really am back!

Di xxx

33

9th May

Dear Molly,
I'm so exhausted. I returned home this evening and the first thing my mum said was, "Oh, you're back," almost as if my re-appearance was somewhat of an inconvenience. I was quite upset about it to be honest. Now I know my mum isn't the most affectionate person in the world, but she could have at least pretended to be pleased to see me especially since she'd made such an effort to try and persuade me to come home in the first place. At least Gina the little spaniel gave a grateful bark when I walked through the front door. Ruby ignored me.

Maybe it's just my changing hormones but I seem to burst into tears any time I've got the tiniest excuse. I haven't been like this since I was a toddler but now the taps are always ready to be turned on. Whenever. Wherever. Another hazard of pregnancy. I can't even watch the news now without bawling if I hear about a fatal car crash or a house fire. Why doesn't anybody warn you about how emotional you become during pregnancy? Why don't people prepare you for being a blubbing wreck for the entire nine months? No wonder men don't carry babies! The whole population would probably come to a complete halt if they did!

Anyway, I arrived back home unannounced and Mum proceeded to work herself into an unnecessary tizzy because since I've been away she has been using my room as a makeshift laundry room and she had left a huge pile of ironing on my bed. Dad was in the TV room by the fire, watching some antiques show which he seemed fascinated by, but at least he had the good grace to say it was nice to see me. Jayne barely greeted me because she was rushing out the door in a cloud of Poison perfume to meet her boyfriend, but she still managed to make some sarky comment about me being a drama queen and that I'd had the whole country out looking for me. I think that's a bit of an unfair exaggeration to be honest with you. I mean, there was hardly a nationwide helicopter search for me. And the West of Ireland is hardly the outback of Australia.

I made myself a cup of tea, helped myself to a slice of apple tart I found in the fridge and brought the food up to my room. I removed the pile of newly washed bed-linen, put it on the floor and started unpacking.

I've hidden the diary that I found because I'm not sure if I've got my head around all that Molly stuff yet. It brought me so much sadness reading about that young girl who must be my great-aunt. It's one thing reading a work of fiction but this was real life. One thing's for sure, I need to know more. I need to know what happened to young Molly. Where did she go? Who helped her? What happened to the baby? I feel it's now my mission to find out.

D xx

34

11th May

Dear Molly,
Today I asked Mum about the other Molly. She kind of bristled and said that Granny's youngest sister had gone to work in England at a very young age and that had been that. She had never come back to Ireland and Granny and our Great-Auntie Noreen hadn't kept up contact with her.

"But I thought she went to Dublin?"

"She went to England after a bit in Dublin," she said vaguely.

"Whereabouts in England?" I asked but Mum appeared not to hear the question and continued her ironing.

I asked if Molly had been pregnant and Mum looked horrified and said, "Where did you hear that?" and then said that in those days it was very common for people to send their children over to England to work and that Molly would have been very well looked after because she'd been working for a Catholic priest, and she would have been well fed and everything and able to see the doctor free of charge if she ever became sick. The way my mother spoke about it made me reluctant to reveal anything more about the secret diary I found. However, I did ask her if Granny had ever spoken about Molly. Mum just shook her head firmly and said that I was being silly asking so many questions about something that had happened such a long time ago.

I decide to let it rest because I know that Mum and Granny had never really enjoyed a close mother-daughter relationship and the truth probably was that Mum didn't know very much about Molly herself.

I didn't want to upset her by dragging up the past. But I could not rid my memory of dear little Molly who went to England all those years ago. What had happened to her in Dublin with the nuns? What became of her baby? Was it a boy or a girl? Did she give it up for adoption or did the baby live with herself and the priest in England? Did I have an English uncle or aunt? So many questions and no answers to any of them. Yet.

My memories of Granny are still pretty vivid. She died when I was just twelve years old but I remember her being a very serious, austere kind of woman with pursed, proud lips. She was tall and stiff-looking and always had her hair pulled back severely into a bun and I remember once saying to her, "Granny, do you ever let your hair down?" and she said, "No, I don't, little girl. Not ever."

Little girl. That's what she used to call me. And not in a particularly affectionate way. I think what she meant was that she never let her guard down, and indeed she always seemed cold and secretive to me. It seemed to me that she was devoid of love. She only had one daughter and that was Mum. I think the reason Mum is quite aloof with me a lot of the time is because of her relationship with her own mother. She only ever hugs me in a crisis situation and would never dream of giving me a compliment just for the sake of it. I used to get upset about it but now I realise that it's not her own fault. It's probably because she just doesn't know how to be affectionate.

I remember being at the swimming pool one day and all the other kids were jumping into the pool going "Mummy, look at me!" and all the other mothers were wearing warm, adoring smiles on their faces and encouraging their kids to jump in. Whereas my mother was sitting on the same bench but with her head stuck in a book and no matter how many times I tried to get a nod of approval or a shout of "Well done", none was forthcoming.

In time I got used to it. There were no-shows at school plays and often she'd forget to collect me from piano lessons. It was almost as if she sometimes forgot she had a third child. She was even supposed to come to my graduation but then the day before the ceremony herself and Dad got last-minute flights to the States to visit my brother and passed on their regrets to me.

Mum said to me one day that she shouldn't have had any more children after Jayne because although she had managed to lose the baby fat after having both Tony and Jayne she'd never totally regained her figure after having me. She's had an eating disorder for as long as I can remember and as a result I think Jayne has too. Jayne's always recommending slimming treatments to Mum and vice versa. Their love of dieting kind of bonds them over black tea with sweetener.

When Granny died, Mum never even grieved. At least if she did, it wasn't any way apparent. I never met my grandfather who died when my mother was a baby. I once asked Mum what he was like and she said she didn't know. The reason I'm telling you all this, Molly, is so that you can try and understand my background a little. I hope you can make some kind of sense of it because I sure as heck never could.

Diana x

35

15th May

Oh Molly, I know it's been days since my last entry but I feel like my whole life has been turned upside down since I last wrote to you. First of all I went back to work and it wasn't at all as bad as I thought it would be. I've been in meetings all this week and then our first show on our new set will be broadcast next week.

Everyone was really nice and even though I would question the sincerity of my work colleagues, especially Eileen who must be furious to have me back on the scene, at least they all seemed pretty supportive to my face anyway.

I had a rendezvous with a brand-new stylist who then brought me into town to try on clothes for my new show and, guess what, I'm going to be allowed to keep them! Great PR for the shops and designers of course if I'm seen plodding about the town in their stuff. This is a huge relief. I mean, just the thought of having to spend lots of money on maternity gear was killing me so it's nice to know I'm going to get it for free. The downside is that all the clothes are awful. Of course I know we've come a long way since the days of the hideous dungarees our mothers wore when they were expecting us but the stuff that's around at the moment isn't exactly to die for either. And what's the story with flowers and hearts being on all maternity blouses? Yuck! Is there some kind of fashion conspiracy against expectant mums that I don't know about? It's not cheap either, especially when you're paying for something you know you'll never want to wear again once the sprog has arrived.

When I stripped down to my undies in the maternity shop, the stylist's eyes nearly popped out of her head when she saw how big my boobs were. Like, if you didn't know any better, you'd swear I'd undergone plastic surgery to make them this big. But although they're huge they're not very attractive. They've got lots of tiny but visible blue veins going through them and my nipples have doubled in size too. I need a great big supportive unsexy maternity bra to hold up my bust. As I said, ridiculously unsexy.

You're probably thinking it's so unfair. And, yes, it is rather unpleasant to have fat feet, horrific heartburn and bloated boobs and never-ending nausea all at the same time. But there are a few tiny positives to being up the duff. For instance, my hair is seriously glossy. Cheryl Cole better watch out. At least my hair is real. It's so lustrous and shiny that when I was in the hairdresser's during the week, she – shock, horror – even commented to me that my hair was in great condition. And she must have been telling the truth because normally hairdressers just bang on and on about your hair falling out because they're trying to sell you some expensive product they're going to earn commission on.

So the nice hair is a bonus. And my skin is quite nice too. Radiant, somebody described it as. It's the hormones, apparently, which keep your skin and hair in great shape. But then somebody else said that your hair falls out dramatically just days after you have the baby. Well, that's something to look forward to then. Along with sleepless nights and endless nappy changes with nobody to help me. Yippee.

Also I feel him or her kick on a regular basis now. It's so exciting to actually feel my baby move. It makes it all so real. That I'm actually going to have my very own baby.

Sometimes I wish I could phone Roger to tell him. I wish I could share all this with my unborn baby's father. I'd love him to put his hand on my stomach and feel the baby move too. Wishful thinking on my part – there's no chance of that ever happening.

I'm going to cut to the chase now, Molly, because you're probably wondering what I have to complain about. After all, the only thing I've told you in this diary entry is that I felt my baby, went to the hairdresser, got new clothes, received plenty of good wishes from my work colleagues etc. So I should be relatively happy. Right? Wrong. So wrong!

Two days ago was probably the worst day of my life. Seriously that's no small exaggeration. Even as I'm writing this I feel extremely jittery because writing down my feelings makes them frighteningly real, like I'm facing up to them and not blocking them out like I thought I'd be able to do.

I was in the hospital for my twenty-week scan which is the really important one. I should have done it over two weeks ago, of course, but my work crisis and sojourn in Galway made me forget. That's the one where they give you a photo of the foetus and it's absolutely petrifying. I had a nightmare the night before. I dreamed that I went in for my scan and they saw a kitten on the screen instead of a baby. I remember asking whether the kitten was a boy or a girl. In my dream I heard somebody say he was beautiful. But at least, I suppose, they didn't say he was the image of me. I was screaming silently but nobody could hear me. Where was my baby?

Who had taken him? Why were they covering it up? Had I been the victim of a massive baby scam?

I woke up drenched in a cold sweat. After that horrible nightmare the last thing I wanted was to go into the maternity hospital all alone. Suppose something was wrong with the baby? I needed emotional support. I needed the father to be there with me.

I tried to get back to sleep, difficult at the best of times when you're carrying something the size of a football in your belly.

I woke at eight and, taking a deep breath, with a shaking hand I rang Roger. The first thing he said to me was that he was already in work and that it wasn't a good time for him. I took another deep breath and then told him I was going in first thing to have my twenty-week scan and that I'd really appreciate if he came in with me as the child was half his. The silence at the other end of the phone was deafening. In fact it was so prolonged that I even wondered whether he had hung up on me.

"Hello?"

"I'm still here," he said darkly. "I can't come with you. I'm sorry."

I felt myself crumble but I wasn't going to show it. Instead I took a deep breath. "Okay, that's fine," I said. "Bye, Roger."

I put down the phone with a heavy heart, rubbed my hands over my tummy protectively as tears spilled down either side of my face. They kept rolling and soon I was in convulsions. I had never felt so desperate in my whole life. Was I only the person in the world who wanted this little life growing inside of me? Surely my child deserved both a mother and a father?

"I love you so much, darling," I sobbed to my swollen tummy. "And Mummy's going to be here for you, no matter what. I'm going to be strong for you and we'll be a little team. You and me against the big, bad world."

So I pulled on a hideous vomit-coloured maternity top that I'd picked up in a bargain bin somewhere and dragged my hair back into a tight bun. I got the bus into town wearing a beanie hat and a scarf. I didn't wear any make-up. I didn't want anyone to recognise me off the TV and, looking as awful as I did, they surely wouldn't.

When I went into the hospital I asked the porter at the door where I should go. He directed me up the stairs. I was almost shaking as I mounted the steps, my stomach feeling like it was wrapped up in knots. I felt jittery, uncomfortable and so emotional that I didn't want to wait around. The sooner it was all over and done with the better. The waiting room was kind of packed with mums-to-be and their partners, and on a table in the centre of the room were a few old dog-eared magazines, most of which I'd already read and didn't want to read again.

There were six couples, a black girl who looked really young, maybe about eighteen, and myself. I sat among the other people and just stared at the ground. I didn't want to catch the eyes of any of the couples holding hands when I was going through everything all by myself with nobody to hold my hand. I didn't want to see the excitement in their eyes nor did I want them to see the loneliness in mine.

What if something goes wrong, I wondered over and over again as I fidgeted furiously with my fingers. What if there's something wrong with the baby? There won't be anyone there to comfort me or to tell me that we'll get through all this together. Doesn't the baby's daddy even care? Doesn't he want to know whether it's a boy or a girl? How can he be so blasé about something as important as this?

I felt my tummy self-consciously, willing the handles on

the clock on the wall to move forward. People were slowly moving in and out of the waiting room as names were being called. It seemed that they would never call mine.

Then a nurse appeared at the door.

"Diana Kay?"

Everybody stared as I stood up. "That's me," I said with a brightness I certainly didn't feel, and followed her out of the room.

As we were walking down the corridor she said in what I thought was a very loud voice, "Are you here by yourself?"

She might as well have bellowed the question from a megaphone as far as I was concerned. I nodded, gulped and fought back the tears. I was sick of crying. There was no point in making a scene. I could do this by myself. I had to stay strong.

I followed her down the corridor as if in a trance. Half of me was dreading seeing the scan but half of me was a bit excited. Was it a boy or a girl? Should I ask or was that bad luck? How could I not know? I'd need to start buying a few things for the hospital overnight bag. In pink or blue. If I didn't know, I'd have to stick to yellow. Yellow is such a safe colour for a baby.

I'd seriously have to start thinking of baby names too. I'd been thinking recently that if I was having a baby girl I'd call her Victoria. I think it's a lovely feminine name. But then, when I said the name to a few people, some of them loved it and some of them hated it. And they were all pretty vocal with their opinions.

"Everyone will call her Vicky," somebody said. I never thought of that but it was true. My friend Vicky had been christened Victoria but she hated her full name. Thought it was stuffy and pretentious.

"Or Tori," said another.

"I don't like that name at all," said another friend, quite definitely. "Reminds me too much of Posh Spice. I can imagine her being delivered with a scowl on her face, wearing Gucci shoes."

After that, I resolved not to tell anybody my baby's name until I've actually chosen a name for definite. If you've already made up your mind nobody's going to say they hate it. But if you haven't made up your mind, and are still on the fence, then it seems that everyone will try and get you to change it. They'll say they went to school with a horrible girl with that name, or that was the name of their ex who was a total bitch. You just can't please everybody.

Anyway I walked down the corridor and was asked to wait outside another room for a few minutes. Then I was called into the little room and a kindly woman of around fifty introduced herself as the sonographer and asked me to lie on the bed and pull up my top. At least she didn't ask me if I was on my own or not.

I pulled up the hideous maternity smock and the sonographer smeared some of that sticky clear liquid all over my tummy. It felt really cold. I stared at the screen monitor beside me in nervous anticipation.

At first the vision was a bit blurry but then I could make out a head. I nearly fell off the trolley-bed in excitement. The sonographer also pointed out the hands – yes, there were two of them – and feet (ditto!). I even saw the spine.

"Is it a boy or a girl?" I asked in trepidation. At least there was only one baby in there anyway. Recently I'd been almost wondering if I was expecting twins because my tummy ballooned in size all of a sudden but, in hindsight, it was probably just the butter croissants – my most recent craving!! In an ideal world of course I would love twins. So handy to have a ready-made family and all that, but as a single mum with no man on the horizon I'm not sure how I'm even going to cope with one never mind two!

"It's hard to tell," said the kindly sonographer, peering at the screen through her glasses.

The baby was moving. I couldn't believe it. It was a real baby. A little human being. A tiny person. Inside of my body. And it was mine! I suddenly became overwhelmed with joy.

"It's a boy," she said suddenly but in a very definite tone of voice.

I felt my heart give a little leap. "Are you sure?"

She pointed to the screen. "There. That's the scrotum."

I couldn't see anything. "It's really a boy?"

"Well, you can never be one hundred per cent accurate," she said.

But girls don't have scrotums, I thought.

That's mad. I'd been pretty sure I was going to have a girl. The sonographer printed out a couple of pictures but to be honest they were a bit blurry. You couldn't make out his facial features or anything. I wouldn't be scanning them and posting them up on Facebook for sure. Not that I'd do that anyway. It's too much. I was just delighted to have them for myself. It was living proof that I wasn't just a fatty!

"Everything seems fine," the sonographer said, giving me warm smile.

The relief that washed over me was enormous. My little baby, that little innocent life growing inside me, was going to be okay. He had the right number of feet and hands. I couldn't believe how lucky I was. It was up to me to look after myself now. If I was stressed and unhappy the baby might be able to feel it. He had to be given every fighting chance.

I sent God a quick message of silent thanks and then rubbed all the sticky goo off my belly with tissue paper.

Before I left I also got to hear my little son's heartbeat. It sounded like a train! I wanted to rush out and buy my own stethoscope so I could listen to his breathing forever. I was so in love with my little man and I hadn't even met him yet.

Once outside on the street, I was dying to tell somebody about the scan. I rang Vicky but her phone was off so I tried Selina instead.

"I'm having a boy," I said enthusiastically. Bursting with undisguised pride.

"Who's this?" she answered suspiciously.

"It's Diana." Who did she think it was? "I've had my twenty-week scan and it's a boy."

"Wow! Sorry, your number came up as private there for some reason. A boy! I couldn't imagine you with a little boy."

"Me neither," I agreed. "I'd convinced myself I was having a girl!"

"So what did it look like?"

"It looked like a baby. A real baby!" I said excitedly.

"Listen, I have to go, I'm in work," she said in a hushed tone, "but let's go out to tomorrow night. You, me and Vicky. The champagne's on me."

I reminded her I was pregnant.

"Well, one glass won't kill you. My sister had a glass of cider every evening when she was pregnant and her husband is a doctor."

"Oh. Well, maybe one glass then."

I suppose she's right. One glass can't do much harm. Mind you, I think I need a stiff drink after what I experienced next. Even as I'm writing this I can't even believe it actually happened. I mean, I still think I might just be having a very bad dream that I'll still hopefully emerge unscathed from.

There I was, standing out on the street after my phone call to Selina wondering who I should phone next. I knew Jayne would be in work so I phoned Mum and told her it was going to be a boy.

"I hope he's a good boy," she said. "My school-friend Maura had three boys and they were all quite bold in my opinion. They never stopped whingeing."

Jesus, could she not just be happy for me?

"But Tony was good as a baby, wasn't he?" I said.

"Well, he was a bit of a handful."

And just as I was about to reply, I saw him. Him. Yes. I could hardly believe my own eyes. It was Roger. No mistake about it. He turned the corner and he was talking on his mobile phone. For just a few seconds time stood still. I was rooted to the spot.

He seemed distracted and didn't notice me at first. My heart just melted with joy. He looked so well. Very handsome and clean-cut, wearing a navy suit and a pale blue shirt with a silver tie. He looked tanned and healthy as though he'd just returned from a few days in the sun. I told Mum I had to go because I'd just spotted Roger. She sounded surprised. Almost as surprised as I felt. I had to cut her off though.

I couldn't believe he had come after all that had happened. But just seeing him made me want to forgive him everything. I could forget the past if only to keep my baby's daddy in my future.

But that feeling of elation was to be short-lived. Roger looked up and caught my eye and the colour literally drained from his face. He approached me as if in slow motion.

"What are you doing here?" I heard him ask.

I felt bewildered. What was I doing? Was he serious? The world seemed to start spinning. Didn't he know exactly what I was doing? Hadn't I told him I was coming to the hospital for my twenty-week scan? Isn't that why he was here? He was late of course, very late, but better late than never.

"I thought you'd be gone home by now," he continued, looking at his watch.

And I just stared at him, dazed. None of this made sense. None of it. What was he doing here if he hadn't come to see me, and in any case why would he deliberately try and avoid bumping into me? Why? We were going to have a son together. A darling baby boy. We were bringing an innocent life into the world. It was a miracle.

I looked up at him and, with all my strength, mustered a faint smile. I rubbed my tummy lightly with the palm of my hand and said, "Don't you want to know what it is?"

"Don't. Please, don't, not now," he said.

"Don't what?"

He started to walk away from me. I stared at his retreating back in complete disbelief. "Where are you going?" I said, raising my voice, feeling self-conscious and vulnerable.

"I'll explain later," he said, shuffling off.

But I wasn't being fobbed off just like that. I could feel myself becoming hysterical. Had he come to support me and then got cold feet and changed his mind? I followed him and still I didn't understand what on earth was going on. But I had to find out. He hurried away but I caught up with him. He entered the maternity hospital. I couldn't understand why.

Then he turned around and snapped, "Will you please stop following me? You're making a fool out of yourself."

And the look in his eyes scared me. I swear I could see hatred in his eyes. Sheer naked contempt for me. As if I was an unbearable thorn in his side that he just couldn't extract. And I didn't get it. Because I'd never done anything mean to him in my life. My only crime had been to fall madly in love with him when he didn't want me to.

"Why are you behaving like this?" I asked him, and

despite myself my eyes filled with wretched tears. And then, like a character from a bad, unsettling dream, SHE came around the corner.

"What's been keeping you?" SHE snapped at the father of my child, before noticing me standing a few feet away, my hand protectively on my tummy. The teenage girlfriend's jaw dropped as we both looked at each other in absolute shock.

"What are YOU doing here?" she asked me then, her voice a mixture of indignation, rage and disbelief.

I could hardly believe my eyes. Roger's teenage girlfriend stood in front of me as the rest of the world suddenly spun on its axis. She still had the same pinched face that I remembered her having the first time I ever saw her in a nightclub possessively clinging onto Roger's hand and looking smugly over at me at every opportunity. The only difference now was that today she wasn't as skinny as I remembered her. Actually that's a bit of an understatement. She was a lot bigger, especially around the tummy area. I'd say she was at least four months gone. A month behind me, maybe.

Diana

36

18th May

Hiya Molly,
I always thought it would be more fun to have a baby girl because I'm girly and feminine and love the colour pink. But some of the baby-boy clothes in the shops are really cute too. Most newborn clothes are dotted with smiley teddies and cute bunnies and rainbows. Then I noticed from about nine months onwards, they feature cars and JCBs and Bob the Builder and stuff on the front of them. God, little boys really grow up so fast!

I've bought a lot of blue and some yellow stuff too. Jayne says it's extremely unlucky to be buying baby stuff before the baby is born but I'm not superstitious like she is. Jayne is the type of person who would never walk under a ladder, refuses to work on Friday 13th and would never drive a green car.

The way I look at it, though, is that I'm not tempting fate, I'm merely trying to be practical and prepared. I haven't gone so far as packing the hospital bag though. Mind you, I'm going to try and organise that soon although it must be weird packing clothes for a little person who hasn't even been born yet.

By the way, I started back live on air again this morning. I'm glad that I had a few days to calm myself down and get my act together before I faced the live camera again. The show was a huge success because we had that lovely lady, Peggy, back in again with her son whom she hadn't seen since he was a baby. I felt like Oprah. I wanted to ask Peggy so many questions, so after the end of the show I asked her if I could take her number and whether she would meet me for lunch or even coffee. I'd hoped she wouldn't think I was a weirdo for asking. But to my relief she said that it would be very nice indeed.

There was a lot of media interest in today's show and a couple of photographers came out to take pictures of myself with Peggy and Peter and then some photos of me on my own. My boss thought it was a great way to announce to the world that I was back. He's always looking for publicity for the station. Media whore. Incidentally, what's the name for a male whore?

Of course it's great now that I don't have to hide my bump and pretend any more. Also, people no longer find it that strange when they see me wandering around with a plastic bag constantly at the ready. At first I was, admittedly, afraid people would ask me who the father-to-be was, but luckily nobody has so far. I'd say people wonder all the same. I'd say they presume it was just a one-night stand and they're gossiping freely behind my back.

Or maybe the general consensus is that I went to a sperm bank or something. Or whatever. Ha, ha, I don't even know if they HAVE such a thing in Ireland. But the funny thing is that I don't particularly care what anybody thinks any more. I really don't. Because I need a job and I need money and this is something I can do, and something that I'm good at. I have a baby on the way to support now which is more important than the opinions of people I don't even know. A little life is growing inside me that's going to develop and burst into the world and need his mummy to look after him. Because God knows his dad has so far proved he has no intention of doing that.

D x

37

20th May

Molly, I sent Roger an email and told him that we were expecting a boy. He didn't reply for three whole days and then he sent a brief email with an abrupt question, "When are you due?"

That was two whole days ago and I still haven't replied because I don't know why he has asked me that question. Is it because he wants to be at the hospital with me, or because he wants at all costs to avoid being at the hospital on the day to avoid a scene as mortifying as the last one? Maybe his new girlfriend is thinking of changing maternity hospitals altogether so we don't end up on the same ward on the same day. That would be just too embarrassing for everybody, wouldn't it? To be honest I'd be delighted if she went somewhere else. Like to the moon.

Imagine if her baby came a bit early and she ended up in the same ward as me, surrounded by her family and friends, and Roger was also sitting there, proud as punch, with a big bunch of flowers on his lap and I was lying across the way with my baby and no man and no flowers.

I still haven't told anybody that the father of my child is actually expecting two babies at the same time. It would feel weird telling people that, you know, because they would probably automatically think I was expecting twins and then I'd have to explain the whole sorry saga to them. This is one nightmare that just doesn't seem to end.

The one I'm dreading breaking the news to the most is my mum, to be honest, because deep down I've a horrible sinking feeling that she thinks Roger and I will end up getting back together by some miracle and that we'll get married and live happily ever after. As if there'd even be a remote chance in hell of that happening!

Dad, on the other hand, doesn't want us to get married. Anything but, in fact. He said it to me when Mum was out shopping the other day. He can hardly bear to hear the sound of Roger's name. I'd already guessed that my father didn't rate him very highly. In fact I can see Dad visibly wince whenever Mum mentions his name and it pains me. I always meant Dad to be so proud of me and I hate to think that I've let him down now.

If Dad had his way I'd say he'd probably banish Roger and all memory of him to the very ends of the earth. He was there the day I came home after my scan, the same day I met my ex and love rival at the hospital. He witnessed me collapsing in the hallway afterwards. He was the one who picked me up as I lay there howling like an injured animal when the horror of what had just happened to me finally sank in. He saw me writhing around the carpet clutching my tummy, the tears streaming down both cheeks, convinced that my heart was going to break in half. It was my darkest hour. I don't think they come much darker to be honest. And only for the fact that I'd looked up and seen the misery in my poor father's face and knew that I had to pull myself together, I don't know how I'd have got through that evening. My father's a living saint.

I told him about the scan and how I'd had to go in by myself because Roger wouldn't accompany me. He gave me a hug and said everything was going to be okay and that it was great news that I was going to have a boy. He said my baby would be like his second son and he couldn't wait to teach him how to play golf. Jayne and Mum were out late-night shopping, unaware of the entire ordeal, and Dad and I later watched some football game in front of the fire, sipping tea and nibbling on fruitcake. It was the closest I'd ever felt to him, but I also felt he'd aged ten years that evening. And it was all my fault.

Of course I didn't have the heart to tell him about Roger's other pregnant woman because I didn't want to risk him having an on-the-spot heart attack. I decided to keep that particular tragic detail all to myself. And not tell anybody how she had almost swung at me when she discovered I was pregnant.

In fact I vowed never to tell anybody how my love rival had started roaring and screaming at Roger in the middle of the hospital car park like a deranged fishwife who had lost the plot completely, nor how she had spat at my feet in disgust before I took a step back and threatened to call the police and report her for harassment. I won't tell anyone any of this because I don't think it fair to involve others in the miserable fiasco. I am in shreds, I am barely keeping it together, but everyone has their own worries to contend with. Especially Dad. In recent months he's lost a lot of bank shares on the stock market that he had been relying on as part of his pension. He doesn't talk about it but sometimes I see a fear in his eyes that I've never ever seen before. Dad was never a Flash Harry. He's always been sensible and on top of things, so why is he now being forced to share the pain of the economic crisis? He's never been unable to provide for himself and Mum. She doesn't even seem to notice how he's lost the spark he always used to have in his eye. But I've noticed. It's been gone quite a while. Now I have to figure out how I'm going to bear my own burden by myself without involving other people. Everyone has their own cross to carry.

D x

38

26th May

Dear Molly,
Sorry I haven't written in quite a bit. Work has been quite hectic, which is a good complaint really. When I'm busy I don't have time to wonder where it all went wrong and indulge in bouts of self-pity. But sometimes it can be stressful, like yesterday when we had a young mother on our show accompanied by her severely autistic son. It was really hard doing that interview but the mum was so surprisingly upbeat about everything. Meeting people like that is so inspiring. It also makes you feel selfish for moaning about your lot.

On the downside, I've also had to venture out to quite a few functions in the evening. I didn't miss any of that razzmatazz when I was holed up in my great-aunt's little remote cottage to be honest. Most of the so-called glitzy functions are quite boring really, especially when you're not drinking and feel you look like a whale standing beside other girls who have shown up in their teeny-weeny and sometimes see-through outfits, elbowing each other out of the way in an almost frantic bid to get their picture taken.

Sometimes I'm so wrecked after work all I want to do is crawl into bed and curl up under the warm duvet with a hot chocolate and a trashy magazine. The last thing I want to do is make small talk with people I don't know, hold a glass of acidic wine that I can't drink because even the mere smell of it would be enough to make me throw up, and stand in my high heels listening to a coma-inducing speech about a product I couldn't give a fig about.

Dan says it's good for me to get out and about, however, and have my picture taken at functions so that people don't forget about me. So even though I'm pregnant and would much rather watch Coronation Street with a box of chocolate biscuits, he still says I should make an appearance at one function a fortnight anyway to keep my face out there. It keeps me in tune with my public apparently but I'd beg to differ on that one. I don't think the, eh, public, makes much of a fuss over you when you're pictured out and about. After all, this is Ireland and it's not the type of place where anyone makes much of a fuss over anybody or anything. I was even at a film premiere with Bono once (I mean he was there too, not with me) and people were muttering, "There's your man from U2," as if he didn't have a name. We don't fawn over people in this country just because they're on telly or whatever. Which is good, I suppose.

Anyway, because it fairly kills me to stand around in high heels chit-chatting at these events, I just tend to pop in and out before the movie or fashion show or the dreaded speech starts. That's usually enough to keep the PR girls happy because they just want names at their functions to put on the press releases for the papers and magazines. They don't actually care if you stick around once you get your photo taken.

They don't always get it right though. I mean, I've been at

launches where the only person I recognise is myself, and then the next day I read in the paper that Colin Farrell and Liam Neeson apparently attended the same gig. And I'm like, am I going blind or something? They were not there.

Jayne can't understand why I sometimes moan about having to go out. She says she'd love that type of lifestyle. But I don't think she would really. It's just so false and meaningless. I'd rather have a nice bath and curl into bed reading Molly's diary again. You know, I think I've read it about twenty times at this stage. It humbles me over and over again. Makes me think that no matter how shit I think my own life is, she had it a hundred times worse.

BTW, I'm meeting Peggy tomorrow. I'm taking her to The Westbury Hotel for tea. I just want to chat a bit more to her about what really happened and why she didn't see her son for all those years. I'll keep you posted.

Diana x

39

27th May

Dear Molly,
The Other Woman is having a girl. I found out last night. You're probably wondering how in God's name I happened to stumble across this information but no, Roger didn't tell me, which of course would have been the polite thing to do.

The truth is that it was killing me not knowing so I went onto her Bebo page where she has a profile photo of herself and Roger cheek to cheek, and her Bebo skin was all childish with pink hearts and stuff on it. In her status update she had written 'Me n Rog havin grl, XXX'

In a weird way I felt relieved. If it was a girl there wouldn't be so much competition between the two children in later years. Roger may decide in the future that he has enough love for both of them. But for the moment he hasn't an ounce of love for me or our unborn child and I cannot understand it at all. Really I can't. I ask myself, day in, day out, what on earth I ever did for him to treat us like this.

So my baby is going to have a half-sister six weeks or so

after he is born. Really you couldn't make it up. It's like something out of an old episode of Dynasty. Stuff like this doesn't happen in real life to people, does it? Well, obviously it does, but it's all so surreal. Why can't I just be married to a normal bloke who is only expecting one baby at a time? A man who cherishes me and gives me foot massages when I'm tired and fetches me a sick bucket when I'm about to puke. Most pregnant women have loving partners like that, don't they?

I would honestly prefer Roger to be a callous bastard with no interest in women and children than to know that he's worshipping another woman in the same condition as me. I'm sure she's forgiven him by now for impregnating me in a moment of madness while we were still a couple. Sometimes I think it would be easier for me if Roger was gay or something, but the fact that he's playing happy families with another girl while I stare at the walls night after night, trapped in my own loneliness, wondering what on earth the future holds for us, just kills me.

She's even going semi-private, not public. Semi-private is for people who don't want to share a ward with the rest of the riff-raff. Like myself. At least that means we won't end up in opposite beds if she delivers ahead of time.

I'd love to be semi-private myself. In fact I'd like to go completely private and have my own private bathroom after I give birth and everything. But I'm not prepared to bankrupt myself for that privilege. Must remember to invest in several pairs of ear-plugs and pack them in my hospital bag though. If sharing a ward with several noisy newborns, I can expect to get zero sleep and more than likely I'll lose the will to go on.

Anyway I'm off to meet Peggy now. Chat later, xx

8.49 p.m.

Dear Molly,
I met Peggy earlier. She told me her whole story. It was so fascinating and completely shocking at the same time. Somebody should really write a book based on her life. She was sixteen when she got pregnant.

She was raped, Molly. Yes, raped! She told me herself. I nearly fell off the chair in horror when she told me. I asked her whatever happened to her rapist and she said she never saw him again after the party. The night she conceived. It was her first time to have a drink. And to have sex.

I asked if her son Peter had ever tried to locate his dad and Peggy shook her head and said that he had never tried, or even wanted to know him because he had abandoned him and hadn't been a father to him.

"Would you ever tell him the truth?" I asked, squeezing the dear lady's hand, trying to come to terms with what she must have gone through. Up until now I would have found it hard to believe that anybody had had it tougher than my poor Great-Auntie Molly. But no, here was somebody who had carried a much heavier cross. All by herself. Had she told anyone? Her mother, even?

Peggy looked horrified. "God, no, love, she would've killed me for taking a drink."

It was hard for me to get my head around it all. The woman gets drunk. The woman has sex. So does the man. Man gets off scot-free. Woman goes to prison. Sort of. To repent. For both of them.

"More or less," said Peggy, nodding, when I expressed my views to her.

"But that's outrageous, it's scandalous!" I said, pouring her another cup of tea.

She sighed. "Not much has changed. I mean, socially it's more acceptable now to be a single mother as you know, but there's still girls out there being sexually assaulted every day of the week. And they won't report it because they'd have to go to court and relive the nightmare. And sometimes when you're intoxicated you –"

I waited for her to continue.

She took a sip of her tea, then put down her cup and said, "Sometimes when you've had too much to drink you don't remember."

"But YOU remember?"

"Yes, I do. Like it was yesterday. He patted my head and said 'Good girl' afterwards as I wiped myself clean and then got dressed and walked home in the dark all by myself, crying. I never saw him again."

I was so stunned by her revelation that I was flummoxed. Imagine going through something like that all by yourself at the tender age of sixteen!

"You could still prosecute," I said, knowing that I was clutching at straws, but trying to think of something, anything. "It's never too late. I mean, I read all the time about priests and teachers and people like that going to jail years after the abuse they inflicted on their victims. Have you any idea where he is?"

Peggy nodded with a sigh. "I know," she said. "And I can't prosecute. He's dead."

"Oh."

"Yes. He died in jail."

"Oh my God!"

"He got thirty years."

"For what?"

"Rape."

I was confused now. "So he was convicted after all?"

"Not for what he did to me," said Peggy, shaking her head sadly and taking a hanky from under her sleeve. She stared at it for a very long time until she spoke again. "He raped another woman some years after me. I don't know how many other women he raped, who like me were too afraid to come forward. Only God knows that. But one woman did come forward. He'd beaten her up so badly that she permanently lost her hearing in one ear. He left her on the side of the road, poor mite, bleeding from her injuries. She was a student up from the country training to be a nurse."

I couldn't believe what I was hearing. This was so, so shocking. Like something you'd read about on the front page of the paper. What a monster! How could somebody be so evil?

"But it wasn't your fault," I said, struggling to find the right words. The pain etched in the old woman's lined face was almost too much to bear.

"Oh yes, it was. If I'd told somebody, he might have gone to jail earlier. Then the others would have been spared the same ordeal."

"You can't blame yourself over something like that. I know it's really terrible, but you didn't know what to do. You were sixteen. At sixteen you're still a child. When I was sixteen I still had all my teddies on my bed."

"Did you?" Peggy clasped her hands thoughtfully and then gave a faint smile. "As a matter of fact, so did I."

Diana

40

1st June

God, Molly, I hate all these bloody hospital visits. I just can't stand them. Firstly they take forever and ever and secondly the public waiting room is always so overcrowded with people sneezing and talking loudly, and thirdly I hate being weighed in front of a hundred people and the midwife shouts out your weight so that everyone can hear. It's so, I dunno, intrusive or something. I wish to God I could afford to go private. I mean, I wear a hat pulled far down on my head every time I go in and try and avoid eye contact with the people sitting opposite me in the waiting room.

Lots of them are foreign and probably wouldn't know me from Adam but sometimes I see Irish people staring at me as if they're trying to figure out where they know me from, and I become all paranoid. Or maybe I'm just paranoid all the time. I mean, as if those people seriously give a shite! They're all leading their own lives and don't give a hoot about me. Jesus, that's what TV does to people. Seriously, every single person I know who works on telly thinks the whole world is on their case from morning to night. And the truth is nobody cares. That's one of the reasons I wanted to escape to Connemara and never come back to Dublin again.

Anyway, this afternoon I was at the hospital, queuing yet again, with a urine sample in my hand and a woman in front of me turned around and shrieked, "Oh it's you! Oh. My. God." (Most Irish people don't make a fuss about celebrities. She was one of the 1% who do.)

I wanted to die. I mean, I had absolutely no make-up on and I had my hat pulled so far down my face I could hardly see where I was going, and still somebody recognised me. About one per cent of me was a tiny bit flattered – it's proof that some people do actually watch the show – but the other 99% of me wanted the floor to open up and devour me. The woman who, like me, was probably about six months pregnant, stuck out her hand for me to shake, which was a bit awkward as I had my pregnancy hospital folder in one hand, and my small tube of warm pee in the other. I put the pee in my pocket while I shook her hand, thinking that really things don't become much more surreal than this.

When I first got word about my TV job I must admit that I had visions of red-carpet events and celebrity parties, and getting my hair and make-up done for free and wearing all these specially commissioned, stunning designer dresses at award ceremonies. But not in a million years did I ever imagine that I'd meet my biggest fan in the hospital waiting room of a maternity hospital.

We were in the queue waiting to get our injections done and I really was dreading that bit. I always feel faint at the sight of a needle anyway. Needles just put the fear of God in me. In fact, I hate them so much that once the magazine where I have my column asked me if I wanted to go to India on a press trip with all expenses paid and I turned it down because of all the injections I'd have to get before leaving. Yes, seriously, I turned down first-class flights and all because the thought of all those anti-malaria and anti-all-the-other injections was enough to terrify the bejaysus out of me.

So on this occasion, strange as it might seem, I was kind of glad to have this nutty fan rabbitting on about the TV show as it kept my mind off what was going to happen next. I was so busy answering her random questions (i.e. Question: What's Colin Farrell really like? Answer: I don't know) that I didn't even notice the time fly and suddenly I was at the top of the queue and there was this really evil-looking nurse glaring at me, her needle poised like a dangerous weapon in her right hand. I wanted to die there and then. I was petrified. I knew by the look in her eye that she was having a bad day and was determined to take her fury out on somebody. Call me psychic but I also knew that person was going to be me. I was about to turn around and run away but then something stopped me. I'd better stay and get it over and done with, I thought. I mean, I'm supposed to be having an epidural in a few months when the baby comes along and that's a big thick needle that's going to go right into the middle of my spine. So why am I shaking like a leaf over a tiny prick that's only going to go into my upper arm? Cop on, Diana, I chided myself – even little kids get injections and don't make a fuss.

I took a deep breath and told myself to be a brave girl and just get on with it, but nevertheless, despite my bravado, when the hostile nurse jabbed my arm in revenge for I don't know what (maybe she'd been dumped by the man of her dreams that morning), I squealed like a baby. It hurt. It really hurt so much that I wanted to punch the nurse as a form of retaliation. But I didn't. I was dignified about it and just sat there while she put a plaster over the spot of blood. But I knew when I got home the bruising would be massive and that my battered skin would go all the colours of the rainbow. I just knew it. All thanks to that silly bitch!

D x

41

6th June

Molly, I met Peggy again today. I really want to keep in touch with her. And she trusts me. We trust each other in fact. We tell each other things we wouldn't dream of telling other people. I went to her home. She lives in a little terraced cottage a few minutes' walk away from Phibsboro village. Walking into it is like entering a different era. There's no central heating and she has just a lone electric heater in the tiny kitchen. She has a cat called Cuddles who is orange and black and could sincerely do with going on the Atkins Diet. And she collects owls. She has lots and lots of owl ornaments everywhere. I asked her why she'd started collecting owls in particular and she said she couldn't remember, it was just one of those things.

There was a sepia photo of a smiling toddler, framed on the wall. Cute, innocent face. Full of wonder.

"That's Peter," Peggy said proudly when she saw me looking at it. "One of the kinder nuns took it of my boy and gave it to me just before he was sent to America. I've taken it with me wherever I've gone and it has always been my prize possession. I used to keep it under my pillow and cry myself to sleep."

Tears sprang up in her eyes and I could feel my heart wrench. "How old was he when you separated?"

"He was two years and nine months. He had the most beautiful smile a child ever had. His little smile could light up a whole room."

"How often did you get to see him when you were working in the laundry?"

Peggy winced. I could feel her pain almost as though it was my own. Was it wrong of me to be asking so many questions? Why did I feel an absolute compulsion to know absolutely everything that happened? Was I just digging up old painful memories unnecessarily?

"We were allowed to breastfeed our babies because it was the cheapest way of feeding them. When we weren't feeding them we were busy washing and ironing. It was hard even to play with our children because we'd be so tired from standing on our feet all day and our hands would be bleeding from all the manual chores we were required to carry out."

Peggy held out her hands. True to her word, she had the roughest skin I'd ever seen on a lady's hands.

"Do you remember the day Peter went away?"

"Do I remember? I'll never forget it, love, I remember it like it was yesterday. I was in the laundry with the other girls and it was just another day. The head sister called me into her office and I didn't think anything of it. I found her staring at me coldly through her glasses and then I knew she was going to tell me the news that would break my heart. She gave a stiff smile and said, 'We've found a very good family for Peter in America. It's an answer to prayer.'"

"Oh God."

"I know, love, it was my worst nightmare come true. I

was about to lose my precious son, the only thing I had that was worth living for. Although they wouldn't give us much play-time together, the bond between us was incredible and he knew me and loved me and was able to talk to me in his little childish babbling kind of way. He was my whole life. He was the only thing that kept me going. He kept me sane."

I couldn't believe what I was hearing. I couldn't believe the amount of suffering this poor woman had endured. And I kept thinking of little Molly and whether she had been mentally tortured in the same way.

Peggy turned to face me. "Would you like another cup of tea, love? Maybe a biscuit?"

I told her I was okay. My half-drunk cup of tea was stone cold at that stage but I didn't mind. I was so gripped by Peggy's story. None of this had come out on the TV show. On our show, when Peggy had been a guest, she had been quite vague about the whole thing as if she couldn't quite remember what had gone on. Of course she'd generated enough interest to get the phones hopping with callers and the press had jumped on the bandwagon, but she hadn't spilled the beans like she was doing now. What she was telling me now, my God, you couldn't make it up!

Maybe Peggy had been a bit intimidated by the TV cameras and the lights and the buzz of the studio. Or maybe, indeed, it had been easier for her not to delve too much into the past. After all, Peggy had spent most of her life in a home for abandoned women, followed by a job as a cleaner in a girls' school. No surprise then that she wasn't at ease with suddenly being thrust into the spotlight.

The show had focussed more on Peter really, who had grown into a fine, articulate man who had a family of his own now back in America. It made for great TV but I'd genuinely had no idea about the true story behind the story. Now I was finding out fast. And I was gripped.

"When I looked into Peter's big blue innocent eyes when he was a baby," Peggy continued, "and he looked back at me full of hope and trust and love, all I saw was my son. I didn't see his criminal father who would never know him. He was my son. Mine. One hundred per cent. And when they took him away from me, by Christ but they took away my soul."

"How long did you get to say goodbye?"

"Not long. Maybe two hours. I went to the shops with him walking along beside me holding my hand and I bought him a bouncy ball and a couple of bags of sweets. I think he thought it was his birthday or some kind of special occasion. He was so happy, and I remember him laughing, but my heart was breaking in two."

I shook my head in wonder. The story was wretched. It was hard to imagine the cruelty of it all. "But could you have escaped?" I suggested. "The two of you could have got on a bus or something and gone away?"

Peggy just gave me a look. "Where would we have gone, my dear? My family didn't want to know. We couldn't have gone to live with them because of the shame. The only person who stayed in contact with me was my mother. She came to visit about four times a year and would bring teddies for the baby. My father never knew she visited us. She'd pretend she had a doctor's appointment and would get the train."

"What?" I was aghast. Oh God, to think I'd been going around the last few weeks feeling completely miserable for myself! Now I felt guilty. The abuse some people had to suffer behind closed doors in Ireland. Because of the perceived 'shame'. It was enough to make you sick.

"There weren't too many options for girls like me back then," Peggy went on. "I had no money and nowhere to bring my son up. It wasn't like it is today where single mothers get houses and everything. There was nothing for fallen women. No social welfare. People didn't want to know. It was best if we all went to England where they could forget about us." She then looked down at her empty cup. "I suppose I'll make another pot of tea. Would you like a cup of tea?"

"I'd prefer a drink," I said truthfully. "Is there a pub around here?"

Peggy said nothing for a minute and I nearly bit off my tongue in horror. Oh no! What had I just suggested? This same woman had confided in me that she had been drunk the night she'd been raped. And here I was suggesting she should go to a pub! What kind of ridiculous monster was I? I almost expected her to throw me out of her little cottage.

But then, just as I was getting ready to apologise profusely, and accept whatever punishment was coming, Peggy's face broke into a smile.

"I know a great place around the corner. The barman's a pet and I'd murder a brandy. Just wait and I'll get my coat."

Di x

42

7th June

AHHH! NoooOOH! Oh, Molly, I found my first stretch mark today! What a very unwelcome surprise. I nearly died when I saw it. It was like a big silvery spider on my left hip. Yuck! Up until now I'd thought I'd get away with having none. I really hoped I'd be one of the few, very few pregnant women who escape their pregnancy stretch-mark free. I'd even tried rubbing in special vitamin E oils and various creams and soothing body-butters all over my tummy like they say you should do in all the pregnancy books. But alas it was to no avail. Nothing worked. I think it's to do with genes. Mum said she got terrible stretch marks with me and Jayne. I asked her whether Granny had also had stretch marks and she said she didn't know. Granny had never once discussed childbirth with Mum and my mother had to find out all her information from the local library!

I really hope that one day my son will be grateful for this never-ending endurance test his mummy is going through right now: the swollen feet, the heartburn, the weird dreams, constant nausea, constipation, the fact that I have to pee constantly and that my flat tummy is now a thing of the distant past with probably no intention of ever making a comeback to its former glory. I hope he'll be aware of all these sacrifices I've made for him, especially when I'm old and he's contemplating bundling me into an old folks' home to eke out the rest of my days.

On the upside, the ratings for my show are rising according to the latest JNLR figures and of course I'm thrilled about that but, most importantly, my boss is also very pleased. He says under normal circumstances I'd be in for a pay rise because of the show's success, but due to the recession I must still take a pay cut the same as everybody else. When he brought me into his office to tell me this in private I almost burst into tears. Okay, I know and understand that the whole country is suffering due to the greedy bankers but this news brings the reality home to me, that me and my little boy won't ever be able to move into a nice apartment like I was hoping for. I haven't enough of a deposit saved. It all seems so ironic really. There are hundreds of thousands of empty properties lying all over Dublin and, indeed, the whole country, and I have a job, but I still can't afford to live in any of them. Isn't it crazy? Isn't it just mad the way all of these banks got bailed out by the government, i.e. us, and yet when I went into one of them the other day looking to apply for a mortgage I was promptly shown the door? Well, obviously not so bluntly but I was still refused a mortgage on the grounds that I was only with the television station on a contract and therefore had no security. Security? They're looking for people with secure futures? In this day and age? It's a joke. I mean NOBODY is secure with the mess the country is in at the moment. Not one of my friends has a secure pensionable job.

Thank God my parents are still alive and living in Dublin. I honestly do not know what I would do without them. I'd be homeless. I'd be like, well, poor Peggy was all those years ago. Pregnant and nowhere to go.

You're probably wondering how our trip to the pub went. It was pretty enjoyable actually. The barman knew Peggy's name and everything. He knew her tipple was brandy. I had to tell him mine was whiskey though. One cube of ice, thanks.

He kind of looked me up and down, and I got a bit defensive and said, "Yeah, I know, but I still want a Jameson."

Then he got embarrassed and said, "I wasn't judging you 'cos you're pregnant, love. I just thought I knew ya."

Peggy told him I was off the TV and so he gave us the round on the house. He said it was the first time he'd ever had a celebrity in the pub. Then it was my turn to be mortified. After all, the last thing I'd call myself is a celebrity. I certainly don't feel like anything resembling a celebrity since being turned down for a mortgage by a snooty banker in a suit. And I sure as hell don't feel like a star when I'm queuing with my urine sample in the maternity hospital. The very word 'celebrity' makes me cringe a bit. It's very overused.

Still, I very much enjoyed my whiskey and Peggy certainly seemed to enjoy her brandy and there was a homely fire burning in the corner. It was really nice actually because the conversation up until that had been pretty harrowing. But Peggy said to me in the pub that it had been quite therapeutic to talk about it so openly to somebody she now trusted, and that she wished she'd told somebody years ago.

I know this sounds very silly but I asked her if there was a woman in the Magdalene laundry called Molly. And she said there were two Mollys actually. When she told me this I nearly fell off the chair in excitement. Imagine if my great-aunt had been in the same home as Peggy! Imagine if she was still there and I could find her? But my excitement was unfortunately short-lived.

"There was old Molly and young Molly," Peggy remembered with a far-off look in her eye. "Old Molly died of pneumonia sadly. I was very upset when she died as she'd been like a mummy to me when I first arrived and she was very good to little Peter and even knitted him a couple of cardigans to keep him warm."

"And what about the other Molly?" The words caught in my throat. I was nearly beside myself with excited anticipation. What if she actually knew my great-aunt? What if they were long-lost friends?

Peggy grimaced. "Poor Molly. Poor, lovely, lovely Molly."

I could feel the colour drain from my face. What had happened to Molly? Did Peggy really know her? There can't have been too many Magdalene laundries in Dublin. Had some terrible tragedy befallen her?

"Molly was very special."

"In what way?"

Peggy suddenly looked vague. "She was one of God's children."

I found myself frowning. God's children? What was Peggy talking about? Was I missing something here?

"Molly had Down's Syndrome. We all loved her. We looked after her. She was so sweet and child-like."

"But why was she in the Magdalene laundry if she had Down's Syndrome?"

Peggy shrugged, with the nonchalant air of somebody who has seen so much in her lifetime, so many failings of the human race, that nothing would ever surprise her. "Darling, she had nowhere to go. Just the same as me."

"Did she not have a family?"

"We all had families. At least, we all started out with families. But not all of us ended up with them."

When I got home this evening I felt kind of drained to be honest. I was still no closer to finding out what happened to my Molly. Had she been separated from her child at a moment's notice the same way Peggy had been? I couldn't imagine how that must have felt. What was wrong with this country that they had to export all their bastard children to England and America? It was disgusting. It was cowardly. Thank God Peggy and her son had found each other and rekindled their relationship. But so much precious time had been lost in between. Peter had no memories of his mother from early childhood. And he was American. He spoke with an American accent. He didn't even consider himself Irish and it wasn't surprising really since Ireland hadn't wanted him. This country had rejected him outright and he wasn't prepared to forgive and forget.

Not that he's bitter or anything. On the contrary in fact. Peter is a lovely affable man who went to live with a nice middle-class family in Boston, set in a lovely part of the world, and he lived a relatively nice life with private education and drama lessons and holidays in the Caribbean. He was a precious gift to a professional couple in their forties who had longed for a child of their own but hadn't been blessed with one. Funnily enough, soon after Peter went to live with them, his adopted mother became pregnant and Peter had a brother. His life was normal. He hadn't really suffered at all, not really. Not like his mother had. She had paid a terrible price for being in the wrong place at the wrong time with the wrong person. And, God, how she had suffered.

I've kind of become obsessed with her story now because she tells it like you're watching a film or something. Like you're there going through the motions. You're just dying to find out what happens next. Of course I know what happened in the end. In the end she was reunited with her son. But I feel like I'm hearing Molly's story too. How many women were there altogether in these laundries? Did anybody even know?

How many more thousands of women had similar tales? And were 'saved' by the religious communities? How many? I'm sure most of these stories had no such fairytale endings.

My sister Jayne thinks my obsession with Peggy is all a bit weird. She doesn't know many older people, though, so she wouldn't understand. Older people don't tend to come in for leg waxes and massages. I tell her that I get more spiritually from my conversations with Peggy in one afternoon than I do in a month of drinking cocktails at press launches. I told her about finding Molly's diary and asked her what I should do about it, and she looked at me like I'd grown a second head.

"What should you do about it? What do you mean what should you do about it? It's none of your business, Diana."

And that was a bit of a slap in the face for me because for the first time I had to question my motives for my new obsession. What WAS my obsession with single mothers all about? Was it because I was about to become one myself? Maybe I was on a wild-goose chase thinking I was going to find Molly after all these years. Maybe I should leave Peggy alone too and not try and get her to drag up her past again. Was there was something inherently wrong with me? Should I be seeking some sort of therapy?

Mind you, unless I'm totally kidding myself, Peggy seems to look forward to our get-togethers as much as I do. I've been telling her all about Molly's diary. She seems very interested in Molly, as though she's some kind of kindred sister. I would have liked her to read Molly's diary herself but her eyesight is poor and her reading glasses aren't strong enough. Sometimes I read bits out loud to her. I don't feel like I'm betraying Molly though because it was such a long time ago, and Peggy wouldn't be telling what was in the diary to anybody. You could trust Peggy with your life.

Sometimes I wonder if poor Molly is dead. I know it's an

awfully depressing thing to think about but sometimes I dream about her being dead and that her child is still travelling the world searching for her, heartbroken. And I wake up in a terrible sweat and then can't get back to sleep again. I feel such a strong connection to both Peggy and Molly but at least I can chat to Peggy and look her in the eye and reach over and touch her hand. I can't do that with Molly who is like a ghost who haunts me every hour of the day. Maybe Molly is dead. It's highly likely. Maybe she died a broken woman, estranged from her darling child.

What must it have been like? To give up your precious, helpless bundle of joy? To people who you had never met before? Had Molly even got to hold her child and grown to love him or her? Had they bonded? Like Peggy had with her son before he had been cruelly snatched away from her? Had she got to feel its skin against hers and smell its unique baby smell? Or had her child been taken away immediately, as soon as the umbilical cord had been cut. Had her breasts leaked unwanted milk? Had she rubbed her empty tummy in despair? The same tummy that had been 'home' to her own flesh and blood for nine months and now was left with no further purpose?

I can't even imagine what it was like for those two women. But Peggy was here and had got some sort of closure. What happened to Molly? I am going crazy thinking about her. I now read her diary obsessively. I know it word for word at this stage. I am feeling guilty for being pregnant and knowing that some religious order isn't going to 'arrange' things for me. Jesus, what is wrong with me?

Diana.

43

10th June

Dear Molly,
Mum isn't talking to me. We had a big argument this evening when I asked her if Granny had ever mentioned Molly.

"You asked me that before," she said without even looking up from her Woman's Way magazine.

"And you never gave me a straight answer," I countered, ignoring Dad's look of warning. I didn't understand what the big deal was and why she was so keen to avoid the question. Granny must have spoken about her little sister at some stage. It would have very been odd if she hadn't. That would be like me never talking about Jayne. Or her never thinking about me. Your sister doesn't just disappear off the face of the earth like that.

"You're like a broken record," my sister grumbled as she sat reading the newspaper at the kitchen table. "What business is it of yours what happened to Granny's sister? You need to move on with your life."

That's Jayne for you. Practical as the day is long. Move on. Don't get stuck in the past. She's right, you know. In some ways I'm envious of her no-nonsense attitude. Jayne takes after Mum in that she's not really into getting sentimental about things. For instance, I'm a total hoarder. I collect theatre stubs, train tickets, airline tickets, photographs, birthday cards. You name it, I keep it. I once tried to make up a charity bag to give to the poor but I agonised so much over every little item of clothing (some of which I hadn't worn for well over a decade) that I decided it wasn't worth the pain and I just wrote a cheque to the charity instead. Jayne is forever making up charity bags. In her case it's probably more to do with de-cluttering her wardrobe and having her room spotlessly clean than helping the needy. She has a rule and that is whenever something new comes in something old must go out. I think it's brilliant in theory but I just can't do it. In fact I'm the complete opposite to Jayne. I can't have enough stuff and when I get wind of the fact that she's doing up another monthly charity bag, I can be found lurking out in the landing desperately waiting for her to go to the bathroom so I can have a good old rummage and see what I can salvage for myself.

Everyone says that after you have a baby the first thing you want to do is fire out all your maternity clothes or put them on top of a bonfire and burn the lot because you're so sick of the sight of them. I bet you I won't though. I bet I'll still be wearing my maternity clothes months after the baby is born. Not because I won't have lost the weight but because deep down I'll have myself convinced I still have a use for them.

"I'm just curious to know what happened to Molly," I protested. "What's wrong with that? I just think it's sad that she went away and never came back. Did she ever write or send Christmas cards or anything?"

Then the oddest thing happened. My mother's face crumpled, she burst into tears and then ran from the room.

"Look what you've done now," Jayne accused.

I was gobsmacked. What had I done wrong? Not in a million years would I ever intentionally hurt my mother. Granted, we don't have the closest relationship and my mother wouldn't have the warmest nature ever but I respect that she can be a bit aloof at times and that's just the way she is. I know she means well.

"I didn't mean to upset her," I said.

Dad turned to me and said, "Diana, I never want you to bring up Molly's name to your mother again. Is that understood?"

"But why?" I asked, not pleased about being spoken to like a naughty schoolgirl. Suddenly I was fifteen again.

I was greeted by a wall of silence which hung between us awkwardly. Nobody spoke until Jayne suddenly looked up from the newspaper she was reading. "What's Roger's surname, Diana?"

I was so wrapped up in the uncomfortable scene that had just taken place that it took a few seconds for me to comprehend the question.

"Who?"

"Roger. You know, the guy who, like, knocked you up," she said sarcastically.

"Matherson," I said frowning. "His surname is Matherson. Why?" Why on earth would Jayne want to know his surname?

"That's what I thought," she said. "It says here that he just got engaged."

Diana

44

14th June

Dear Molly,
Now my editor at the magazine has asked me to take a pay cut. Okay, I know it's only a five per cent cut, and I shouldn't be complaining when half the country is losing their jobs, but I'm so broke.

I mean, where am I going to live? Where am I going to put my little baby? I feel like the Virgin Mary looking for an inn, only I don't even have Joseph for support! I bought a little Moses basket the other day with a pale yellow bonnet on it. I got thirty per cent off because it was the last one and it was on display but it's perfect. It's so cute – the bonnet is frilly with little teddies on its perimeter. It seems big enough only to fit a teddy bear, not a real live human being. I fell in love with it as soon as I saw it in the shop window but the baby will only sleep in it for six weeks and then where will he go? He can't sleep in my bed. In all the books it says that it's not a good idea to have babies used to sleeping in your bed because then they want to stay there forever.

I've seen parents have terrible trouble with toddlers

throwing tantrums on that programme, Supernanny. That's my guilty fix now by the way. Supernanny. It's replaced my former addiction to Judge Judy. And if I have to be honest, it's made me realise that I never want more than three kids. Jesus, how do parents cope with the noise levels?

I know all about the Naughty Step now, and having to stoop down to my kid's level when I talk to him so that I don't intimidate him. God, yeah, I'm kind of an expert already and I haven't even given birth yet!

I'm worried about my ever-decreasing finances though. I'd love to get even a little one-bedroom apartment somewhere. Obviously having a house is the long-term dream but it seems so far off-limits right now. I have visions of one day having a proper nursery filled with fabulous toys and gorgeous kiddie furniture. And I also want a garden where we can play together in the summer. Baby and me. Mind you, with the dreadful weather we get every summer, I'm probably just kidding myself.

I wonder if Roger will offer to help financially with the baby. I mean, he should of course, but he hasn't offered and I haven't asked. Yet. In a moment of madness I sent him a text congratulating him on his engagement. I got no reply, not surprisingly, and then I felt like a fool afterwards. I started imagining himself and the child bride tittering at my text and feeling sorry for me. The spurned pregnant ex.

I think Mum has calmed down with me a lot since I've stopped asking her about Molly. She bought a little blue baby hat and mittens in Dunnes Stores last week, which I thought was a sweet gesture. Maybe deep down she feels sad for me, now that she knows Roger has got engaged and there is absolutely zero chance that he will whisk me up the aisle and finally make an honest woman out of me.

Dad said to me that I will have to discuss maintenance

with Roger. He says it's my child's right and that I am not asking for money for myself but for my son. I know he is making perfect sense. I just hate having to put my hand out, like I'm grovelling. I think I'll write him a letter. A civilised letter, once the baby is born. And if he doesn't comply and agree to support his son, well, then, I'll have no option but to take him to the family court. I hope it doesn't come to that though. Fingers crossed that we can make some kind of civilised deal before we resort to going down the legal route. I'd hate the stress of all that.

I'm trying to be grown-up about the whole thing and, sometimes, when I'm being completely generous in spirit, I envisage inviting my baby's half-sister to come over to play in a few years' time. My imagination, of course, doesn't stretch to family holidays and taking a big caravan on a road trip through the South of France during the summer with all of us on board, but I can't see why we can't all live together in harmony.

I don't know why Roger would prefer everything to be so nasty. Is this going to continue forever? All this animosity. The bitterness? It shouldn't be a competition between myself and Roger's child bride to see which kid can win their dad's affections the most. Although sometimes I feel physically sick at the reality of the situation I've found myself in, mostly I try and put all those ill feelings aside for the sake of my unborn. He deserves every chance. I had a mum and dad who loved me and every child deserves the same. But how can I communicate with a man who won't communicate back? Roger never answers my calls or texts. And by never replying he makes me feel like some kind of stalker for trying to contact him.

I think he ignores me as a way of belittling me. Maybe it's all a game to him. But is it always going to be like this? Every birthday and Christmas? Every school play? Every teacher-parent meeting? Every school sports day? Is he even going to come to the baby's christening or will it simply be a question of me going up the aisle with the baby in my arms? Alone.

Maybe Roger will want a joint christening with his other child. That would be interesting. I'd like to see the priest's face on that occasion. Or maybe we could have the child christened at his forthcoming wedding and their wedding cake could double up as a christening cake? Right, enough of the sarcastic comments. It's not even funny.

BTW I'm getting bigger every day. My bump is quite visible now and I need to sleep with a pillow under it to prop it up. My breasts are huge but are gravitating towards my belly with the weight of them when I don't wear a bra. Really gross. I'm wearing the most hideous-looking bras at the moment because you're not allowed to wear bras with underwiring when you're pregnant because they can cut off the circulation of blood. I've got dimples on my upper thighs too – the first dreaded signs of cellulite – and I'm also getting the most horrific bouts of heartburn. Jesus, I'm like a bloody walking pregnancy cliché.

Seriously though, it was Jayne's and my joint birthday the other night (yes, we were born on the same day two years apart!) and my dad offered to take us all out for a meal en famille to a local curry house. I decided to go for spicy vegetables and not only did I spend twenty minutes in the loo before we left the restaurant, I had heartburn for the whole night.

It's getting to be a right pain now. Baby's head is on my bladder from morning to night. I was at a big black-tie work function the other night and I had to go to the bathroom no less than four times during the speeches. Yes, four times! I felt so self-conscious getting up and down like a yo-yo and excusing myself. I wish to God I didn't have to go to any work-related functions at this stage. Why can't people understand that I just want to stay at home and rest?

Women just keep coming up to me, gleefully telling me about their own ghastly birthing experiences which make me break into a terrified sweat. They always finish by saying, "It's worth it in the end though," or "I'm sure you'll be fine." Men just always look extremely uncomfortable and excuse themselves swiftly to go to the bar after wishing me luck. Also, the fact that I never ever have a partner with me makes it all the more awkward. Normally I don't mind being single, but right now I'm so lonely I'd like a bit of male company. Some chance of that though, huh? I mean who on earth would want to date a pregnant thirty-year-old woman?

Also, I've noticed that Vicky and Selina aren't ringing to suggest girls' nights out any more. Not that I blame them. They're still single and looking. If the three of us were sitting up by a bar, I'd be like a spanner in their works. Men would jump to conclusions and think my friends were trying to get themselves up the duff too. So the invitations are sparse. But don't get me wrong, they're still lovely to me and text me regularly to see how I am and suggest coffee or lunch. Just not nights out.

The viewers are lovely too. I get lots of well-wishes from people who watch the show, especially other pregnant women. It's so sweet. It's good to know I'm not alone. Especially as I actually am.

Diana

45

17th June

Dear Molly,
I went to see Great-Auntie Noreen today. I hadn't seen her for a couple of months although it's really been on my mind that I should pay her a visit. First of all I wanted to thank her for letting me escape to her adorable cottage at a time when I desperately needed to escape. Really those couple of weeks away were a lifesaver towards helping me regain control of my life again. But I also had another reason for visiting. And that of course was that I wanted to find out about Molly.

Now I know that Mum wants me to forget about Molly altogether and I don't want to go against herself and Dad, especially as they've been so kind and supportive to me throughout the pregnancy, but after a lot of thought and much soul-searching I decided I must at least try and find out what happened to my great-auntie. Imagine if she was still alive and living alone in squalor and thought she had no family to call on? Imagine if she spent every Christmas alone in a damp, dingy flat somewhere crying her eyes out?

Then after I find out what happened to her, maybe I can

move on and try and focus on the present which is really what I should be doing. All this obsessing over Molly can't be any good for my state of mind. But after reading Molly's diary I feel like it's my duty to do something. I feel I was meant to find that diary. I just can't let go. Even if I wanted to.

I find myself in production meetings thinking about her. Even sometimes I'm on live TV discussing something serious and topical and my mind will wander. Like the other day we were tackling the very sensitive issue of children who are stillborn. Obviously as a presenter you're not supposed to get overly emotional about subjects but, as I was interviewing a woman about her experience, I suddenly started wondering if Molly's child had been born dead? Imagine if that had happened and she'd been over in England with nobody to support her. My eyes welled with tears and I was mortified because I was getting more upset than the interviewee. I just about held it together before the show wrapped up and then I ran to the Ladies' and bawled for about ten minutes.

Anyway today was my day off so I went out to see Noreen which is something I'd been planning to do for ages. They told me when I arrived that she was in her room so I made my way down the dark gloomy corridor of the nursing home where they have eerie pictures of the Virgin Mary and all these saints on the walls. Noreen was pleased to see me although at first I think she thought I was Jayne. I asked her how she was. She said she was fine but could be better. She also said she was tired of the nursing home. She said wanted to go back home.

"To Spiddal?"

"Yes, that's where I was always happiest. I don't like it here. I don't trust the other women here. They're shifty. Dorothy in the room next door is always trying to bully me."

My eyebrows were raised. Had there been an incident? Was there anything I should know about? And what could I do to help? Maybe I should speak to somebody in charge. I didn't want to think my great-auntie was feeling vulnerable with nobody to turn to.

Noreen sat up in her chair and pulled her blanket up around her thighs. She frowned and told me that Dorothy had been pestering her to join the Thursday night bingo.

"And I wouldn't dream of it," said Noreen quite definitely. "I much prefer to read a book. And that's another thing. Dorothy took my favourite Agatha Christie novel and never gave it back to me. I had my name on it and everything."

"Are you sure about that, Auntie? You can't go around accusing people of stealing, you know."

But Noreen was adamant that Dorothy was the thief in question. I began thinking that it probably would be the best thing for Noreen if she were to return to her old home. Mind you, if Noreen were to move back there, she'd need some live-in home help. Maybe I could find somebody to live with her? A nice Filipina nurse, maybe.

I asked her whether she'd had lunch. I thought it might be nice for us to go out somewhere in the car and stop off for something to eat. But when Noreen couldn't remember whether she had indeed had lunch or not, my heart sank. If her memory didn't even stretch to a few hours ago, what hope had I of getting her to recall the past? A time when her little sister Molly was in her life?

I rang Reception and they confirmed, quite indignantly I may tell you, that yes, Noreen had indeed had lunch and had enjoyed cream of mushroom soup, followed by chicken, potatoes and peas, followed by lemon jelly and vanilla ice-cream, which of course was way too much information but I think they thought I was accusing them of starving my great-aunt. As if!

I asked her then if she fancied going for afternoon tea somewhere. Her face lit up and she said that would be great. She said she loved getting out of the nursing home for a break as it was like a prison in there. I could totally see where she was coming from. I hope I have nice children one day who will let me live with them and not lock me away in some home and forget all about me.

On the drive to the hotel, I told Noreen I was pregnant. I came straight out with it. Of course I expected her to be totally shocked but she wasn't.

"I'm delighted for you," she said calmly.

In fact she said it so calmly I wondered if she had heard me right. "But I'm not married, Auntie Noreen," I said nervously.

Without flinching she answered, "Maybe you're better off, dear. I never got married myself."

"Why didn't you?"

"I never met the right man," she said matter-of-factly.

I parked the car right outside the front door of the hotel as it had started to rain and I didn't want Noreen getting wet. I helped her out of the car and escorted her into the warmth of the hotel.

"Do you know something, Auntie?" I said with a resigned sigh. "I met the right man but he's with the wrong person."

"My dearest Diana," she gave me a withering look, "if he's not with you right now and you're carrying his child, he's obviously not the right man for you."

I thought about her reply. She made total sense. Of course she did. Wise woman. I suppose deep down I knew that Roger was a complete cad for abandoning me when I was expecting his child but I refused to indulge in horrible thoughts about him. Part of me did not want to accept that my baby's father was an irresponsible prick. That in some way implicated me. Because I was the one who chose him.

We removed our coats and took a seat by the roaring log fire, making sure there were no kids around as Noreen had made it clear she didn't want to be sitting anywhere near boisterous children. I totally agreed. I mean, I know I'm going to have my own child soon and all and I can't wait to be a mummy, but other people's kids really do my head in, especially if they are running around hotels or bars while their parents get sloshed. I simply cannot understand how parents take their kids to pubs on Sunday and stay there all day. It's a disgrace. So selfish of them. There's plenty of other things they could be doing en famille. What was wrong with the public park?

Noreen and I ordered afternoon tea and it came with all the trimmings – crust-free, delicate, fluffy white bread sandwiches, strawberries, different-coloured cup cakes, fruit cakes, scones with homemade jam, and to boot, the manager sent us over two glasses of champagne with his compliments which I was thrilled about. You see, there are definite perks to being on the telly!

As my great-auntie was in such good form I decided to just go for it and ask her straight out what happened to Molly.

Noreen stopped eating and looked extremely surprised by my question. Then she put down her fork carefully and frowned. "She went to England," she replied. She then patted her lips with a starched white serviette and started eating again.

"And?" I pushed her.

"And that was that."

"Did she not even write letters?" I asked, determined to get somewhere today with my line of questioning.

"Not to me, no."

"To anybody?"

"She wrote to my mother, I believe, but I never saw the letters. Mammy used to burn them in case Daddy read them. My mother rarely discussed her with us, so I don't know what was in the letters."

"Why did Molly go to England, Noreen?"

Noreen visibly flinched before answering. "To work for a priest. It was a well-paid job. And a respectable job too. It was very difficult for girls to get jobs in those days. Especially if they weren't educated or skilled. It wasn't like it is now."

"But what happened to her baby?"

"Who has been talking to you?" Noreen eyed me suspiciously over her teacup.

I told her I'd found Molly's diary in the attic and had read it. As I told her I felt my cheeks burn. I suddenly was overwhelmed with guilt. Maybe I shouldn't have pried.

"You shouldn't have read it. It wasn't yours to read." Noreen looked quite cross.

I stared at the ground, my cheeks burning. I knew it wasn't any of my business and that reading somebody's diary was the lowest of the low. But I couldn't help it.

"What was in the diary?"

"Just about her getting pregnant and that. But then the entries suddenly stopped. It was like she just vanished."

I could see naked pain on my great-auntie's lined face and I had to ask myself silently for the umpteenth time why exactly I was doing this? Why was I making those closest to Molly uncomfortable? Why was I forcing them to relive the misery that was Molly's disappearance? And what kind of self-indulgent monster was I?

"That's exactly what happened. She went to Dublin and the nuns took her in. They gave her work in the laundry until she had the baby and then they found her a priest in London."

"Did she take the baby with her to England?"

"Ah Diana, it was all such a long time ago," Noreen sighed.

But I still couldn't let go. I finally felt I was getting somewhere. Closer than I'd ever been. If only I could just put the last few pieces of the jigsaw together.

"But you must have heard. I know pregnancies outside marriage were supposed to be shameful back then, and everything was brushed under the carpet but you must have known. You were her older sister! Surely you were curious?"

It was almost an accusation. I wondered how much Noreen really knew and why she was being so secretive about it. Why did nobody want to talk about Molly at all? Her only crime had been to get pregnant. I just didn't understand it.

"She didn't get to keep the baby. That wasn't the way it happened in our day. She nursed her little girl for two and a half years or more and then they were separated. Molly stayed on with the nuns a while longer in order to earn her boat and train fare to get to England."

I was appalled. A wave of intense shock mixed with sadness washed over me.

I found my voice eventually. "Oh my God. That's so, so sad. So pitiful. I actually can't imagine how difficult that must have been." I tried to visualise Molly saying goodbye to her little girl. "I'd say the little mite was beautiful."

"Yes, she was."

"Did you see her?"

"Yes, I did."

"Was she gorgeous? Molly must have really bonded with that child. She wouldn't have been able to help herself. I already feel bonded to my baby even though he isn't born yet. I talk to him all the time and sing to him. I love him so much."

"Molly knew she was going to have to give her daughter up at some stage. There was never going to be another way. That's what happened in those days. Molly wasn't under any illusion as to what was going to happen to her. She was a realistic child."

A child. That's exactly what she'd been, Lord love her. What she must have gone through. The pain and suffering! I smothered a fresh scone with butter and nibbled at it thoughtfully.

'But still. Knowing it was going to happen wouldn't have made it any easier. I don't believe that for a moment."

"Well, as I said, it was a long time ago. Things have changed now, thank God."

"Thank God is right," I agreed.

Imagine if things were still the same and I was sent up to the nuns to wash and iron bed linen while Roger married his child bride and they lived happily ever after in a nice house with two cars in the drive? Can you imagine how unjust it would be that you'd be condemned to a life without your child just because some fellow had had his wicked way with you and then decided he didn't want to marry you? The scariest thing was that this went on in Ireland not so long ago. We're only talking three generations here, and it didn't stop there.

"Did Molly's baby look like her?"

"Very much so. In fact they were the spit of one another."

I was intrigued. "So did Molly give her a daughter a name or was she even allowed to do that? The new parents might have changed it anyway I suppose."

Noreen suddenly had a very far-off look in her eye. "She gave her a name, yes."

"What was it?"

She hesitated before answering.

"Please tell me," I begged.

"You're putting me in a very difficult situation, Diana. I don't know if I should."

I didn't understand why not. I really didn't.

"Please?"

"Her name was Rosemary."

"Rosemary? Really?" I was quite startled. "How funny that she was called the same name as my mum. What a coincidence!"

And Noreen didn't bat an eyelid. Just continued to stare into space. And then it hit me with extraordinary clarity. My mouth went completely dry and I suddenly went so cold that goose bumps appeared on my bare arms.

"Oh my God," I said in a very slow, disbelieving voice that sounded quite foreign even to me. "My mum was that baby, wasn't she? Mum was Molly's illegitimate baby?"

She didn't answer me. Just looked sad.

"Noreen?" I croaked, barely able to get the words out. "Tell me the truth, I'm begging you. Is Mum, was Mum –?"

Noreen met my eye. "Yes," she said, reading my mind. "You're right. I might as well tell you because you're like a dog with a bone trying to get information out of me. Oh Lord, all I want at my stage in life is a bit of peace and quiet. My sister, Molly, was your grandmother, Diana. There you have it. Your mother, Rosemary, was her precious baby girl."

D

46

19th June

Dear Molly,
I haven't slept well for the last two nights. I know I pushed Noreen to tell me the truth but now that I know it I'm not sure I know how to deal with it. I can't discuss things with Mum because Noreen made me promise I wouldn't divulge what I had found out. Apparently Mum went looking for Molly when she was eighteen. She got a boat and train to London and located the house where her biological mother and my real granny had worked as a housekeeper.

The priest that had employed her had since moved parish and another priest told my mother that Molly had been dismissed for getting pregnant again and he didn't know where she was. When Noreen told me that, I swear I nearly dropped off the chair in shock. I couldn't believe that Molly would have let that happen to her a second time. Who on earth was the father of the second child?

Noreen had no idea. All she knew was that Molly had left the priest's house under a cloud and that she had brought even more disgrace upon herself. I was stunned to hear it. So where did my granny go then and more to the point, where was she now? I wanted closure. I needed it and I wasn't getting it.

I'm more worried than ever now about Molly. Was she a down-and-out somewhere on the streets of London clutching a bottle of wine in a doorway? Surely not. Winos never survive very long with the freezing winters anyway. God help them. They don't stand a chance. Had she starved to death? Her body found in a gutter somewhere? Had her second baby survived? Did that mean now that Mum had a brother or sister she'd never met? Had I cousins in England? Gosh, it must have been such a shock for my mother when she found out that she wasn't an only child like she'd always thought. No wonder she'd reacted the way she did when I started asking about Molly. My poor mum.

It also came as a shock to me to discover that the woman I'd always known as 'Granny' had never been my granny at all. We hadn't been terribly close of course. Not the way some people are to their grannies, and her relationship with my mother was often, at times, strained. Noreen said that the two of them had always had their ups and downs, and things had been especially difficult between them when my mother found out at the age of sixteen that she'd been adopted. She resented Granny Ita for a long time for not having told her the truth.

I'm sure it hadn't been easy for Ita either. She'd worked long hours as a midwife in a Galway hospital in order to support them both. She never remarried nor had any biological kids of her own. As far as Noreen could recall she never even had a boyfriend after her husband died. Now that I think about it, I realise what an extraordinarily selfless woman she must have been to have sacrificed her whole life to raise my mother by herself.

I'm sitting at the desk in my room writing this. I used to lie in bed scribbling my thoughts to you, Molly, but now my belly has got so big it just gets in the way of everything. I've ballooned further in the last few days. I don't go out any more at night because I'm afraid of drunk people bumping into me. I'm also afraid of sober people bumping into me. I mean it's obvious that I'm pregnant now and you couldn't miss the big tummy on me, but, although the majority of people will keep the door open for you, or get out of your way if you're holding onto a rail going up the stairs, there are still some very ignorant people about. Like the other day I was going into the dry-cleaner's and this woman was coming out and she pushed past me, and there I was holding the heavy door open. I was so outraged that I muttered "Asshole" under my breath. She swung around and looked shocked and then just swanned off like she thought she was the queen or something. And then the other day I was on the Luas and nobody stood up to give me a seat. I'm not saying that I demand to be handled with kid gloves or anything, but I'm sure when I wasn't pregnant that I would have given up my seat for somebody who was. Then again, I shouldn't be complaining. I'm lucky. I know I'm lucky. No matter what happens, I'm going to get to keep my kid when he's born. Unlike my poor, poor granny.

Jayne said the other day that she would do a Yummy Mummy massage on me for free. Then she said she'd get one of her therapists to do it as any time she does anything in the salon for me we end up talking, or should I say arguing, and it's not relaxing at all. I'm really looking forward to my treatment actually. I've been so stressed lately this is a real treat. It would cost a fortune if I was to pay for it myself.

I immediately accepted Jayne's kind offer before she had a chance to change her mind. It's such a rarity for Jayne to offer me something for free that I'm grabbing the opportunity with both arms. Maybe she's mellowing as she's getting older. I think her new man has been a calming influence on her anyway. His name is Clive and he's a successful partner in a big accounting firm. It's not surprising that he has a good job. Jayne really wouldn't be remotely interested in wasting her time with somebody who wasn't a good catch. She could never understand why I fell for Roger. Anyway, being in love really suits her. She's not as peevish as she used to be. She even brought me an expensive-looking cellulite cream home from the salon the other day to rub into my upper thighs. She gets sent samples all the time and as she explained while presenting me with my free gift, she has no use for cellulite creams herself. She wasn't being nasty or anything even though it would be easy to think that. She just has rather an unfortunate manner.

My new column came out today. I mean, it's the same column but I'm now writing about pregnancy rather than dating. Both the editor and I felt it wasn't appropriate for me to be writing about dating anymore. So anyway, in my column I was ranting about how difficult it was being pregnant and single, and that all pregnant women should have at least one special person in their lives to administer TLC to them when they're feeling down. Little things like impromptu foot massages or flowers mean so much. Well, the column was written a couple of weeks ago because the magazines usually work way in advance so I'd completely forgotten about it until today. The day I wrote it I'd been feeling particularly vulnerable and sorry for myself. I found writing down all my thoughts very therapeutic. I then emailed it off feeling much better about myself and thought nothing more of it. Until this afternoon.

I had just wrapped up filming and was about to go into my daily production meeting when my phone rang. I quickly checked to see who it was, because I was in a bit of a hurry and didn't want to be wasting time talking to somebody if it wasn't urgent. When I saw Roger's number flashing I nearly died of fright. I mean Roger never ever rings me. I was so shocked I couldn't answer. Best if he left a message and then I could dissect it in my own good time. But all during the meeting I found it hard to concentrate on what Dan was saying. I was nodding and made small grunts of agreement where appropriate, but although I was there in body, my mind was a million miles away. What did Roger want? Why would he contact me just out of the blue? Had he had a change of heart? I didn't want to get my hopes up but it did cross my mind that perhaps he wanted to get back together with me. Maybe he realised that I was the one after all. Maybe he'd had a falling out with the child bride? But did I really want him back? He'd have to do a lot of apologising first. I might be pregnant and not feeling very attractive but I wasn't a complete mug.

In the end it turned out I was wrong on all counts. Roger had no such notion of us re-forming and becoming a couple again. In fact, quite the opposite. I didn't even get to speak to him.

I waited until the production meeting, which seemed to go on for ever and ever, finally ended. Once I was outside the building and in the safety of my own car, I fished out my phone and listened to my message. It was pretty brief. And Roger's voice was anything but warm and friendly.

"It's Roger," he said in a fairly menacing tone of voice. "I've just read your column where you are so obviously having a go at me, and I'm wondering what the fuck you think you are playing at."

Diana

47

20th June

Oh, Molly, I reckon I didn't get more than a couple of hours' sleep last night. Between vivid nightmares and having to use the loo either to pee or throw up every half hour it ended up being a pretty restless night.

Now that the time is nearing I suppose I am fretting a bit about the whole experience of giving birth. But then I have to constantly remind myself that millions and millions of women have given birth to healthy babies and that if the pain was so utterly dreadful, then those same women would never have more than one baby, would they?

It's the fear of the unknown really. I said to Jayne the other day that I was thinking of delivering naturally with just gas instead of going for the full epidural which is kind of taking the easy way out, according to some.

You see I'd read this Mother Earth type article in a pregnancy magazine the other day, written by a woman who'd had four babies one after another. With the first baby she'd had an epidural and then went naturally for the subsequent three births. Said it made her more in touch with her femininity. I was telling Jayne about it. Jayne has developed a slight interest in my pregnancy now. I think since meeting her Mr Right she's become a little broody.

"Do you think I should have an epidural?" I said as I poured myself my tenth glass of grapefruit juice that day.

"I dunno," she shrugged. "Would you have root canal work without an injection at the dentist?"

"Of course not!"

"Well, then, I don't think going through unnecessary pain would make you feel more like a woman. That's just daft. When I'm having my babies I'll be asking the doctors for absolutely every painkiller there is going."

But lots of women do it on gas alone. I think I might give it a go. I'm still not sure though. You hear horror pregnancy stories all the time. There's a pregnancy/parenting type website that I'm always on where people discuss their birthing stories. Some are so gross they'd put you off eating for a week. I've heard of people being in labour for a full thirty-six hours – eeek! And I've listened to stories where women say they were ripped to bits down there and couldn't sit down for days afterwards, and that peeing afterwards was absolutely agonising.

The other thing I'm dreading, of course, is the sheer indignity of it all. Lying there spread-eagled with complete strangers working between your legs. I was even worried that they might bring in some medical students for the experience but then my GP said that if I didn't want any students there, then my request would be honoured. Thank God for that.

I don't know who my birthing partner will be yet. To be honest I can't think of anybody suitable. I won't ask Jayne because I don't think she'd really like to be there. I'm sure she would come if I asked, out of a sense of duty, but I don't want to push that duty on her. My mum would attend, I suppose, but she's very squeamish.

I don't want Dad to be there. It would be too awkward, and of course, it's out of the question that Roger might want to attend the birth of his own son. I'm still actually reeling from the venom in his voice when he phoned me about my column. I mean, I didn't even think he read the magazine. Somebody must have tipped him off. No doubt the child bride.

I never rang him back because I didn't want him yelling at me and upsetting me, but he phoned me again that night and attacked me for slandering his character. He said that if I wasn't careful I'd be getting a solicitor's letter from him in the post, which I thought was a bit drastic. What does he want from me? Would he prefer that I didn't work? He knows that my job is in the media, and that in a recession I'm bloody lucky to have a column at all.

Instead of crumbling like I usually do at the sound of Roger's voice I managed to keep my reserve and told him in no uncertain terms that I was going to continue with my column in the fashion that I was happy with, and that from now on he should mind his own bloody business. At first I was greeted by silence. Stunned silence, I believe. I honestly don't think Roger thought I had it in me to stand up for myself. But I'd had enough of his bullying. He'd pushed me too far this time. I mean, he'd already tried his best to ruin my personal life but I wasn't letting him get away with interfering in my career now too. Dickhead.

He went on to mutter something about involving him and I said right back, "Sure, I didn't even mention your name. I never mention you, Roger. Not to anybody outside my family anyway. Why on earth would I?"

I think he was quite taken aback and abruptly he said he

had to go. I was almost shaking as the call ended but I'm glad to say I did feel a sense of personal satisfaction as I bade him a curt goodbye. I had finally stopped letting him treat me like a doormat. And it felt amazing.

D xxx

48

25th June

Molly,

I asked my mum if she wanted to be my birthing partner and she didn't exactly jump for joy and admit that she'd been secretly hoping I'd ask her all along. But she did say that she would accompany me.

She said she'd probably wait outside, and come in afterwards to give me a bit of support, and of course meet her new grandson. I told her it was fine if she waited outside. Actually it suits me better if she stays outside with a book or something. It'll just be reassuring to know I'm not all alone on such a momentous occasion.

To be honest I don't particularly want any family members in the delivery room itself with me. If I'm going to be yelling and screaming like a crazy fishwife I don't particularly need an audience. Leave your dignity at the door. Isn't that's what they say about childbirth?

I wonder will Roger be at the birth of his other child? I bet he wouldn't miss it for the world. He'll be there acting as the doting dad in front of the midwives. Trying to impress them.

He'll probably bring along a video recorder. Incidentally, I wonder what people do with the videos that they make of their offspring's birth. I mean, honest to goodness, you're hardly going to invite friends and neighbours round to watch it on a Friday night with a bottle of wine now, are you? And you're hardly going to show it to your teenagers in later years. People are extraordinary, really.

It's been a mad week so far. I find myself getting very tired now and need to lie down quite a lot at intervals. I've stopped going out socially altogether. God, I wish that I had a proper permanent job so I could go on maternity leave and take to the bed watching Oprah and Judge Judy for the next couple of months. I'm totally in the mood for watching trashy chat shows and not having to tax my brain too much. I never realised that thinking could be so exhausting until I got pregnant. I do draw the line at Jeremy Kyle, however, because I find all that shouting about DNA and stuff quite wearisome. And also it's a bit too close to the bone.

But in TV-land there's rarely a perk such as maternity leave. As I'm on contract I'll have to work right up until the due date if I want to keep getting paid. Let's just hope my waters don't break live on air! I have an absolute fear of them breaking in a public place. Like at work or in Dunnes Stores in the middle of the fruit and veg aisle or something. With some supervisor rushing off to get one of those yellow hazard yokes that indicates a wet floor to people so they don't slip.

Actually I was out shopping the other day for maternity bras because I've gone up yet another cup size. Yes, I'm officially ginormous now. But at least I look like a proper pregnant person now instead of an obese woman. Anyway I had to get new bras, comfy granny knickers and stuff I need for the hospital like heavy-duty sanitary pads, a nursing bra and ointment for cracked nipples. Very sexy, not.

I was so depressed about having to spend my hard-earned money on all this awful stuff instead of treating myself to a slinky black going-out dress, that I decided once I'd finished my shopping I'd treat myself to a large pizza and a beer. The little Italian restaurant I went to, just off Grafton Street, was empty and I was shown to a seat at the window by an exceptionally charming waiter. The smell of delicious food drifting from the kitchen area got my taste buds very excited. My sense of smell is really strong now. It's not often for the best though. For example the smell of petrol makes me want to retch so I need to steer clear of filling stations if at all possible. Also, if I'm on a train or a bus and there is one single person on it with BO I can smell it as if my face was buried in their underarm – gross! The other thing I cannot do now is walk down Henry Street because of the amount of people who walk down it puffing fags. If I'm walking behind them the cigarette smoke goes right in my face and I feel like gagging. Yuk! I never noticed before how many pedestrians smoke on Henry Street!

Chip shops are also a killer. The smell of grease – bleurgh! Anyway the good thing was that the smell in this little restaurant was making me hungry, not sick. It was so nice not to feel sick for a change. I couldn't wait to tuck in.

"Today we have a special offer. A free glass of house red or white with every main course," the handsome sallow-skinned waiter said with a warm Mediterranean smile.

How cute, I thought. "That's a great offer," I said, delighted I'd come in. "I'll go for a large veggie pizza with all the trimmings, and a red wine."

In fact red wine was even better than beer, I reasoned with myself. Red wine is supposed to be good for you. Healthy, even – in moderation of course. And it was free on this occasion, so you know, no contest.

"We 'ave soft drinks too if you prefer. Cola?"

"No, no, I'm fine with the wine," I said. Then I relaxed into my seat, glad to put my feet up. It was so nice to have nothing to do for a change. I really should keep counting my blessings, I thought. I had so much to be thankful for. This led me inevitably to think of Molly and Peggy. I made a mental note to meet up with Peggy again soon and fill her in on my latest news. Peggy doesn't have a mobile – so annoying – and she never answers her house phone. I think she can't hear it unless she's standing in the hallway right beside it.

So, anyway, there I was sitting by the window enjoying my delicious piping-hot pizza and especially enjoying picking the pieces of pineapple off it to savour on my tongue, when this guy walked past the window. This really tall, very good-looking and remarkably familiar man. He was exceptionally well-dressed in a navy suit (bet it was Armani), with an expensive-looking briefcase under his arm. He happened to glance in through the window just as I was gazing out. Our eyes met. Briefly. And the next minute I saw him walking in.

I went back to my pizza, trying to place him. Where the hell did I know him from? I took the first sip of my red wine and felt it trickle smoothly down my throat. It went down an absolute treat. Yum! I felt I deserved it after what I've been through the last few weeks.

Then, about a minute later, I looked up in surprise. There he was. The guy. Standing right in front of me. In the restaurant. Jesus, he was a ride. Startling green eyes and a perfect, square jaw. His skin was lightly tanned as if he'd been away on holidays somewhere sunny.

"Diana, isn't it?"

I could feel myself blush like a giddy schoolgirl. Shit. How did he know my name? What was his name? How did I know him? I shook his outstretched hand, my mouth full of pizza.

Now it was his turn to look awkward. "Sorry," he said in

a deep voice. A deep, sexy voice. South Dublin accent. "I shouldn't disturb you when you're having lunch."

I swallowed quickly and wiped my mouth with a napkin. "Oh no, not at all. It's great to see you. Sit down. Have you had lunch yourself? They're doing a great offer – if you order pizza you get a wine on the house."

"So the waiter told me as I was walking past, but unfortunately I've had lunch already."

"Have a glass of wine then," I said, surprising myself.

"Oh go on, you've twisted my arm," he laughed.

Lovely white teeth, I noted. "The wine might not be on the house though."

The good-looking bloke shrugged. "I don't mind paying for it," he said, laughing. "I might actually have an ice-cream too seeing as it's Thursday."

I still couldn't figure out where I knew him from or what his name was. It was killing me. After all, he knew MY name so I reckoned it would seem rude if I asked him his.

The waiter came over and gave him a big broad smile. I gulped in embarrassment. Oh God, no. He obviously thought this man was the father of my child. And suddenly it dawned on me that this handsome stranger who somehow knew my name didn't even know I was pregnant. How would he? The table we were sitting at was fairly high, covering most of my bump, and I was also wearing a big loose cardigan.

He ordered his wine and offered me another glass which I declined.

"You're being sensible," he laughed. I laughed back.

"I don't see you out and about much these days? Not since that night in Krystle anyway."

And then it dawned on me. Krystle. Oh God yes, I remembered him now. He tried to chat me up and I ran to the bathroom to puke and never saw him again.

"I've been lying low," I said which wasn't exactly true. "Listen, you'll have to excuse me, I'm so embarrassed. But I've completely forgotten your name."

"It's John," he said. "Not that hard to remember."

I didn't know whether he was being smart with me.

"Actually," he said, his face breaking into a broad grin, "I might not have told you my name. I know you didn't tell me yours but I found out from somebody what it was. You seemed to be in an awful hurry to get away from me that night as far as I remember."

If only he knew! He probably presumed I was off to meet my rich boyfriend or something, instead of going off to find somewhere safe to throw up my dinner.

"So, are you out this weekend?" he asked with a twinkle in his eye and I suddenly realised with a fright that he was flirting with me. It felt very odd indeed.

Men usually didn't chat up girls who were seven months pregnant. Then again, he didn't know, did he? I hoped I wasn't being deceitful by not telling him.

"No, I'm just going to have a quiet one this weekend. Work's been a bit hectic. I'll probably read a book or watch a DVD or something. Very boring, I'm afraid. What about yourself?"

"I'm going back to Krystle on Friday night because it's my mate's thirtieth. I've been working in London for the last couple of months so I haven't been out in Dublin in God knows how long."

That would make sense. He's been away. He hasn't seen my TV show. He hasn't Googled me either. If he Googled me he'd know I was pregnant.

He told me a bit about himself. He works in IT. Very dull. His words, not mine. He lives in a flat in Notting Hill. I'd say he makes good money. He said London was great if you had money and if you didn't it was no fun at all as the cost of living in the capital was so high.

He said he'd been over in Dublin for the week doing business and that he would be flying back to London on Monday. He said he was taking the rest of the day off because he'd been working flat out and needed to unwind. That day's business meeting had gone surprisingly well. By the way, was I free to go on to the Shelbourne for another drink? Yes, I was free. But I wasn't going. I was afraid to stand up and reveal my bump. And at the same time I was ashamed of myself for feeling afraid.

"I'm meeting my mother," I lied, looking at my watch. "So I'll just hang on here a bit if you don't mind."

If he was disappointed he didn't show it. "Are you doing a bit of shopping?" he enquired brightly. He eyed the plastic bag I had on the table. Thank God it wasn't see-through.

"Yes, I hope to pick up a few more bits and pieces," I said hurriedly, at the same time wondering should I come clean about the pregnancy. I wasn't sure how to go about it. I mean, should I have stood up and said, 'Nice to meet you and, by the way, just to let you know, I'm up the duff'?

I shook his hand, still sitting down. And then he was off.

I finished my wine, savouring every last drop, and thought about going to visit Peggy. I rang her number but as usual nobody picked up. After a bit of internal debating, I decide to go home instead. I was tired now and my bed was calling.

I went to pay for my meal but the waiter shook his head. "No, no, no," he insisted.

For a brief moment I wondered if it was on the house. Had he recognised me from the TV too just like the barman in Peggy's local? But then he cleared things up for me. Well, sort of.

"Your husband paid for it," he said. "*Ciao*!"

Diana xx

49

30th June

Molly,
My baby is a total party animal. Yes, the Lord have pity on me but as soon as I lie down for the night, he seems to want to go disco-dancing and the DJ in my tummy doesn't stop spinning the discs till about 4.00 a.m. Sheer torture.

Mind you, the madness will soon be over when baby pops out. I can't believe we're actually going to meet in a couple of months. I'm so excited. I wonder what he looks like. Is he cute? Does he look like me or Roger? With any luck he'll look like me. Not that I think I'm gorgeous but naturally I'd rather see myself in my child than Roger.

It'll be weird not feeling like a house any more but to be honest I'm sick of this pregnancy lark. It drags on forever. My baby gets a lot of hiccups too, it's mad. When he gets the hiccups (usually at the god-awful hour of 2.00 a.m. or thereabouts) my whole body jumps. Baby often gets the hiccups if I drink so I'm trying my best not to drink anymore. It doesn't sit well with him. He particularly seems to hate champagne and goes bananas if I have a glass.

Mum asked me the other day why I even drink the odd glass

of champagne when I know it makes me so sick. I replied that I'm sick every day and every night anyway so I might as well. But I think I'll give it a rest now. I can drink champagne once Baba's here as a welcome-home treat. It'll be something to look forward to. All the pregnancy literature (and believe me when I say I devour it!) advises mums-to-be to get plenty of sleep in the final stage of pregnancy because once the baby comes you sure as hell won't get much of a chance to sleep then. But it's not so easy for me. I work full-time. Also the TV is always on in our house in the evenings and it's always loud as Dad's quite deaf. I need ear-plugs.

I find I'm tossing and turning a lot now in my sleep, trying to find a comfortable position for the bump. It's also tiring walking around and driving. I went out to see Noreen in the nursing home today and treated myself to a taxi-ride there and back. Noreen was in a bad mood. She'd been squabbling with Dorothy again. Apparently Dorothy had robbed her bridge partner, a woman called Alice. It all sounded a bit dramatic.

Noreen had her hat and coat on when I arrived. "I presume we're going out?"

"I didn't bring the car this time," I apologised.

"So we're not going out?" Noreen looked indignant. Old people can be very belligerent when they want to be.

I felt guilty then. "There's a café across the way. We could go there."

"Well, it's not my favourite place but it will have to do, I suppose," she grumbled as I took her arm and led her out of the nursing home by the arm.

If one of us falls, I thought to myself, the other doesn't stand a chance. It took us about half an hour to cross the road (actually that's a bit of an exaggeration but it did feel like forever!).

Noreen stuck up her nose at the simple menu. "I hate

lasagne and I hate chips," she announced, loudly enough for the whole café to hear.

"Why don't you get soup of the day and some brown bread, then?" I suggested.

We asked what the soup of the day was and were told it was mushroom.

"Oh God, I hate mushroom," said Noreen.

"What about a panini then, with ham and melted cheese?"

"A what?"

"Or a baked potato with beans?"

"I'll go for that so. And I'll have a cup of tea also."

I'd a feeling today wasn't going to be the easiest of days. Noreen seemed in funny form. She had convinced herself that some of the other residents of the nursing home had it in for her and were ganging up on her. I thought I'd better have a word with the head sister when we got back, just to see if I could find out what was going on.

"I'd like to go to Spiddal," said Noreen as we waited for our grub.

"What, now?"

"No, of course not. Not right this minute. I'd need to get organised and my hair needs setting. It's a holy show."

"You've an appointment with Veronica tomorrow. I checked before we left."

"Veronica doesn't speak English."

"But that doesn't matter, Noreen. She knows how to do your hair nicely."

"I need a change of scenery. I'm depressed in that place. Nobody speaks English."

"Were you happy in Spiddal?" I'd never had much of a chance to ask Noreen about her youth before.

"Well, I suppose I was. We didn't have much money – my father, your great-grandfather was a fisherman."

"I know that from Molly's diary," I said. "But what about your mother? What did she do?"

"She stayed at home and kept the family going. Daddy was very fond of the drink so our mother had to hide his money so she could buy food with it. I remember it well. Sometimes she'd hide it under our mattresses because she knew Daddy wouldn't ever think of looking there."

Noreen's long-term memory was excellent even though her short-term memory left something to be desired. It gave me hope that she could recall so much.

"Why did you all leave Galway and move up to Dublin?"

Noreen stirred a lump of sugar into her tea. "I'm not really sure. We were never given a particular reason but I think it was something to do with Molly. You know, people were talking. You can imagine what it's like living in a small village where nothing much happens, especially during the winter."

I could well imagine. People talk even in Dublin and that's a capital city.

"We moved up to Dublin and Daddy got a job working on the docks as a labourer. He'd go down every morning that he was sober which wasn't very often. Sometimes he'd get work and sometimes he wouldn't. It just depended. Lots of men used to go down so there was fierce competition. There were no guarantees. There was no such thing as social welfare back then either."

I drank it all in. God, times were tough back then, weren't they? Our generation really doesn't have clue. We're all moaning about the recession now and the fact that we have to give up our penchant for Jimmy Choos and fancy cocktails in five-star establishments, but we don't know what it's like to starve.

"Noreen? You know the way lots of people from Ireland emigrated back then to places like England and America?

Well, why didn't your family do that? Your father would have got work somewhere else."

Noreen grimaced. "I know. My father really wanted to go. He hated this country. But my mother refused to leave. She said she'd never live anywhere else and that if he wanted to go he'd have to go without her. She knew he'd never go alone."

"Why do you think that was?"

"Molly, of course. Mum would never leave as long as her youngest daughter was slaving away, pregnant, in the laundry in Dublin. She used to visit her on the sly and write letters to her."

"Isn't it ironic then that Molly went to live in England herself then?"

"It is ironic."

"Did your mother never see her again? After she went to England?"

"She did. Just the once. Mammy went to London as soon as she found out she had cancer to say goodbye to Molly."

At that point Noreen's eyes filled with tears and my heart felt it was being squeezed by a tight fist.

"Oh God, how awful!"

"It was a tragedy alright. My father was inconsolable when my mother got the diagnosis. The cancer had spread to all the vital organs and she was told by the doctor that she had only six weeks to live. In the end she got seven and a bit."

A lone tear escaped down her cheek. I felt wretched for her. Life was unbearably sad. Or death, rather.

"Did your father mind her going over to Molly?"

Noreen shrugged. "He knew nothing about it. He never ever forgave Molly for bringing shame on the family. Ironic, really. When half the time he was out of his mind drunk and couldn't provide for us even though he was head of the household."

"So what did your mum tell him? That she was going on a holiday?"

Noreen gave me an almost pitiful smile. "Of course not. She lied through her teeth as per usual. Told him she was going to see a cancer specialist in London who was able to cure people. It gave him such hope."

"But no such specialist existed?"

"No. Nobody could have saved her. She was riddled with the damn disease. But she was a woman on a mission. My mother was so strong and proud. She wanted to say goodbye to all three of her daughters personally. Said that was the only way she could die in peace. She wanted to take your mother with her. But Ita said no. She said the overnight boat and train journey would be far too long for a little girl. And anyway she didn't want your mother getting confused and asking questions."

The tears were flowing now. Down both our cheeks. Unstoppable.

Noreen stopped for a moment and sipped her tea. "It's gone cold," she said.

"Would you like a refill?"

"I would, thanks."

We waited for the refill and took a bit of time to dry our tears. "I'm sorry for bringing it all back, Noreen," I said, placing my hand over her dry bony one.

"Don't be sorry. I should have spoken about it years ago but I wasn't allowed. Ita didn't want to talk about it. And neither did my father. I've been bottling my feelings up all those years."

After a moment's pause I said, "So your mother went to London alone, knowing she was dying?"

"She did. And Molly was distraught and said that she had brought bad luck on all the family. It was awful the way poor Molly punished herself. My mother came back home and said she could die in peace now that she had seen Molly. She really really loved her youngest daughter. I always suspected Molly was her favourite. She was so bright and beautiful."

"It must have been sad that Molly couldn't have gone to the funeral though."

"On the contrary. She was there."

I sat up straight in my chair. How was she there? Had the hatchet finally been buried?

Noreen shook her head, however. "No. That's just wishful thinking, I'm afraid. Of course, that's the way it should have been but Molly didn't stand with the rest of the family in the church. She stood at the back by herself. Nobody saw her, except for me. My father didn't see her. She was wearing glasses and her hair was cut quite short and dyed black. It was winter and most of her face was covered with a thick scarf. She was almost unrecognisable."

"You recognised her though."

"Of course. I'd have known Molly anywhere. I went up to her and gave her a hug. I asked her to meet with me later and she said she couldn't because she was staying up in a hotel in Dublin and then going back to England early the next day."

Noreen paused for breath. I could tell she was getting upset again.

"I was worried about her. I thought she looked very pale. She admitted she hadn't been well and had been throwing up all that morning. It was probably just a bug, she said. She had wanted to pay her respects and also catch a glimpse of her little girl. She didn't go up to her because she didn't want to draw attention to herself. I think that must have been the last time she ever saw your mother, Rosemary."

"How sad."

"Yes, very sad. I felt very sorry for her having to go back to a hotel in Dublin by herself. But it turned out she wasn't by herself after all. She had, well, company."

"Company?"

"Yes, the priest whom she was working for."

"He'd come over to Ireland too? That was very nice of him. At least she had somebody to support her at such a difficult time."

"Hmm. If you wanted to call it support."

I frowned. I was confused. Why had Noreen's demeanour suddenly changed? What was she holding back from me?

Noreen looked at me straight in the eye, her face now showing clear signs of distress. "Oh Diana, can't you put two and two together? She was his mistress as well as his housekeeper. His mistress! And what's more Molly was expecting his child at our mother's funeral."

Diana x

50

1st July

Molly, I'm obsessed with Brie cheese. Seriously, it's not funny. I literally find myself dreaming about it. Only because I know I can't eat it. Every time I'm in the supermarket I feel myself drawn to the cheese aisle and I have to steer myself away from it. I don't know why pregnant women aren't supposed to eat it but there's some medical reason, I suppose.

It's such a shame that I can do so little to cheer myself up. I used to drink gallons of coffee, now the smell of it makes me want to gag. Same for all caffeine. I also used to drink Diet Coke. Now I'm on Lucozade. Did I tell you? I've swapped grapefruit juice for Lucozade. One day it made me sick so I switched to Lucozade. Now I drink that from morning to night. Like I'm hung-over or something.

But at least I don't nibble at coal. Or scoop ice from the freezer. Or eat jars of gherkins. Like some pregnant women apparently do.

I've recovered from yesterday's ordeal. Almost. It actually took a while for the initial shock to hit me. As Noreen was making her startling revelations, it felt like the walls of the tiny café were closing in on me. Crushing my brain. I was flabbergasted. How had that happened? My granny had had an affair with a priest? But I thought she had left the priest's house and gone to work somewhere else. Where would she have gone though? Did Noreen have any idea?

"No," my great-aunt explained. "When Molly left the priest's house she didn't leave a forwarding address."

"Did she not?" I said, feeling very disappointed. How could somebody just vanish into thin air though?

Noreen could obviously see how distressed I was becoming. "Maybe, darlin', you should just leave it be. You're very vulnerable right now. You should be looking after yourself at this late stage of your pregnancy. You need to protect that little fellow growing inside you. He's depending on you to be strong."

"But it's my granny we're talking about. We can't just forget about her. She was your little sister."

"It was a long time ago."

"But . . ."

Noreen closed her eyes as if it was all becoming too much for her. "I'd like to go back to the nursing home now," she said before I could go any further.

It was the first time I'd ever heard her say something like that. And it made me feel wretched. I don't know when to stop, do I?

Diana

51

12th July

Dear Molly,
My mother told me today that Jayne would be moving out. From now on I'm going to have my sister's room, which is great because it's a lot bigger than mine and she has a fine double bed as opposed to my single one.

"There'll also be a lot more room for your cot and all your stuff," Mum added enthusiastically.

I'd been in the kitchen ironing a blouse for work. A hideous lime billowing yoke that makes me look like a green hippopotamus. But hardly anything else fits now. I can no longer squeeze into my earlier pregnancy tops. I can't even breathe in them.

I wasn't really listening to Mum at the time. She goes on about nothing an awful lot and I tend to zone out. I'm really not interested in local gossip like Mum is. I do say hello to the neighbours and I'm polite but I don't want to get involved in their lives. Not the way Mum does. She's always talking about them. And she's always talking about myself and Jayne to them. She must drive them round the bend.

I kept ironing without saying anything. I was thinking about a pram. I hadn't got one. I wondered how much they were. No doubt they were hideously expensive.

"She's moving in with Clive," she said with a slight sniff. "Not that I approve, but they're all moving in with each other now, all the young people. I don't know. Morals seem to be flying out the window."

I wondered if she knew who was she was talking to. Maybe she was mixing me up with somebody else. I hung my hideous top on a hanger. I was exhausted. Ironing just one thing is exhausting these days. I hate the way the steam rises in my face, making it all sweaty. I hate the way the iron is so heavy and I need to ask somebody to help me fold up the ironing board and put it away. It makes me feel so feeble.

"That's funny. I was talking to Jayne before she left for work this morning," I said. "And she never said anything."

"Maybe she forgot."

I stared at my mother. "How could she have forgotten? When's she moving out?"

"Next Monday."

"So soon? Obviously she's been planning the move for some time. It's just odd that she didn't mention it to me, that's all."

My mother's gaze flickered. "I think she didn't want you getting upset."

Now I was insulted. Why would I mind Jayne moving out? If anything I'd be pleased to have more room for myself and the baby. Did she think I'd be jealous or something? Surely not. As if I'd be so small-minded and peevish. "I couldn't give a fig if she moves out," I said belligerently. "But I do think it would have been normal for her to let me know herself."

When Jayne came home that evening from work I asked her straight. "Are you moving out?"

She looked at me shiftily, like she had been caught out doing something wrong. "Yes, I am. It'll be a bit crowded here when your baby arrives. I wouldn't want to be getting in the way."

I raised an eyebrow. "Of course you wouldn't be getting in the way," I objected. "There's plenty of room in this house."

Jayne sighed and grabbed herself a chilled can of Heineken from the fridge and took a gulp. "I need this," she said.

"Where are you moving?"

"To Monkstown. We've bought an apartment there overlooking the sea. It's very nice. We'll be having a housewarming after we move in, you can see the place then."

We? My eyes nearly self-ejected from their sockets. Was I hearing things? Herself and Clive were buying a property together? Already? That was crazy. They barely knew each other. And it cost a fortune to live in Monkstown. Jayne was always moaning about how broke she was, how she never had any money for anything.

"When did all this come about?"

Jayne sank into the sofa and used the remote to turn on the TV. She obviously didn't want to discuss it. "We decided ages ago," she said dismissively, eyes firmly fixed on the screen in front of her.

"But it's not like you're with Clive long-term."

Jayne swung around towards me, an angry look flashing across her face. "Don't you even think about giving me a lecture! You're having a baby with somebody you're not even going out with!"

I was stung. Where had that come from? I thought it was a low blow. I left the room and went outside. Dad was in the garden tending to the plants.

"How are you, love?" He looked relatively pleased to see me. Well, at least somebody was.

"Jayne's not in great form, is she?" I said.

Dad doesn't like taking sides. It makes him feel uncomfortable. "We're all under a lot of strain these days," he said gently, digging at a patch of soil. "The recession has hit everyone."

"Well, obviously it hasn't hurt her pocket too much if she's buying a pad in Monkstown. I mean, I know property prices have come down and everything but still."

"They got quite a bargain, though. It was a repossession sale. The banks sold it on the previous owner."

"I wouldn't buy a repossessed home. It's bad luck. I'm surprised at Jayne. She's normally so superstitious. Did she tell you how much they paid for it?"

"Yes, she did," he answered, not giving anything away.

I was amazed that my sister had actually confided in Dad about the price. She's normally so secretive about everything, especially when it comes to her finances.

"She had to," he added, almost as an afterthought, "because I was the guarantor."

"That was nice of you."

"Well, they wouldn't have been able to buy it otherwise. The banks are slow to lend to first-time buyers no matter what they say."

I didn't know what it was but I had a hunch that he was keeping something from me. Why was everyone being so secretive about Jayne's apartment?

I decided to probe. "Even with you being guarantor, though, I'm amazed that they got a loan without proving they had a substantial deposit saved first. But maybe I'm wrong. Maybe the banks are becoming a bit more generous."

Dad laughed out loud. "I don't think so. Without the help of Clive's parents and your mother and myself, they'd never have got their hands on the keys."

I stood still in my tracks. Mum and Dad gave Jayne a deposit. But how? They had no money. They were broke. Dad had lost a load of shares recently.

I know for a fact that he hasn't been sleeping recently because he's been worrying so much about his pension. I know all this because Mum told me. Mum also had to cancel her annual golf membership in the local club this year for the first time, and they both decided not to go skiing last Christmas with their friends like they'd always done before. Bearing all this in mind, how in God's name were they able to help Jayne finance the purchase of her plush new Southside pad?

"How much did you give her?"

"Ah, love," my father said wiping his brow with the back of his hand, "I don't particularly want to discuss something private like that. When your turn comes, you'll be helped out too. You know you will."

When my turn came along? How in God's name would I ever afford to be able to buy a nice luxury apartment on one income?

I went back inside the house. Jayne was still in the sitting room watching TV3's Xposé. I noticed she had opened a second Heineken. Funny that. Jayne doesn't normally drink beer. Always says her worst nightmare would be to grow a beer belly. This house move must indeed be stressing her out if she's using beer in the evenings to help her relax.

"Dad says he and Mum helped you with the deposit for your new apartment. That was really decent of them, wasn't it?"

"Yeah. And?"

"There's no need to get defensive. I was only just commenting. I was just wondering where they came up with the money."

"They sold the boat."

"What?"

"Yeah, they never use it any more anyway."

I was amazed. "But they love that boat! Sailing is a passion of theirs. You know it is."

My sister was getting more and more irritated. I could see by the glowering expression on her face. She took another slug of beer. "They needed to sell it. Do you know how much it costs to moor a boat in Dun Laoghaire? It's crazy money."

"That's not the point. They loved that boat."

"That IS the point. Jesus! They couldn't afford to keep it any more so they were going to have to sell it sometime. They're not millionaires, you know."

"Did you put pressure on them to sell it? Is that why you didn't tell me about buying the apartment?"

Jayne swung around, her face flushed. I wondered if it was the effects of the two beers she'd just gulped down or whether she'd sat outside earlier on her lunch break and caught some sun-rays.

"Are you accusing me of harassing them? Are you? What's wrong with you? I thought you'd be happy for me. Fat chance of that."

"Well, if you thought I'd be happy for you then why didn't you tell me ages ago that you were moving out?"

"I don't know why I'm being interrogated, Diana. I'm excusing you this time because I'm allowing for the fact that you're seven months pregnant and your hormones are all over the place. If I didn't know that I'd think you were jealous or something."

I went to bed then. I needed to get away from my sister in order to calm down. I just couldn't believe she'd do something so sneaky behind my back like try to persuade Mum and Dad to get rid of their boat so she could buy a cosy love nest with Clive. She barely knew the man!

When I got up at around nine o'clock after a bit of sleep, I felt momentarily better. I decided I shouldn't really be fussing about Jayne. Whatever arrangement she made with our parents wasn't really any of my business. So I decided to apologise. I knew Mum and Dad would be out playing bridge so this would be a good time to talk to her. I found her in the kitchen eating a salad, with a gold-fish-sized bowl of white wine beside her on the table. What was it with all the drinking all of a sudden? Jayne rarely consumes alcohol. She's a complete health freak.

The radio was on so I went to turn it down.

"Leave it alone," she said, almost growling at me. "I'm listening to that."

"I just wanted to say something to you," I said, switching it off.

She looked up obstinately.

I sat opposite her at the kitchen table. I was so tempted to pour myself a glass of wine too but I decided against it. "I'm sorry for having a go at you earlier, Jayne. I am delighted for you that you've got a new place."

"No, you're not," she suddenly snapped, taking me by surprise. "You're not remotely pleased for me. You cannot be pleased for anybody at the moment, Diana. I don't know what's got into you. When you're not having a go at Mum, you're upsetting Dad or going out to Noreen to annoy her. Today it just happened to be my turn."

I was totally taken aback. "That's definitely not true," I said in my defence. "Okay, I know I sometimes open my mouth and speak my mind without thinking, but I never deliberately mean to hurt anybody."

Jayne picked up her glass of wine and moved away from the table.

"Don't you even want to talk?" I asked, feeling hurt.

"What's there to talk about? Do you want to know the truth? The reason I didn't tell you about me and Clive moving in together was because I thought you would be upset and I didn't want to rub my happiness in your face."

My mouth fell open in surprise.

"And," she continued on her rant, "you have proven me so right. I know things are tough for you at the moment, and I've been there for you. We all have. But being jealous of everybody will not make things any better for you, Diana, whatever you may think!"

Before I could answer back, she'd left the kitchen slamming the door behind her.

I burst into tears. I couldn't help it. Is that what they all thought? That I was jealous and spiteful and only concerned about myself? I was dismayed. I continued to sit at the kitchen table for what felt like a very long time with my head in my hands. I tried to ignore the questioning little voice in my mind which wouldn't go away. What if Jayne was right? Was I really trying to poke my nose into everybody else's lives in order to avoid accepting that my own life was a pitiful mess? No, surely not. No, no, definitely not. Well, hopefully not.

Di xx

52

15th July

Oh Lord, Molly, there's panic at work. Complete pandemonium. Due to an additional fall in advertising revenue, the powers that be have warned of more staff cutbacks. It's a really worrying situation that we're faced with because there's a skeleton staff running the whole operation as it is. I don't know where they are going to down-size, but I'm worried that I'll be let go if I take any time off at all to have a baby. I'm only on contract so I've no legal rights. I am almost hoping that I'll have the baby on a Friday night so I can go back into work on the Monday. The atmosphere is one of total doom and gloom. People tiptoe around as if they're walking on slabs of ice. They look so worried and fraught and they all have mortgages and it's been on the news that mortgage interest is going up soon. So many people who bought houses in this country in the last few years are in negative equity and now can't see the wood for the trees. It's so depressing.

Mum has kindly offered to look after my newborn for the first six weeks or so but then she says I'll have to get a nanny.

She says that the nanny can have my old room which is fantastic.

I honestly don't know what I'd do without my parents. There is no possible way I would be able to still work and look after the child myself. I still think it's unfair that Roger's life, unlike mine, isn't really going to change that much at all. He won't have to take any time off work. He can just carry on as usual as if nothing's happened.

I'm trying not to think about him at the moment though, because when I think about him I get stressed and feelings of intense resentment overcome me. The fact that his girlfriend is probably being pampered to within an inch of her life doesn't help either. He's probably waiting on her hand and foot and bringing her breakfast in bed every morning. It makes me ill just thinking about it. I haven't heard a peep from him at all. You'd swear I'd gone and got pregnant all by myself behind his back judging by his behaviour towards me. I discovered the other day that he'd even deleted me as his friend on Facebook. How sad is that? Like, what age is he? I don't even want to confront him about it because I wouldn't give him the satisfaction of letting him know I even noticed. Why of all the men in Ireland did I have to pick him to be my child's daddy?

Anyway, since I don't have too long to go now and I'm desperately trying not to lose my job, I've been considering different forms of childcare options. God, getting somebody to look after your pride and joy doesn't come cheap, that's for sure. A full-time nanny costs approximately four hundred euro a week. How I'm going to come up with that after tax I do not know. I'll be working just to pay the nanny but what other choice do I have? Give up my job and stay at home? Where else would I get work in the middle of a recession? There are no jobs going in the media. It's probably the worst-hit industry at the moment along with real estate. Excellent, capable, qualified, gorgeous-looking TV presenters are at home twiddling their thumbs at the moment. They're probably on social welfare because they feel they're too famous or overqualified to work as a shop assistant or as an office temp. High-profile journalists are teaching English as a foreign language. I met one such girl the other day. She was on our show recently talking about what it's like being a mother of twins. She now teaches Brazilian students at night in a college in town twice a week. She used to do all the fashion and beauty articles in the magazine where I have my column, but she took a break when her little boys were born. The editor now gets her nineteen-year-old PA to do the fashion and beauty instead. Cutbacks, how are ya! These are seriously scary times we're living in.

After looking into agencies which seem to charge quite a substantial amount of money to get you a nanny, I decided to post my own ad up on the internet and see what happened. I expected to get a few replies but when I got over a hundred of them I was stunned. My God, I didn't realise how many people out there wanted to work as nannies. It took me almost a whole day to sort through all the online applications. Obviously a lot of people out there can't read because I had specifically asked for a female and quite a few males had applied. I couldn't even imagine having a male nanny! Can you imagine putting him in my old room? Mind you, if he looked like Brad Pitt . . . Only joking!

There were a fair few applications from weird-looking people who had piercings all over their faces. Big turn-off! I don't understand why people would do that to themselves. Of course I did ask for photos to be sent along with the CVs because I think you can tell a lot from a photo. If somebody has a nice smiley honest-looking face then you'd imagine they'd be nice to your kids. Mum said I should try and get an Eastern European girl because apparently they work harder than other girls and would be happy to do housework too. She also said to get a thin girl because thin people aren't lazy. I thought she was being funny but she wasn't.

As soon as I told people in work that I was looking for a girl they were all more than willing to give their opinions.

"Don't get a Brazilian girl," said one of the cameramen, himself a father of four. "We have one and she's out partying until dawn every night of the week."

I made a mental note of that. Definitely don't want a party girl with a constant hangover.

"Stay away from Swedish girls," said Delia who works in the accounts. "They'll only go after your man when you're not looking."

I reminded her that I didn't have a man.

"Oh, well, then you'd probably be alright," she decided.

Everyone seemed to agree that Italians were very good with children although when it came to cleaning they weren't so enthusiastic. And apparently French girls spend all their time in their rooms. I dunno, it all seemed a bit racist to me. Surely all nannies are different? Surely it depends on the person and not where they come from?

I whittled the applications down to about ten. You seriously wouldn't believe some of the odd replies I had got. One German girl sent me a photo of her and her female friend. They both had shaved heads and tattoos on their shoulders. Said they didn't mind if they didn't get paid or anything, just as long as they could be together. Delete, delete, delete. Honest to goodness!

It's hard interviewing over the internet. There are things you need to be aware of. I'd been warned about scams, where a girl says she'd love to come and work for you in

Ireland and, you know, she sounds ideal but she's a student and doesn't have the money for her airfare. Would you be so kind as to forward her some money in advance? Really, you have to be so wary these days.

I decided to interview a girl who was already living in Dublin. She had been with a family for nine months and wanted somewhere closer to town. She called around to the house but she didn't smile once and when I asked her about the last family she worked for she told me she thought they were a bit boring.

I didn't think she would suit.

The next girl I met said she had a boyfriend who would like to stay overnight sometimes. I explained that because I lived with my parents that would be very impractical. She also said she was allergic to dogs. We have two. Next!

Then I met up with another girl in town. She was only interested in discussing pay and didn't ask me anything about myself. She said she was saving to go on a round-the-world trip and was only looking for a family for about six weeks or so. She admitted she hadn't any experience with babies even though she'd said in her CV that she had.

Two other girls that I was also supposed to meet with in town simply didn't bother showing up. So much for that! After two days of searching for the perfect nanny I was no better off than I was when I started. It was almost worse than online dating. Everybody seems perfect until you actually meet them.

Mum said I'd be better off waiting until the baby was a few weeks old. She said then I might be able to get somebody in late September, a student maybe for the academic year, who was hoping to learn English. Like an au-pair. I thought this might indeed be an option. An au-pair only worked thirty hours a week but only got one hundred euro pocket money as opposed to a proper salary. More affordable. And if my mum could help me mind the child as well, that'd be great. It would mean I could save my money for a deposit for a home of our own.

I know prices of property are coming down but I still can't afford one in an area that I'd like and I don't want to raise my son in my bedroom. I want my own place and to feel like I'm my own boss. I dream of a nursery for my little boy, painted blue and yellow maybe with cute Bob the Builder curtains and a cot full of teddies. I don't care how hard I have to work for it and how much I have to save. I desperately want my own home and sharing is not an option. I'm not a student who can kip in with other young people who leave dishes mounting up in the sink and leave beer cans and cigarette butts in their wake. And anyway I can't think very many people would even want to share a place with a single mum and her baby.

In the meantime I need to make even more cutbacks. I don't spend very much anyway because my hair and make-up is done for free in work and we also get the papers/ magazines free of charge too. I don't buy coffee because you can bring your own jar into the canteen and stick your name on it, but I do buy my lunch in the canteen. Maybe I should start bringing in my own sandwiches. I've noticed a lot of people doing that recently. But I dunno, I'd feel so miserable making room in the staff fridge for my bread all wrapped up in tin foil. God, why did I not save up in the last few years? Why did I spend crazy money on things like a designer white bag? I bet NOBODY buys white bags anymore. We're all about black. We're mourning the so-called boom years. And just when the recession hit us out of nowhere, I somehow thought it was a good idea to bring a baby into the world? If only I had a rich man. If only I was still slim and not pregnant. Then I could have answered John's flirty Facebook email that he sent the other day. He asked me if I was around next weekend. Around? Yes, I'm round but not available. I'm afraid to go anywhere now in case my waters break.

D x

53

29th July

Molly, I haven't been to a single ante-natal class. I know, I feel very guilty about that. At my last hospital appointment the midwife asked me in a very loud voice whether I'd attended any of the classes yet. I said I hadn't got around to it. The thing is, I don't really have the time to be coming into town to do the classes. They're free of charge but you have to book in advance. I haven't booked. To be perfectly honest I don't want to sit around in a circle with a lot of pregnant couples. I think as a single person I'd stick out like a sore thumb.

Maybe I'm being paranoid but I just don't want people feeling sorry for me. A friend of mine said she went to the classes and a fake tit was passed around so that people could practise how to breastfeed. Also a video of a woman giving birth was shown and a couple of men went pale and had to leave the room. After hearing that I was seriously put off going to the classes.

Nonetheless I told the midwife that I had indeed booked into the ante-natal classes and was very much looking forward to them. Anything for an easy life, really. Then I came home and had a bath. I didn't enjoy it as much as I used to enjoy my baths. You see, even though I've had to give up most of life's pleasures in the last few months such as cheese, whiskey and sauna sessions at the gym, I've still relied on my nightly bath for a bit of comfort and something to look forward to. But now, sadly, the water in the bath no longer covers my bump. So even though the rest of me is nice and warm beneath the soapy water, my poor bump is cold and miserable, looming out of the bubble bath like a lone mountain over a lake.

I didn't stay in the bath long. Just a quick dip. Then when I got out I wrapped the biggest bath sheet I could find around me, and got into bed. Just before I turned off the light I gave my mobile a quick check. Normally the only messages I get these days are from random people asking, "Have you had the baby yet?" It's so annoying. Like, if I had the baby I'd tell people, not keep it a big secret so I wish they'd stop asking. It's not a race against time for goodness' sake! But on this occasion there were no such annoying texts. Just a lone message. From Roger.

'Ring me. ASAP. Please.'

It was the word 'please' that really got to me.

So unlike Roger.

What on earth was going on?

D x

54

1st August

Well, Molly, I met my ex-boyfriend at the Four Seasons Hotel. When I initially replied to his message he insisted that we meet face to face. He had sounded very strained and distant on the phone and wouldn't tell me what was wrong with him.

Immediately I presumed he had lost his job and was going to tell me this bit of information so that I wouldn't be expecting child support off him. One thing I was sure about was that he wasn't just contacting me for a friendly little catch-up. He'd made it clear time and time again that he and me were not to be. And I couldn't think why on earth he'd want to see me now.

It took me ages to get ready. At the moment I'm living in a velour pink Juicy Couture maternity tracksuit which is the most comfortable thing I own, but it's not really suitable for The Four Seasons Hotel which is where Roger wanted to meet up. I had recently bought an evening dress to go to a TV awards thing but I couldn't possibly have worn something that fancy to meet my ex for a coffee. Oh, the dilemma of it all! Hardly anything in my wardrobe fitted, but in the end I went with a simple, black maternity jumper and my navy maternity jeans. I put a pair of Chanel-type sunglasses on my head to make me look semi-glamorous. Luckily I'd just happened to get my hair highlighted the day before so I didn't have any unsightly roots but I have gone darker than usual because with a newborn baby I don't want to even have to think about hairdressers for the first few weeks of his life.

Anyway, even though I looked as wide as a wheelbarrow, I kept telling myself that it didn't matter a jot because Roger was the person responsible for making me look that huge. It's not like I was just being lazy on the couch stuffing myself with fruitcake for the last few months.

I made sure my face was nicely made-up, however, with lashings of mascara and I put some deep red lipstick called Vixen on my lips to make me look confident and sexy. Why I still felt the need to impress Roger, I didn't know. But I did.

He was reading a copy of the Irish Times, or at least pretending to, when I walked in. I spotted him immediately even though he was seated at the far end of the lounge with his back to the entrance as if he didn't particularly want anybody to see him. I felt nervous approaching him from behind. I couldn't imagine what he'd want to see me for.

I tapped him on the shoulder and he flinched.

"Hi," he said, turning around to face me. His eyes were unsmiling and he looked tired.

"Hi," I said back and took a seat.

"You're getting very big now," he said, eyes firmly fixed on my belly.

"I know." Was that supposed to be a compliment?

The waitress came around. I said I'd have a tea. Although I could have murdered a straight brandy right at that very minute.

"How are you?" he said.

"Fine," I lied.

"You look well."

"Thanks."

I remained non-commital.

"It's good to see you," he added.

I stared blankly. Did he expect me to reciprocate? Tell him it was good to see him too? I tried in vain to read his face. This was too confusing. Couldn't he have phoned instead of dragging me all the way here? Enough with the mind games now, I thought. I was suddenly furious at him for inconveniencing me. I was short of breath and tired. This was my one precious day off.

"I believe congratulations are in order, Roger," I said coldly. I wasn't going to sit there and pretend we were long-lost buddies. Like everybody else in Dublin I knew he was getting married to the child bride. "I don't know if you got my text about –"

"Oh, there's no need to congratulate me."

"No? Oh. I read somewhere that you were engaged. In fact it was an announcement in the Irish Times. I was wondering if it was going to be a shotgun wedding or whether you were going to wait until after both babies were born. That might be a bit more sensitive."

Roger held up a hand to stop me with a pained expression on his face, as if he were Simon Cowell from the X-Factor and I was singing out of tune.

"Stop the sarcasm, Diana, let's try and behave like adults here."

I gulped. Was he giving out to me for being childish? He who had walked out on me when I was pregnant to date some silly kid just out of school? Was he seriously for real?

I was about to open my mouth when he started to speak.

In a very low voice. As though he were afraid somebody else would hear. He leaned towards me with his face uncomfortably close to mine. If I'd stuck my tongue out I could have licked his face. Not of course that I'd dream about doing such a thing but it's mad the way the strangest thoughts run through your mind at the strangest of times.

"Diana, I've been doing some thinking."

I raised an eyebrow. Oh?

"I realise I haven't been there for you much."

Much? Was he completely taking the piss? He hadn't been there for me AT ALL!

"But I want to make amends. I want to be there for you more." Then he halted. As if even he didn't quite believe what he was saying himself.

I tried to open my mouth to speak but I couldn't. The room was spinning. My ears were ringing. I found myself gripping onto the arms of my chair with my fingers.

"The thing is," he said hesitantly, "the thing is that I don't want you to get your hopes up."

Miraculously, my power of speech suddenly returned and I cleared my throat. "Believe me, Roger, I don't have any hopes for the two of us. I have no emotions left for you whatsoever." I eyed him steadily so he would know I meant business.

He looked gobsmacked. Totally taken aback.

Did he think tormenting me was fun? None of this made sense. Why had he wanted to meet me so urgently? So that he could tell me not to get my hopes up again? As if I'd be so foolish as to get my hopes up. It had taken me long enough to pull myself together and realise that I was facing this difficult journey alone.

"I see," he said and hung his head in a deflated kind of way. "I didn't realise there was nothing there at all."

At that moment I felt a satisfying surge of power rise within me. He was losing his cocky edge. Finally. Well, good. I'm not sure where I was getting my strength from but I sat up straight in my chair, drained my cup of tea and said, "I do hope that we can be friends for our kid's sake as I think it's for the best, but I can't believe you thought that I was still pining for you when you were sharing another girl's bed and I was alone in my bed expecting your child. That is just ridiculous, Roger."

"The whole thing has been a bit of a rollercoaster, I agree, but –"

"A rollercoaster?" I felt myself getting hot. I needed air. "No, Roger," I found myself saying. "It's not like that at all. A rollercoaster ride has ups and downs. There have been no ups in this sorry situation. Only downs. Now, really, I need to go home. I'm tired."

"Can I give you a lift?"

"No, thanks. I've parked my car outside in the car park."

"Can I at least walk you to the car then?" he said, reaching out to touch my arm as I stood up. Like I was an old woman incapable of getting to my own two feet instead of a healthy woman who was merely very pregnant. I let him pay for the beverages. And he escorted me to the door protectively which I found a bit awkward. Why had it suddenly become so important for him to be involved in my well-being and safety?

At the door, a few people were coming into the hotel, so we waited until we had some space to make our exit. But through the glass I suddenly noticed that one of the people entering the hotel was John. Yes, that John! God, I hadn't seen him since that day in the restaurant although I had sent him a private Facebook message thanking him for paying for my meal. He'd sent a fairly flirty reply suggesting that we should hook up again sometime but I never answered. When you're heavily pregnant it doesn't seem right to be flirting with men who aren't the father of your child.

I lowered my eyes as he stepped into the hotel lobby. Too late. He'd seen me.

"Diana!" he said in a surprised tone of voice. I think the surprise soon turned to shock as his gaze wandered downwards and fell upon my tummy. "Oh my God," he said. Such a teenage-girl thing to say, I thought.

"Yes, I'm pregnant."

His hand flew to his mouth. He really did look stunned. And he probably felt like a bit of a fool for blatantly flirting so much with me. "I didn't know, you know, when we were in the restaurant."

I felt Roger's grip tighten on my arm. The nerve of him!

John looked at him in bewilderment. "And you must be the lucky dad-to-be," he said, holding out a hand for Roger to shake. "Congratulations."

At this point I'd have given anything for the ground to open up and swallow me. The whole scenario was unreal. Like a scene in a bad movie. I didn't want so much drama in my life.

John must have thought I was some kind of twisted freak for leading him on. Even though I hadn't meant to do anything of the sort. I hurriedly said goodbye and exited, Roger in my wake.

"Who was that?" asked Roger when we were safely out of earshot.

"John," I said giddily, walking on ahead of him. I didn't want him holding my arm anymore as if I was some piece of property he'd just rescued from the Lost and Found box.

"Yes, but who is he?"

"Just a friend," I said cryptically. I didn't feel I had to elaborate. What business was it of Roger's?

"He seemed to be very surprised to see you were pregnant. Were you out with him recently?"

"Yes, we had lunch together a while ago," I said cheerily, suddenly realising that Roger might be just the teeniest bit jealous. "He's great company. Good-looking chap too."

I didn't quite know where my new surge of confidence was coming from but I allowed myself to enjoy my little victorious moment. After months of all the mental torture Roger had put me through, all those feelings of loneliness, rejection and despair that he'd subjected me to, I felt I was entitled to a few moments of smugness. And John was indeed a good-looking fellow. He'd looked exceptionally handsome today in a smart charcoal-grey suit and bold, turquoise tie. Tall, broad, clean-shaven and with a sun-kissed face, he'd looked a damn sight sexier than Roger anyway. And the hilarious thing was that deep down Roger knew it.

I stopped by my car. "Well, it was nice to see you again," I said, offering my hand instead as he went to give me a kiss.

Roger had a weary look on his face. As though this wasn't the outcome he'd been hoping for. "Are you free this weekend?"

"I'm free every weekend," I said, looking him straight in the eye. "Not that you seemed to notice these last few months. But what do you think pregnant women do in their spare time? Go out disco-dancing? Mountaineering? Ice-skating?"

"I wish you wouldn't be so sarcastic."

"Me too. I wish I wasn't sarcastic either. It would be great to be more upbeat about the whole thing. But put yourself in my shoes and you might realise it's not as simple as that. I'm not a tap that can be turned on and off to suit you, Roger."

He looked at me awkwardly. I don't think he knew how to deal with the new Diana at all. Where was the old meek Diana who didn't mind putting up with whatever crap that was thrown at her?

"So you're turning me down?"

"I don't date men with girlfriends," I said. "Unlike some people."

"I'm not with Lee anymore."

I felt like I'd been hit by a train. What?

After a moment I found my voice again. "I see," I said quietly not even really registering what I was saying. My head had started to pound.

"She's gone now. She said she needed space. I'm single."

Gone? What was he talking about? That Lee girl was his fiancée and the future mother of his child. How could she be gone? Just like that? What the hell was going on? I was not capable of taking in this information. I needed to sit down again. I was overwhelmed with exhaustion.

"So you're not engaged any more?"

"That's right."

My eyes closed.

Suddenly everything went dark.

I'm exhausted now. I'll tell you the rest tomorrow.

Diana

55

2nd August

I made front page news, Molly. Yes, I know! It must have been a very slow news day indeed. But somebody in the maternity hospital must have called one of the newspapers.

I came around to hear Roger discussing his "partner" with one of the nurses. It was so confusing. Why would Lee be here too? And then I realised in a muddled haze that Roger was in fact talking about me. And that the last thing he'd told me before I passed out was that he was no longer with the child bride.

Roger and the nurse stopped talking when they saw I was awake. The nurse started patting my forehead with something cool and damp. I felt woozy. As if I'd been out on the tear for three weeks. Then I noticed Roger was crying. What was going on?

I struggled to stay awake. I heard somebody mention the loss of a baby. I felt myself being seized by a strange terror and instinctively tried to place the palms of my hands on my tummy but one of my hands was bandaged.

I'd broken a finger, but it was on my left hand which is

why I'm able to write to you today. The banjaxed finger is all bandaged up but the pain is something else.

I felt the bump. It was still there. But why were they talking about the baby being gone? I tried to sit up but every bone in my body ached.

"Is my baby okay?" I asked.

The nurse said everything was fine and that I shouldn't talk. I needed to rest and take it easy. But if everything was okay then why was Roger crying? I'd never seen him shed a tear before. I didn't think he even had it in him to cry. I'd just presumed he was a robot made out of pure steel.

I wondered if he was upset because he'd split up with Lee. I wondered if he was expecting me to shower him with sympathy after all that had happened. I'd just fainted and had a serious fall. Surely he didn't expect me to start mollycoddling him right now?

Then again, Roger is a complete narcissist with apparent notions that the whole world revolves around him. Somebody needed to tell him that the world had moved on and that time hadn't stood still since he left me.

The nurse left the room discreetly. Roger sat down on the chair beside the hospital bed and took my hand in his. The good hand. "Our baby is okay," he said, tears streaming down his cheeks so fast I became alarmed. He squeezed my hand.

"What is it?" I panicked.

"It's all been too much," he said shaking his head mournfully. "I couldn't have coped if you'd lost the baby as well."

"As well? Wh – at? Oh, God, no."

"Yes. Lee lost our little girl. And now she won't see me. She's gone away with her sister on a holiday to Australia. She wanted to get as far away from me as possible. She says she doesn't think we can ever be a couple again after what happened. She says that it's not me, it's her, and that seeing me keeps reminding her of –"

But then the nurse came back in again with some painkillers for me and Roger stopped talking.

Di x

56

3rd August

Hi Molly,
Just over one month left. I can't believe it. I'm now the size of a caravan. Or a mobile home, even. Every day just drags on and on. I said to a female colleague in work the other day that I was sick to the teeth of being pregnant. The woman, herself a mother of three tots under the age of seven laughed and said, "You ain't experienced nothing yet. The last few weeks are by far the worst." I nearly cried out loud. I mean, I said to her that I was so tired because I can't sleep and I get up every five minutes to go to the toilet.

She just laughed and laughed, rather sadistically I thought, and said, "You don't know the meaning of tiredness, hun. Just wait until Babser arrives. Then you'll know all about it."

And there I was looking for a bit of sympathy. Fat chance. Nobody cares. But then when I find myself moaning too much, I remember that some women are not as fortunate as myself.

I have to remember poor Peggy, and poor Molly and then there's poor Lee to add to the list of women I feel sympathy for now. I've tried not to think about her loss too much but

I do feel her pain. She must be going through hell at the moment.

A miscarriage could happen to any of us. In fact it does happen a lot but it's not something that's greatly talked about in society. When you meet someone you know on the street and ask them how they are, they're never going to tell you, "I'm fine, just had a miscarriage there the other day."

I suppose it's something that women grieve for alone which is why I understand why Lee has taken time off her studies to travel to the other side of the world. God help her. Although Roger can't understand why she has pushed him away, I kind of do. When you lose something so enormously precious, a piece of you, somebody who you've been looking forward to meeting, somebody who you've felt move inside you, and then suddenly they're not there any more, how can you not grieve? And people try to cope in different ways, I suppose. There's no rule book.

But, what I don't understand, what I really and truly don't understand, is the speed at which Roger came rushing back to me. What kind of man does that? If Lee knew, I'm sure she'd be devastated.

Diana

57

11th August

Dear Molly,
I lost my job today. Dan called me in to his office for a chat and as soon as he did my heart sank. Dan never wants to chat just for the sake of it. Immediately I feared the very worst. I always seem to have a sixth sense about these things anyway.

I was glad I was told in private away from anybody's pitying eyes. It was a relief that I had no audience there to witness me blowing my nose over and over again as I cried myself into a blubbering mess. I was so sorry that I broke down in front of Dan. I knew I was making him feel guilty and I didn't mean to. I knew it wasn't his fault.

"It's nothing to do with you," he said, putting a comforting arm around me.

"I know, that, Dan. I apologise. I'm not myself at the moment," I sniffed, mortified for both of us.

"The show's sponsor has suddenly withdrawn and we can't find anybody else to come up with the kind of money we need to keep a live show going."

He genuinely did look glum when he told me. An

atmosphere of doom and gloom hung in the office. He offered me a cup of tea but I said I needed to get going. I had to figure out how I was going to support this tiny innocent creature growing inside me. The timing couldn't possibly be worse. It was so disheartening that the show was being scrapped, especially as we had all worked so hard to make it a success. There is no Irish show like it out there at the moment.

It was raining when I got into my car. I must have sat for at least twenty minutes in the driver's seat listening to the radio without hearing a word that was being spoken.

Just when I thought things were going my way. Just when Roger and I were trying to sort out our personal issues and be friends again. I'd even taken to looking at properties on the internet recently. That dream had just been snatched away from me in an instant. I was going to be penniless. A penniless single mother. How could this have happened to me?

When I came home and told my mother amid floods of tears, she was outraged. "They can't get away this," she fumed. "Surely there's some law about firing a heavily pregnant woman. You should be able to sue."

But I shook my head helplessly. This had nothing to do with my pregnancy and everything to do with the financial crisis that was rocking the world at the moment. Everybody was suffering. Now it was my turn to take the pain.

"At least you won't have to find an au-pair now," said Mum, clutching at a last miserable straw.

Hmm. That was no great consolation prize. I'd actually been quite looking forward to having a childminder. I'd even started looking at properties with two bedrooms on the internet so that the au-pair could have her privacy in her own room. And it would have been a bit of adult company for me too.

Now I was back to square one. No new home and no au-pair. My dream of moving out and creating a new life for me and the baby had evaporated.

It had all seemed to be coming together in the past few days. Granted, I knew that there was trouble brewing in work and the rumours of shows being scrapped had been flying around for weeks now, but it had still come as a complete shock when the news was told to my face. The most annoying thing was that in spite of us working our asses off to make the show a success it had still all come to nothing.

"At least you hadn't taken out a mortgage," said Mum, still trying to look on the bright side. "At least you're not in negative equity like half the young people out there. People are in financial turmoil right now with no end in sight."

But even her optimistically positive spin couldn't lift me out of my low mood. I couldn't help brooding. How irresponsible was I bringing a helpless little creature into a world where his mum wasn't working and had no savings to speak of? I'd even have to sell my car now in order to buy things like a pram and a cot. I priced some of the baby items online the other day and nearly died when I saw the prices. How can they get away with charging that kind of money? It's ludicrous.

The following evening I decided to meet Roger for a coffee and tell him too. There was a time when I would have been far too proud, not to mention too afraid, to phone him in case he deliberately didn't answer. Now I had no qualms about it. He'd put the ball firmly in my court.

He picked me up and we went to the Merrion Inn.

"Is everything okay?" he asked, looking concerned.

"As far as the baby's concerned, everything's fine," I reassured him.

I still wasn't used to this kind of care and concern from Roger and it unnerved me somewhat. It was impossible to hate him when he was being this nice, but half of me was wondering if he was putting it on. Had he ulterior motives or was it simply guilt that had played a part in his return? And of course I needn't tell you that my friends were warning me to be very careful. "I don't think you need this right now," said Vicky gravely when I confessed to her over the phone that Roger was back in my life again. "He might just be grieving for his other lost child." That had occurred to me. Of course it had. I'm not that insensitive and I felt desperately sorry for his ex. But I also worried about becoming a rebound girl. I wasn't strong enough mentally or physically to start playing games.

I told him I was losing my job and that I was worried. He took my hand and rubbed it gently and told me that everything would be fine and he offered to take me away for a night to a lovely spa hotel to cheer me up.

At first I was a bit sceptical. "You know, Roger, it's lovely of you to offer but –"

"Hey, I don't need to be there with you. You can bring your mum or Jayne if you like. I'm not hoping to try and persuade an eight-month pregnant woman to have nookie with me and pretend it's a treat for her. I mean it. It's a thank-you present from me to you, and an apology for all I've put you through. I want you to relax and zone out completely. Bring a good book. And remember it's not good for our son for you to be stressing out like this."

And then of course I became all paranoid again, thinking that he was only being nice to me now because he wanted his unborn kid to be okay, much the same way as a horse trainer might look after a mare in foal.

"Maybe I'll go on my own," I ventured. "I need time to think about things and I could do with some R&R."

I was testing him and he probably knew what I was up to. But his eyes didn't flicker.

"Sure," he said. "Just tell me a night that suits you in a hotel that suits you and I'll make the booking."

"Okay. I'll see if I can find somewhere decent on the internet this evening. I don't want to go too far out of Dublin in case my waters break and I have to call an ambulance."

He became all serious then. "I want you to phone me the second you think you're in labour, Diana. Do you hear me? There'll be no need to call an ambulance. I'll bring you into the hospital personally myself. I don't want to miss this once-in-a lifetime opportunity to see my son being born."

I felt myself recoil slightly. In recent months Roger and I had become almost strangers to each other. Suddenly I didn't like the thought of him seeing me giving birth one bit.

"I've already asked my mum to be my birth partner," I told him stiffly.

"I see. Well, that's okay then. It's your decision." He looked disappointed but resigned to the fact. He didn't push it on me. "I understand."

D xx

58

12th August

Molly,

I asked Mum today if she minded if she wasn't my birth partner. To be honest she seemed quite relieved to be getting an opt-out clause. Mum, like myself, balks at the sight of blood and needles and stuff. Definitely not the calmest person I've ever met. She didn't punch the air with joy or anything so obvious but I could tell she was happy to pass on this particular task.

She asked me who was going to replace her.

"Roger," I said, then waited with bated breath. I knew that my answer would completely take her by surprise. I haven't mentioned Roger's name to anybody in my family for months now.

She'd been in the middle of ironing and then halted in shock, leaving the iron to rest on one of Dad's best Ralph Lauren shirts.

"Mum!" I yelled. "The iron!"

She whipped off the iron but not in time.

"Switch it off and sit down," I said.

She unplugged the iron and sank onto the sofa beside me. "Well, there's a surprise. Since when have you been back in contact with Roger?"

"Since a couple of weeks. He contacted me to make amends. He's being really nice and, well, caring."

"That's the way he should have been behaving since the beginning," Mum sniffed, clearly unimpressed.

She was right. But I didn't want her to be right. I wanted her to be so wrong. That way I could convince myself that having the father of my child come back into my life was for the best. And that everything was the way it was always meant to be.

"I know, but he has apologised," I countered weakly. "And now he wants to be there for me and the baby."

"And what about the other poor woman who's expecting his other child? His new fiancée? Does she not mind sharing him around?" There now seemed to be more steam coming out of my mother's ears than had come from the iron moments earlier.

Her reaction threw me completely. Maybe I'm gullible but I didn't think she'd fly into such a rage at the news of Roger's reversal. In fact, I'd half-expected her to throw her arms around me and wish myself and Roger well. I mean, she'd hinted enough earlier on in my pregnancy that nothing would make her happier than to see us married. And why had I ever told her about Lee being pregnant? Telling her had been painful – now telling her about the miscarriage would be another ordeal.

"He's not with the other girl now and he says he wants to be with me."

"Does he now? Well, if only life could be so simple. But does he not realise he can't do whatever he likes on a whim, especially when he has two children on the way by two different mothers? I never heard the likes of it!"

I told her exactly what had happened. All that the father of my child had told me that day in the hotel.

Mum took it all in and then waited a short while before delivering her verdict. But when she did give it, she gave it loud and clear. "Roger is a shit of the highest order," she said matter-of-factly.

I went to my room then. To calm down and indulge in a spot of self-pity. I so wanted to tell my mother to leave me alone, to point out to her in no uncertain terms that I had my own life to lead, and now that I was going to be a parent myself it wasn't right that she should still speak to me as if I was a child.

But then, of course, what position was I in to have a massive blow-out with my mother? I depended on her now and she bloody well knew it. If I couldn't stay here I'd be homeless. My baby might be taken into care by social services if I wasn't able to provide a safe, comfortable home for him. I couldn't be unemployed AND homeless. And Roger for all his recent sweetness and offers of support, hadn't exactly offered us the spare room in his house to stay for a few weeks, or offered to help out with the impending night feeds and nappy changes. Either he wanted to be a proper hands-on father or he didn't. He couldn't just be an à la carte dad.

Of course, I know he has a tenant who currently rents out his spare room and that helps pay the mortgage but he could give that tenant four weeks' notice in order to make room for his tiny son. There was still time. And this was an emergency. It was all very well to fish out the credit cards and tell me he'd put me up in a fancy hotel for the night. But that was just one night. Where on earth would I call home for the rest of my life? I couldn't argue with my mother as she was putting a roof over my head. And I was grateful, because unlike poor Molly all those years ago, I was welcome in my parents' house. God only knows how wretched that poor girl must have felt heading off to work for the nuns. It still breaks my heart even thinking about her plight. And I can't stop thinking about her. I'm obsessed. I've also decided to stop thinking and to start doing. I'm going to actively start looking for my poor granny.

Diana

59

13th August

Hi Molly,
I called out to Peggy's house this afternoon to see her. I thought I'd better visit her before I put my car up for sale because it'll be a nightmare crossing the city on public transport with the new baby. I have a to-do list of things I have to attend to before Baba comes along, because I know my life will be turned upside-down when he arrives. The most urgent item on my list is to track down my real granny.

Peggy was very pleased to see me. We went to her local and were given a round on the house again. The barman was ridiculously pleased to see me. He says I'm his only famous regular although Bertie Ahern apparently popped in one time for a pint.

I didn't want to burst his happy bubble by revealing to him that my fifteen minutes of fame were soon coming to a close. Anyway Dan had warned us to tell nobody because he didn't want the media writing about the demise of the show until we'd aired our last episode.

Of course I'd told my parents and Roger but I'd sworn them

all to secrecy. Not even Jayne could know. Speaking of Jayne, the house is so much more peaceful since her departure. Apparently she's happy too with her move so we're all happy. Mind you, Mum's not so happy about it. She thinks if you're willing to live with somebody you should marry them first. She's very old school. But she's had to adapt a bit of course, what with me being a single mum and all.

Jayne still isn't speaking to me, which is ridiculous. I don't need to fall out with anyone right now. I need all the support I can get. All my friends have deserted me. Vicky says she can't help me if I won't listen to her, and insists that Roger is bad news.

Anyway Peggy was in great form. She says Peter is coming over in a few weeks from America and this time he's bringing his two children who she's never met. She says she's really excited about meeting her little granddaughter and grandson, like it's the stuff dreams are made of and says it's all thanks to me. It lifted my spirits to know that I've done some good at least. But I like to think they would have all met up some day regardless of my input. I like to believe in fate and happy endings.

I told her what my Great-Aunt Noreen had said to me about Molly and how she had turned out to be my real granny but that she had got pregnant again for a second time by the priest that she had been working for over in England. Peggy just nodded thoughtfully when I told her. I'd expected her to be scandalised at the story but she was anything but.

"When you've lived as long as I have, nothing at all would surprise you," she said, taking another sip of her brandy.

"But then she left the priest's house, so he mustn't have stood by her in the end. The cheek of him!" I protested.

Noreen gave a wry smile. "Of course he didn't. He probably had several women on the go."

"My poor granny! She must have had two illegitimate children by the age of twenty. And here I am, thirty years of age and struggling to cope."

"You're not really struggling though," Peggy chided. "It's not been an easy ride for you of course, but you're a great girl. Very strong. Very brave."

Brave. That word again. Somebody else had described me as "brave" the other day. I didn't feel brave. I just did whatever I had to do.

"Peggy," I sat up straight, "Peggy, I appreciate the way you listen to me talking about my granny. I'm not allowed to talk about her at home because it upsets too many people."

"Sometimes it's less painful to let things be and not resurrect old hurts," said the old woman.

"But I want the same happy story-ending for my granny as you had."

"I know you do but let whatever happens, happen."

I took another sip of my drink. "But nothing might happen if nobody does anything," I stressed, feeling all buoyed up now. "I want to find out where my granny went to when she left the priest's house, and also where the priest went to. I'm going to go to England to find out. It was a long time ago but somebody must know."

"The priest has probably passed away by now."

"Maybe, but maybe not. If he's alive I'm going to prise the truth out of him."

"Well, good luck, Diana, you're certainly one determined woman. When are you thinking of going?"

Next week, I decided there and then.

Yes. Next week I'm going to find Granny.

Diana

60

15th August

Another visit to Noreen, Molly. She has good days and bad days, and today was not one of her good days.

"They're ganging up on me in here and Dorothy is the ringleader," she said with conviction.

"Maybe you're imagining it, Auntie," I said gently, not wishing to upset her any further and fretting that I'd made a wasted journey out to the nursing home as far as any more info about Molly was concerned.

"I am not. My Agatha Christie novel has not been returned and I know who nicked it. It was my favourite Agatha Christie. Death on the Nile. I've a good mind to call the guards."

Christ alive. I needed to get Noreen out of here. "Get your coat," I said. "We'll go for a drive. I'll tell Reception you won't be here for lunch."

"Oh good." She seemed pleased. "Where are we going?"

"Would you like to go to Powerscourt gardens? We can have some nice homemade soup and scones there in the Avoca café."

Noreen brightened and fetched her coat.

As soon as we arrived into the café and ordered lunch I decided to get right to the point. To be honest I was fearful of wasting the next hour or so discussing the mystery of the vanishing book.

"Noreen, where exactly did the priest live?"

"What priest?" She eyed me suspiciously.

"The one Molly went to work for after she gave up her baby. Where did he live?"

"London."

"But where in London?"

"I don't know. You'll have to ask your mother. I told you – she went to see him years ago. Didn't get her very far though. This soup isn't salty enough. They never put enough salt in the soup. Ask somebody for some salt. Ask that black man there, he's doing nothing."

There was a young foreign man sweeping the floor with a brush. He looked up quizzically. I was mortified.

"I'm so sorry," I said apologetically. "But could we have some salt?"

I didn't want Noreen to get sidetracked. Not now. I couldn't afford to hit a brick wall so early on in the conversation. Especially now that time was of the essence.

"That nice young man's getting the salt for you," I said. "But, Noreen, can you not remember where Molly lived with the priest? I can't ask my mother because I'm forbidden to ask questions about her."

"I understand."

"Can you remember?"

"It was outside London. You had to get a train from Victoria Station as far as I know. That's what Mammy said. I remember the name of the station because it was named after Queen Victoria. Do you know that Queen Victoria only ever had three baths in her life? Once when she was born, the night before she got married and then just before she was buried. Imagine that!"

But I didn't want to imagine it. I needed to know where my grandmother lived when she went to England. How many London suburbs did trains from Victoria Station visit on a daily basis? Thirty? Forty? I needed more information.

The guy came with the salt. "Where are you from?" Noreen demanded in a loud voice. "Africa?"

Oh, God no, I thought.

But the smiley young chap's face broke into a grin revealing many, many white teeth.

"I'm from Nigeria," he said in perfect English. "Do you know it?"

For a horrible moment I was afraid Noreen was going to say out loud that most Nigerians were scam artists and cause a scene. I'd heard her say it not so long ago when she was giving out about one of the night nurses who worked in the nursing home. The night nurse was also Nigerian and that particular day Noreen had been convinced it was she who'd stolen Death on the Nile. All because she'd seen something on the news about a group of Nigerians being involved in a credit-card scam.

"I've never been," said Noreen, pleasantly enough. "But I once knew a man who went to Kenya. On the missions."

"Very nice," grinned the Nigerian as he moved away and I squirmed in embarrassment. Poor chap. It must be lonely for him living so far from home.

"It's very nice here." Noreen drank some more of her soup. "No children. Not today anyway."

"Noreen, can you remember where in London Molly lived?"

"The suburbs somewhere."

I could see I was wasting my time. But at least I knew now that wherever Molly had lived, it could be reached by train from Victoria Station. It was a slight glimmer of hope.

So much for that. I'm deflated but not defeated. I have to think fast. Time is of the essence. Who can tell me? My surrogate grandmother knew but she's dead and Noreen can't remember. The only other person in the whole world who knows is my own mother. And she is sitting downstairs watching TV with Dad having no idea of the turmoil I am in.

What are my options? I can go downstairs and barge in on my parents and demand to know where my real granny ended up. But then I've been warned not to mention Molly. I am torn. This is just desperate.

I think I'll wait until tomorrow. I know for a fact that Dad is entering some golf tournament in the morning and Mum will be at home. I feel uneasy even thinking about how I'm going to approach her, but I'll have to do it. This search for my long-lost gran is eating me up and I have to know. I just HAVE to.

Diana

61

16th August

Dear Molly,

Another day, another effort.

"Mum, I was thinking of going out to Avoca in Kilmacanogue and grabbing some lunch," I said, looking up from my magazine hopefully. "Would you like to come with me?"

"Ah love, I've a million and one things to do."

Mum always has things to do. An endless list that is never completed and always spills into the next day and the day after that.

"Okay, I won't go then. I'll just make my own lunch."

Emotional blackmail.

"I'll go another time with you. Today's not great."

"Okay. Is there any jam in the house? I might make myself some jam sandwiches. I'm too tired to cook."

She gave me a look. I could see she was wavering.

"Get your coat then," she said, "but we can't stay there all day. There are things to be done."

Yes!

We were out in Avoca, parked and seated comfortably

within twenty-five minutes. My tummy was rumbling at the thought of eating my broccoli, black olives, tomatoes and feta-cheese salad.

As it was a weekday it wasn't so crowded. Just pleasant. Lots of ladies. Very few men. Don't think men really meet up with other men for leisurely lunches. They just do business lunches. Or trips to the pub. It's funny being off work now, being one of these ladies of leisure, waking up in the morning and knowing I've nowhere to go – if I didn't spend so much time thinking about Granny I don't know what I'd do to while away my time.

We ate in what might have been 'companionable silence' if it weren't for the state of nerves I was in. I HAD to broach the subject of Molly but I just couldn't get myself to.

"You're not listening to me," I heard my mother's scolding voice.

"Sorry. What is it?"

"I was asking you how your food is."

"It's nice," I said, looking down dolefully at my barely touched plate.

"But you've hardly picked at it."

"I know," I answered miserably. "I don't know what's wrong with me. One minute I'm ravenous and can't think of anything but food, but then once I get it I can't eat it."

"It's because the baby is so big now you don't have room for so much food. I remember being like that." She popped the last forkful of her lasagne into her mouth. "Mmm. That was truly delicious." She looked at her watch. "I wonder do we have time for a pot of tea."

And then I began to panic. Because I hadn't got what I'd come for. And that was to get vital information from my mother.

"Of course there's time," I said.

"But I needed to get to the post office."

"Can't it wait until tomorrow? Is it so urgent that it can't wait? I do want to finish this but I don't want to rush it or I'll get sick."

Mum sighed. "It can wait. I'll have my tea. Will you have a tea yourself? Or a coffee?"

"No, thanks. I'm fine with my tap water. Only drink I seem to be able to keep down these days."

Mum ordered tea. I waited until it arrived. Then I took a deep breath.

"I was out at the other Avoca yesterday in Powerscourt would you believe? With Noreen."

Mum looked surprised. "Auntie Noreen?"

I nodded, trying to sound casual as though I'd just thought of mentioning it. "I thought it would be nice to take her out for lunch. To thank her for letting me use her cottage that time, when I . . ."

"Oh yes, when you were having a bit of a crisis."

Or mental breakdown.

"Yes. I thought she'd like to be taken out of the home for a little treat."

"That was very kind of you, Diana," said Mum in an approving tone. "I wish your sister Jayne would take her out sometime as well. It's nice for Noreen to get visitors."

"Why don't you take her out sometimes yourself, Mum?" I asked, almost as an accusation.

Mum dropped a lump of sugar into her tea and stirred. "I do take her out," she said indignantly. "On Saturday I took her to Dunnes Stores in Cornelscourt and bought her two new nighties and a dressing gown."

"Did you? She never mentioned it."

"I'm not surprised. Her short-term memory isn't the best."

"You can say that again. Mind you, she had a bee in her bonnet about some woman that had taken her book."

"Death on the Nile?"

I laughed. "I've a good mind just to go order a copy on Amazon and bring it out to her."

"Good idea," said Mum. "I should have thought of that myself."

"I find Noreen's long-term memory isn't that great either," I continued, without making eye contact. I was getting there. Hopefully Mum wouldn't realise what I was playing at. Mind you, she was relaxed today. And not as suspicious as she sometimes is.

"Really? I don't find that at all. On the contrary, I think she has an excellent long-term memory."

She took another gulp of tea. She was drinking it too fast.

I decided to go for it. Straight out.

"Mum, she had some story in her head of you going off to Kent and getting a train from Victoria Station to Kent."

Mum's eyes widened in horror. "What?"

"Yes, it was a bit mad alright. Why would you be off getting trains around London? She was adamant you went to Kent from Victoria."

"I never went to Kent."

"That's what I thought."

She gulped down the rest of her tea. Oh God. I was getting nowhere with this. This was a waste of time.

"I went to Reading. She must have got mixed up. I never went to Kent."

"How odd," I said, my heart pounding. So my mother had gone to Reading. To see her mother. Why else? Where was Reading?

"I wonder why she would have told you that," my mother said, eyeing me nervously. "Did she say why I went?"

"I think she mentioned you had some business to take care of."

I could almost see the relief wash over my mother's face.

"That's right," she said firmly. "It was business."

D x

62

18th August

Dear Molly,

Roger was in touch again.

"I thought you might like to come over to mine and share a bottle of wine?" he offered when he rang me yesterday evening.

"I don't really feel like wine," I said. "But I can watch you drink if you like."

"Won't you have anything?"

"Well, if you stick a can of Bulmers in the fridge now and it'll be nice and cool by the time I get there, hopefully I could keep it down."

"So you're coming? Great. I'll light the fire."

He genuinely sounded happy to be spending the evening in my company. And true to his word, when I arrived at his house there was a great big crackling fire in his sitting room. He'd also lit a couple of candles and turned the lighting down low. It reminded me of when we first got together and he was always doing nice little things like that for me. Like running hot bubble baths and buying me Vogue as soon as it hit the shops. That was the Roger I first fell in love with.

It was weird being back in his house.

"The place looks great," I said as he took my coat and propped up the cushions on the sofa for me. He went off to the kitchen and I made myself comfortable. He came back shortly with an iced pint of Bulmers and Doritos cheesy crisps (my favourite!).

"Do you want to watch a DVD?"

I didn't really. I don't really like Roger's taste in films. He's big into sci-fi whereas I'm more of a romantic-comedy girl myself.

"I've got 'It's Complicated'. With Meryl Streep. You like Meryl Streep."

That's right. She's my favourite actress. Can't believe Roger remembered.

It was a film all about a divorced married couple who get back together.

We sat side by side. Not in a romantic way. And we both laughed out loud during the funny bits. It was like sitting beside a stranger in a cinema. Every now and then I'd glance over at his profile when I thought he wasn't looking. He really was handsome. I remember thinking I was glad that someone so good-looking was going to be my baby's daddy.

D xx

63

19th August

Dear Molly,
No insurance company will cover me. Not one single company. I'm too far gone, they say. Only three weeks to go. I rang quite a few insurance firms but nobody would budge. It's so frustrating. Surely everyone knows that first-time mothers always go well beyond their due date. Sometimes three weeks over. I feel I'm being discriminated against. I've still loads of time to go over to England and back. It'll just be a day-trip. I'm not staying the night or anything. I can't believe the attitude of these mean insurance companies.

Oh well, I suppose I'll just have to take a chance and go without insurance. What's the worst thing that can happen? I mean what are the chances of me giving birth when I'm over there? The baby hasn't even engaged yet. No panic. It really is now or never – I've got to go and see if I can find my granny.

Once the baby comes I'll realistically have no chance of going over. Can you imagine what a nightmare it would be travelling with a newborn with nobody to help me?

So I've booked my flight. I'm going tomorrow. I don't really need to pack as it'll just be a day trip. Once I've my comfy flats, and my iron tablets, I'll be laughing. I haven't told anyone I'm going. If Mum and Dad knew they'd kill me, or at least try and certify me. Mum especially would be distraught if she knew I was making the same trip that she made all those years ago as a teen. How awful must it have been for her travelling all day and night on the train and ferry, only to be faced with a massive disappointment at the end of her journey.

I haven't a clue what's going to happen when I get there. Maybe I'll be shown the door too? It's a very real possibility. But I won't go without a fight. I'm not a frightened teen.

Of course I'm not so naïve that I'm expecting to get the ultimate fairytale ending. I'm not the star of an epic movie here. No, this is real life. The last thing I expect is to be directed to my real granny's house where I'll find her perched beside a stove in a little artisan cottage like the one Peggy lives in, knitting a blanket or something.

I don't expect her to embrace me and say she always thought this wonderful day would come. I'm not that foolish. All I know is that I've got to say I tried. That's all I know.

Di

64

20th August

Molly,

I'm on the plane now. And oh my God, seriously, the sweat is rolling off me. The back of my neck is wringing. Thanks be the Lord for my roll-on deodorant or half the plane would be passing out thanks to my BO!

Luckily I'm at the window and there's nobody seated next to me. I'm wearing a massive dark-grey raincoat which I bought in town yesterday. It looks ridiculous on me, but the good thing is that it makes me look obese rather than pregnant.

Thank God for online check-in, that's all I can say. Because I've no luggage, I just printed out my boarding card myself and went straight to the security area. Every second that I walked I could feel myself getting hotter and hotter in my silly-looking raincoat and I kept expecting somebody to come along and tap me on the shoulder and say, "Excuse me, Madam, you're clearly heavily pregnant and a risk to yourself and your unborn child. I'm afraid I'll have to escort you from the airport this instant."

I feel like a stowaway. I mean I checked the airline's regulations on their website and they clearly state that they will not carry pregnant women beyond thirty-six weeks. So I'm like illegal now, right?

Well, I made it anyway. All I can say is, the security was seriously lax. They made me take off the coat but when I claimed to be thirty-two weeks pregnant they just waved me through. Clearly I didn't actually look as massive as I felt. All I need to do now is get home again tonight in one piece. And then I swear I'm taking it easy for the next couple of weeks. No more drama. Just lots of staying in bed reading books and gossipy magazines.

I can't wait.

By the way I had a near escape when the seat belt wouldn't fit around me properly and I had to ask the air hostess for an extension seat belt. Maybe it was my imagination but I thought she gave me a funny look. Mind you, an airhostess isn't going to ask me whether I'm obese or pregnant, is she? They're paid to be charming after all!

This is a short fight. No film or free meal. I've just paid 2.50 for a small bottle of water which I think is a bit steep but it's better than passing out with the thirst, I suppose. I wish I'd bought a newspaper at the airport to read – looking out the window is a bit dull because it's just cloudy out there. Maybe I'll read the in-flight magazine. I'm glad I brought you with me, Molly, as I have been able to spend some of the journey writing to you.

Diana

65

21st August

Dear Molly,

I'm a Mummy.

I know. I'm still in shock myself. It all happened so fast!

And guess what I called my little girl?

Molly.

Diana xxx

66

23rd August

Dear Molly,
Baby Molly was born on the 21st August at 1.07 a.m. by emergency C-section weighing just five pounds five. She is the tiniest, cutest baby ever. She has a little scrunched-up face and has lots of wrinkles, a little like ET.

I don't know who she looks like. Mum thinks she looks a bit like me. Dad thinks she looks like his side of the family, Jayne thinks she looks like an alien in need of Botox, haha!

Please excuse me for not writing too much now but I'm suffering from severe exhaustion. Yesterday I felt fine because I had the morphine drip going into my arm keeping me buoyant.

Today I'm experiencing a massive comedown and my wound hurts. Where has the nurse gone with the Panadol?

I'll write again tomorrow, promise,

Di x

67

24th August

Molly,

Haven't slept in three whole days. So tired I'm almost delusional but can't sleep. They never turn the lights off fully in the ward and there are people coming and going all the time. The noise level is something else also. As soon as one baby stops crying another one starts. It's an endless session of wailing.

The hospital is extremely overcrowded today. When I came in the first night it wasn't too bad and I had a cubicle all to myself with my own hand basin. But then, in the early hours of this morning, apparently an awful lot of women presented themselves all at the same time, and not only was another lady shoved into my cubicle, I even heard from one of the cleaning ladies that there were some poor women sleeping in trolleys out in the corridors.

I wish myself and little Molly could get the hell out of here. I begged the doctor to let me go home last night but she said no, in case my wound gets infected. She says my situation will be reviewed tomorrow. I'm feeling very weepy now. I do hope I'm not getting the baby blues. I read somewhere that most women get some sort of baby blues between days three and five after giving birth.

Maybe that explains why I burst out crying earlier on. Maybe I was being overdramatic but when they wheeled the other woman and her baby into my cubicle, they moved my overnight bag and my flowers (a bunch from my parents and another one from my soon-to-be-former employer, Dan) to the only available space which was under the sink. I felt like a trapped animal in a cage with no privacy, and to make matters worse, the woman's partner sat down on the end of my bed and started to chat on his mobile at around five this morning.

I was so hot. Literally sweating. And all I wanted was my mother but it was too late, or rather too early to ring her. So I just lay on my hospital bed in my damp pyjamas, facing the wall so that nobody could see the tears spilling down both cheeks.

Don't get me wrong, they've been very good to me in here. When I was brought here in an ambulance they were so quick. I gave birth just an hour after arriving here after four attempts at getting the epidural (I kept moving because of the labour pains, which are like horrific period pains multiplied by a thousand, down in the lower back). Eventually the anaesthetist told me that if I didn't stay still I wouldn't be able to get an epidural at all. I nearly died when she told me that. Then after the epidural I started getting very giddy and I told the hospital staff (I think there were about six or seven of them there, along with my mother) that I was looking forward to going to the races later on that day. I don't remember that conversation but Mum told me afterwards that it was quite funny. I bet.

Well, you're probably wondering how Mum ended up in

the hospital. You see, my waters broke as I was sitting on the plane on the way home from London and I was mortified because my seat was wet, and I thought that maybe I'd pee'd. Naturally I didn't want to draw attention to myself. Then when we landed, as I followed the other passengers off the plane, I felt a warm gush of liquid spilling down the side of either leg. To my absolute horror I looked down on the floor and saw I was leaving a trail behind me as I walked along the cabin. Honestly you couldn't make it up. In all my life I don't remember anything as humiliating as this ever happening to me. My tights were wringing wet.

The airhostesses were smiling, saying goodbye, but I kept my head down and didn't make eye contact. Didn't want them to recognise me. Wanted to get to a bathroom as quickly as possible and take off my tights. Wanted to phone somebody.

Soon I was in the Ladies' peeling off my tights. I put them in the bin. My legs were a deathly white colour. I couldn't believe I'd have to walk around in public with white hairy sticky legs.

I got a load of toilet paper and wet it to try and clean my legs. But it was proving futile. At this stage I could also feel a strong pain in my lower back. Almost like I was being stabbed. Oh God, I thought, was this actually happening? Fuck! I was going to give birth in an airport toilet all by myself. It wasn't even funny. Suddenly I began wishing that I'd gone to the ante-natal classes. Or at least a couple of them. Then I'd know what to do and how to breathe. I didn't even know what labour was supposed to feel like. I'd thought I'd loads of time left.

I rang my mum. I just got a voicemail. "Please leave a message!" I could hear her voice chirping.

"Mum," I gasped. "I think I'm in labour."

Then I rang Jayne. We still weren't really speaking but, hell, this was an emergency.

"Are you sure you're in labour?" she asked coolly.

"I don't know," I remember wailing, "but I'm in pain. I'm at Dublin airport. Long story."

"The airport? What on earth are you doing there? Jesus!"

"Please, Jayne, don't even ask!"

"I'm in work but ring Roger and ask him to go to the airport right now. If you can't get him, ring me back. Okay?"

"Okay," I said.

For a few minutes then the pain went. I wondered had I imagined it. Maybe it was just a cramp. I felt a bit silly then. There was no point in ringing Roger and asking him to come all the way out to the airport if it was just a false alarm.

I re-applied my make-up because I thought I looked distinctly pale and then walked out of the Ladies' and followed the crowds all the way to Passport Control. Once I was safely past that, I kept walking merrily along until suddenly I was seized by another absolutely horrific pain. More in my side this time. The agony just seemed to grip my whole body. I couldn't move. I stood frozen to the spot. I knew I was blocking people but I just couldn't move. They moved around me instead. Going about their business. Anxious to get home.

Nobody stopped. But then again, how could they have known what was going on since I didn't even know myself?

Suddenly I was absolutely terrified. Suppose I gave birth here? Right here? On the floor? In front of all these passengers. I looked around for a seat but couldn't see any nearby. I put my bag on the ground and sat on it, bent over, trying to block out the pain. A woman tapped me on the shoulder. I looked up. I remember thinking she had lovely big hazel eyes which I felt I could trust. She was in her mid-forties at a guess.

"I think I'm having a baby," I said, my eyes welling with frustrated tears.

I expected her to be shocked but she was really calm. "It's okay, I'm a nurse," she said.

I remember thinking that I'd been saved by a guardian angel. She took me by the arm and helped me up. My shoes were damp where my broken waters had trickled into my feet.

"I've also had three children," she smiled. "Now," she added taking her mobile from her bag, "the first thing I'm going to do is call an ambulance, and the second thing I'm going to do is call your husband."

I felt mortified as I explained I didn't have a husband, hastily adding, "I think the pain is gone now. I feel much better."

"When was your last contraction?"

"About fifteen minutes ago, I think."

"This is an emergency," she said. "Which hospital are you booked into?"

I told her. She rang ahead. There was an ambulance on the way she assured me.

"Do you have a partner?" she asked as we walked into the Arrivals area.

"Sort of."

Did I? I wasn't so sure. But when I rang Roger I soon found out.

"I can't talk right now," he said, sounding very cold.

I winced. Please let him not treat me coldly tonight. Not tonight. I needed him.

"Roger, I'm in pain. I'm in labour."

"What?"

"Yes, I'm having our baby now."

I was met by silence. I said hello again to make sure he was still there.

"But you're not due until –"

"I know Roger, but sometimes babies just come whenever –"

And then I heard HER voice. It was unmistakeable. "Who is that, hun?"

I hung up. The nurse was looking at me sympathetically. I burst into tears. Once I started I couldn't stop. It had already been the worst day of my life. Finding out about my granny, the shock of it all, the disappointment that I would never ever meet her, and now this.

"It's going to be fine," the lady said. "My name is Mary. The ambulance is on its way and I'm going to come with you."

"I'm so sorry," I said tearfully. "You must be dying to get home to your own family."

But Mary was firm. "If you were my daughter I would want somebody to do the same for her. Do you want to try your mum again?"

I did. She didn't answer. Neither did Dad answer his mobile phone. And then I remembered they played bridge on Wednesday nights. I called Jayne. She said she was making her way to the hospital right now and would be waiting for me.

"Are you in pain?" Mary asked.

"Not right now. I feel fine."

The only pain was in my heart. It was almost worse than the pains of contraction. At least I knew those were only temporary. They would be gone by tomorrow. But the heartache was back. How could he do this to me? How could he not be there for me and our baby when we needed him most?

I don't remember much about the ambulance drive although I do remember the sound of the siren and that we were travelling at great speed. The contractions were coming about every eight minutes or so. And each one was sharper and more painful than before. I lay on my side taking deep breaths just as Mary was telling me to do.

Mary then rang Jayne and asked her to pack a small bag to take into the hospital.

"A dark bath towel, some heavy-duty sanitary towels, very large, comfortable knickers, two loose nighties with buttons down the front and a couple of Babygros. She says all the stuff is in the drawer under her bed. Just the basics for tonight, everything else can wait for the morning. No, she won't need a book. Your sister won't be reading tonight, that's for sure."

In spite of my pain I smiled. Did Jayne really think I'd be lying on my back with my legs in stirrups reading one of the Shopaholic books?

Mary ended the call. "Your sister's going to do that for you."

"Thanks. I really appreciate it. Can you turn off my phone now? I don't want anybody else calling."

I meant Roger, of course. It was late. Nobody else would be calling. I was so thirsty now but the paramedics said it was best not to drink anything in case I had to have a Caesarean? A Caesarean? Why? I wasn't too posh to push. As long as I had an epidural. And I definitely wanted one.

The pain was back. Worse than ever. I wanted to scream. I think I just whimpered instead. I didn't want to be making a scene.

And suddenly we were there. The ambulance parked outside the main door and I was helped to my feet. Jayne was just inside. My mum was there too. I burst out crying when I saw them.

Mary handed me a piece of paper with her name and mobile number on it. "Will you let me know if it's a boy or a girl?" she said.

I couldn't stop crying. There were so many kind, decent people out there, I realised. Even if Roger wasn't one of them.

My mother and sister helped me upstairs where I signed myself in and then a nurse took me down the hall to the delivery room where they lay me on the bed. I was on my own for a bit. In agony. Then a nurse came in and did an internal examination. I watched her face as she did so. At first she looked calm. And then she didn't. I saw her frowning. Then she called another nurse in who did another internal examination. The second nurse also looked concerned

"What is it?" I asked, beginning to panic.

"I can't feel the head," the second nurse said to the first one.

The doctor arrived and introduced herself. I recognised her from my previous hospital visits. She was young and pretty with an earnest face. A face you could trust. She told me my baby was in breech.

"What does that mean?"

"He's feet first. He hasn't turned."

"But I'm in labour," I wailed. Like as if they didn't know!

A group discussion followed. In hushed tones. The doctor asked me if I would like somebody with me.

"I'd like my mother."

Mum came in. The doctor explained about the baby being in the breech position. She then told us about our options. She said we could proceed to theatre and the baby would be delivered within an hour. Or else we could wait and see.

"See if the baby turns?" Mum interrupted.

"I want a Caesarean," I yelled. I wouldn't be able to take the pain much longer.

"It means you'd be kept in for three nights, and –"

"I don't care. I want it," I demanded.

My mother agreed with me. "She'd probably end up having to have a Caesarean anyway, wouldn't she?"

The doctor nodded. "Probably."

"Please, please."

We all agreed unanimously. Caesarean was best.

They gave Mum a gown and a mask so she looked like part of the medical team. The anaesthetist arrived in. All bouncy and friendly. As though we were going to hang out and have fun, and not have a big thick needle stuck into my spine.

"Is this your first?" she beamed at me.

"Mmm, yeah." And my last, I thought. I distinctly remember thinking that I would never go through this again as long as I lived.

She had bright red hair. And dancing green eyes. Attractive and bubbly, she could have been in an ad campaign for the Irish tourist board. I wondered if she had a boyfriend or if she worked such long hours she simply didn't have time for one. Isn't it mad what goes through your mind at the most inappropriate times? She was the kind of woman I'm sure I'd be good friends with under any other circumstances. But right at that minute I was I was terrified of her.

"Now turn over on your side away from me," she said.

I was gripped with terror. I felt I was being sent to the guillotine.

I felt something hard tip my back and I flinched.

"You've got to stay still," she said firmly.

"I'm trying," I whined like a wounded puppy. But the labour pains were coming fast and furiously now. I gasped for air. Oh Jesus, I couldn't go through with this. That's all I kept thinking, that I couldn't go through with it all, that I'd have to give up.

On the fourth attempt she told me that if I didn't stop jigging around she wouldn't be able to give me the injection.

"Okay, I'll try my best," I said.

"Stop moving, Diana." That was my mother. I'd forgotten she was in the room too.

"I'm not moving on purpose. I'm in agony!"

And then I started praying to my dear, departed granny. The woman I'd got to love and adore over the past few months. The woman who I had become obsessed with, and now had to come to terms with the fact that I would never meet face to face. I would never be able to hug her or let her know how much she meant to me.

But she was somewhere. And suddenly I felt she was very close to me.

Molly, I begged silently. Molly, if you're out there, please, please, make everything okay for me. I need you now like I've never needed anybody in my life.

And then I was still. So still I never felt the needle go into my spine. And minutes later, my darling baby girl was born.

Diana xxx

68

25th August

Dear Molly, I'm home! You've no idea how amazing it is to be back in my own bed now with no nurses coming in to give me injections or stick painkillers up where the sun don't shine. It's so nice to have my very own private en-suite and to know that I can turn my bedroom light on and off as I so please.

Little Molly is so sweet. I really, really adore her. Yes, I'm almost delusional with exhaustion since her birth and my stomach wound has made me a practical invalid, but the way she wraps her tiny spindly fingers around mine would be enough to melt the coldest of hearts. Well, except Roger's heart maybe.

I'm sure you are wondering when he finally resurfaced. Well, my daughter arrived as you know in the middle of the night, and at approximately noon the following afternoon my phone rang, and it was Roger wanting to know if I had calmed down yet.

"I have," I told him. "And by the way we're now parents to an adorable little girl."

I don't know how I was able to keep my voice so steady and unemotional but I think the fact that I hadn't slept in God knows how long really helped. I didn't have the energy to be upset and give out to him.

"What?" he said, sounding genuinely shocked. "Why didn't you tell me?"

"I told you last night, Roger," I answered steadily. "I told you I was in labour."

"But I thought you were exaggerating."

"Whatever, Roger. Look, I'm going to try and sleep now. It's been a very long night. Visiting hours for the public are between seven and nine this evening so I might see you later."

And then I hung up. And I switched off my phone because I didn't want the whole ward and their other halves listening in and being entertained by my situation. All the other women here seemed to have partners by their side. Unlike me.

He arrived in that evening, looking a bit sheepish with a miserable bunch of flowers that he'd probably got for half price as they looked like they'd only hours left to live. My parents had just left with Jayne, but Selina and Vicky were there and they both gave him hostile smiles.

"Do you want to hold her?" I asked.

"I don't know," he said, shifting from one foot to another. "She looks so tiny. I'd be afraid I'd drop her."

"Go on," I said gently, feeling slightly sorry for him all of a sudden. He genuinely did look scared. And Selina, Vicky and myself when we're all altogether can be intimidating at the best of times anyway. Roger has said that in the past. He used to always say he preferred me on my own, away from my friends. Just the two of us. It used to make me feel so special, that he wanted me all to himself. And I didn't mind sacrificing other relationships for Roger. Pathetic, really. Look where it got me in the end, huh?

He held little Molly in his arms and looked at her tenderly. For a brief second I felt a pang. Maybe finally seeing his daughter would make him realise that he could love us as a family. Perhaps he'd see that it didn't make sense that we were all apart and not together.

He handed her back to me. "She's beautiful," he said. "Can I come again tomorrow?"

Something inside me crumbled. He looked so sincere. My baby's daddy. I wanted to reach out and hug him. I wanted to tell him to forget the past. That the only way now was forward.

"You don't have to go right away," I said, placing our angel child down into her little hospital crib and swaddling her in a soft, fluffy pink blanket which Jayne had bought as a present.

Vicky stood up as if on cue. "Stay, honestly. Myself and Selina were just going to go off and get something to eat."

But I saw his face, panic-stricken, at the thought of being left alone with me and our baby. And then I knew there and then that we'd never be a family. Not ever. And that I would never waste my time on him again. He didn't have to speak, but he did anyway.

"I've somebody, eh, waiting outside."

"Right." I closed my eyes wearily. "Just go."

Diana

69

28th August

Dear Molly,

I've never felt quite so helpless.

I can't drive. I can't do exercise. I can't play tennis. I feel like a prisoner to be honest. A prisoner who is obsessed with sleep. If I get two and a half hours straight sleep I think I'm doing really well. My breasts hurt. My nipples are sore and cracked even though I put special ointment on them like the public nurse told me.

Today she visited again. Third day in a row. She weighed the baby and said she wasn't putting on any weight. Then she said the baby looked yellow. Then she asked me was I breastfeeding properly and then suddenly grabbed my right boob and shoved it into my baby's hungry mouth. I felt like a milking cow. Then she said she'd be back tomorrow. I wish she wouldn't come back. I'm sick of people telling me what to do. And I'm sick of taking half an hour to walk up and down the stairs for fear I'll rip open the stitches in my stomach wound.

No word from Roger. He texted me the day after his brief

hospital visit to ask me if everything was alright. I never replied. Either he is a father or he isn't. I still can't believe he had his girlfriend outside waiting so he could have a quick getaway. Well, she's welcome to him. I'm not jealous. Just disappointed that every time I look into precious Molly's face I see some of him. They have the same eyes.

It's one thing deleting an ex off Facebook, but it's quite another thing when you look into the eyes of the person you love most in the world and see the person that – oh look, I'm not even going to waste any more time writing about him. It puts me in fierce mood. Hopefully the baby will sleep for another hour. Will get back to you. There's still so much from London I have to tell you,

Diana xx

70

30th August

Molly,

My baby girl is in Intensive Care. Oh God, I'm so upset about it. I can't stop crying. The public nurse called in this morning with her huge big weighing scales and said that little Molly had become more yellow than the last time. Alarmingly yellow, in fact. Practically orange.

I didn't see it. I just thought the baby looked lightly tanned. As if she had been off on holidays in the Caribbean or something. I put it down to her having inherited her father's sallow skin tone.

"You'll have to bring her back to the hospital," the nurse said bossily.

"But I can't drive after my Caesarean."

It was true. I couldn't. And my parents had gone out to this all-day golf thingy. I was home alone.

"What about your partner?"

I was overcome with an urge to thump her. "There IS no partner," I insisted angrily.

"Well, you'll have to get a taxi then or something. Your

daughter is a terrible colour and she's not gaining any weight."

"Should I be worried?"

It was a genuine question but she looked at me like I was a cheeky schoolgirl just caught smoking behind the school shed.

"It is very serious," she scolded.

And then she just left. And I looked at my little baby and dissolved into floods of tears. Then I woke baby Molly, got her dressed and put her into the car seat. I carried the car seat out onto the road and flagged a taxi. The weird thing was that I'd been told not to carry anything heavy, and Molly in her car seat weighed a great deal. We arrived at the hospital and waited in Outpatients for over an hour. Then the doctor saw her.

"She has jaundice," he said. "She needs light therapy. Why is she losing weight?"

"I don't know," I said miserably.

"Are you breastfeeding?"

"Yes."

"Well, stop. You're obviously not producing enough milk. That's quite common for mothers of premature babies. You need to supplement with formula."

I decided there and then that I would stop trying to breastfeed. I had thought I was doing the best thing for her but now it appeared my best wasn't nearly good enough.

I then had to take the baby up to the Intensive Care where they undressed her and put her in a special light box in just her nappy. They put a mask around her eyes so she couldn't see and I started to cry when I saw her in her incubator, looking so vulnerable and helpless.

The senior midwife, a formidable woman, who I'd put in her late fifties at a guess, gave me the choice of going home and coming back in the morning, or finding a bed for me in the hospital so I could stay the night and keep an eye on my daughter. I said I'd go home. As soon as I made the choice I felt guilty though. Was it right for me to go home? Would a better mother have stayed and sacrificed another night's sleep? But, honestly, what good would it have done me to stay? She was in the best place in the world to get stronger and healthier. I hadn't slept for a week now so no wonder I was tempted to catch up on some much-needed bed rest.

I took a taxi home. The driver tried to engage me in chit-chat but I could barely reply to him. I was shattered. A lone tear escaped down my cheek. I kept thinking that I had abandoned my little girl. What if she woke up and was missing her mum? What if she cried and nobody was there to comfort her?

My parents had just got in the door before I did. When Mum saw me she raised an eyebrow. "Where's baby Molly?" And then my whole world seemed to come crashing down around my ears. The floodgates had been opened. The tears were unstoppable. I was a young mum without a baby. I'd come home from the maternity hospital and she was still there. Surrounded by other tiny helpless babies in incubators.

In between heaves of unbearable sadness, I explained to my parents what had happened. Mum made me a cup of tea, and Dad told me to put my feet up and relax.

It was the first time I'd been parted from my baby since the day she was born and I felt I'd left my soul back in the hospital. She had looked so tiny and vulnerable when I said goodbye. That image was ingrained in my brain.

"Will we go out for dinner?" Mum suggested. "Just the three of us and have a nice bottle of wine and then have an early night?"

I must have looked pitifully grateful because the next

minute we were all putting on our coats and heading back out the door en famille. We went to L'Ecrivain which was a real treat. Normally we only go there on special occasions. The food was as always, wonderful, and yes, I indulged in a couple of glasses of vino. Mum and Dad managed to suitably convince me that I wasn't a bad mummy for opting to leave the hospital early, and that everything would be okay. But the truth of the matter was that I wasn't just crying for little Molly. I was crying for old Molly. For what I had lost. And I couldn't shake off the feeling of despair that I would never ever get to see my granny after I had built up such high hopes.

I knew I would be separated from my little baby girl for a few nights but I also knew that I'd be getting her back and she'd be in my arms again soon. Molly never got my mother back. Missed all of her birthdays. Missed her wedding. The births of her children. Oh God, it was all so sad. I couldn't help thinking about this as I nibbled at my food. I kept very quiet all through the meal, but my parents acted like they didn't really notice. They probably thought I was just being over-emotional with my child being in hospital and everything.

But as the red wine warmed me up I thought more and more about Granny Molly. And how I had never met her. And how she had never met me. But I had somehow loved her. Just the way a little girl is supposed to love their granny.

When we got home Dad said he was going to have a nightcap. Mum said she'd join him. And to their surprise I said I'd join in too and have a straight Jameson. I noticed Mum and Dad exchange nervous glances.

"Don't worry," I reassured them. "I'm not going to get manky drunk and start bawling me eyes out. To be perfectly honest, I don't think I've any tears left anyway."

Dad poured me one. A small one.

"Ah Dad," I sighed. "I haven't had a proper drink for eight months."

He made it a double. I gave him the thumbs-up. Then we all sat in front of the TV and watched some Agatha Christie film. Great. Nothing like a murder mystery to cheer me up. Halfway through, as Mum and Dad were trying to spot red herrings, I felt my eyes closing. I decided to go upstairs and have a bath. I hadn't had a proper long bath since my baby was born.

I filled it with bubbles. I decided to take a gossipy magazine into the bath with me and read about Katie Price's latest drama. Anything to keep my mind off things. In the bath I noticed my nipples were leaking milk. Ugh. The nurse had warned me that would happen for a few days until they dried up. She'd also told me to expect my breasts to be painful and had given me an ointment to ease the discomfort.

I sank myself underneath the water. Glorious! I had missed my baths.

I started reading the magazine. I read about Jordan, Posh, Lily Allen, and Jennifer Aniston's latest romance but it was no good. I still couldn't stop thinking about my little daughter. And about Granny Molly. And how she had been abandoned by everybody. At least I had my mother and father and my sister. Who had she had? Nobody. I started to cry.

I got out of the bath and put down my magazine which was now sopping wet. Very slowly I got dressed and put my cotton maternity nightdress on me. I know, it's desperate still wearing maternity clothing after giving birth but nothing else fits and I'm sorry, but I'm not going to try and do a Posh on it and get into a pair of skinny jeans within three weeks. That's alright for celebrities with oodles of money and personal chefs who can whip up miniscule delicious low-calorie dishes. But not for most women.

Mind you, the sooner I get out of the maternity clothes the better. It's not good for the morale to be going around dressed like a sack AFTER you've given birth. And one of the newspapers phoned this afternoon when I was at the hospital and asked if they could have a photo of me and the new baby. At least I had an excuse and said I couldn't pose just yet because the baby had jaundice. But really, I feel too fat to have my photo taken. It's not like I'd even get paid for it anyway. If I was a big celebrity and Hello! was calling that'd be a different matter altogether.

So I got into bed, feeling quite down, even though we'd had a lovely meal and everything. I stared into space for ages. Baby Molly's little crib was beside my bed. Empty. And I was surrounded by lovely pink cards, that all read 'It's a Girl!' But there was no baby. She was in hospital and I was at home. And I was thinking of my granny and how every minute spent with her baby must have been so precious, and how selfish I must be to have gone out to a fancy restaurant eating and drinking when my baby was in a little glass box all by herself. And I thought if my granny were still alive, she'd be ashamed of me.

And then I heard the credits of the film being played in the sitting room which is just underneath my bedroom. Poirot must have found out who'd done it. My parents would be soon retiring to bed. Minutes later I heard a soft knock on my bedroom door and I quickly turned off my bedside light and lay still in the darkness. Hopefully if Mum – or Dad – thought I was asleep they'd go away and leave me alone.

But the gentle knocking continued and I felt like blocking my ears so I couldn't hear it. My pillow was soaked from my tears and I didn't want to alarm my mother. I just wanted to be alone with my thoughts, even if they were such soul-destroying thoughts. This was what it must be like for mothers who lose a child for real. To come home and find all their little baby stuff untouched. The little vests that would never be worn again.

"Diana?"

It was Mum. She turned on the light. "Diana, I was just checking to see –"

"I'm asleep, Mum," I said, turning my face away so she couldn't see that I'd been crying.

She tiptoed over to my bed but I didn't move. I didn't want her to see how I upset I was. I wanted her to think I was fine and to leave me alone with my desperation. She stood quietly by my bed and started stroking my hair. I couldn't say anything else. I was too choked up. Please go away, I begged silently as more tears flowed. Jesus, what was wrong with me?

Mum wouldn't budge. It was as if her feet were nailed to the carpet. How did she know I was so upset? I mean, I'd put on such a great show at dinner, acting all cheerful and everything. Yes, I'd been quieter than my usual self but I'd still thought my performance this evening had been Oscar-worthy.

"I'm fine," I said, my voice muffled by my pillow.

She didn't answer for a while. Then she spoke softly, still stroking my hair.

"I know it's difficult being away from your baby and that it's traumatic and everything," she paused, "and it's also very common to have some baby blues a few days after giving birth when things are overwhelming."

"That's not why I'm crying, Mum," I said as I sat up in bed, rubbing my red eyes and turning on the bedside lamp. "I know I'll get my baby back. I know I'm one of the lucky ones and that makes me feel guilty. Because so many people don't get to do that."

I saw her face pale. And I felt wretched because I knew I'd

been told over and over again not to mention Granny Molly but it wasn't an option for me to stay quiet any more. All the secrets were killing me. If I didn't tell somebody I was going to explode. Suddenly I thought, I can't go through this any more on my own.

"I went to see Granny Molly," I said, looking my mother straight in the eye. "I went looking for her the day I went into labour."

Mum looked shocked. "What? How do you mean? Jayne said you'd gone out to the airport to meet a friend off a flight!"

"I know. I said that just to keep the peace. I didn't want to upset anyone. But I hadn't gone out to meet a friend. I'd been away searching for Granny."

Molly, you should have seen her face! She was dumfounded.

"I know I'm not supposed to discuss her, Mum. But why? I don't understand. She did nothing wrong. She was a victim of circumstances. She was a victim of the times that she lived in. It wasn't fair. She was your mother. How can you refuse to talk about your own mother?"

"She had a choice to come home and she didn't take it."

"That's not true, Mum. Where would she have gone? She was pregnant with another baby. And she still had no man to stand by her. She was penniless and probably died a pauper in some woman's refuge!"

"She didn't."

"What do you mean she didn't? How do you know? None of us know what happened."

My mother gave a defeatist sigh. "I do know because I went to see her."

I was stunned. What? When? Where? I mean, I knew that Mum had gone over to England years ago but . . .

"I went to see her eight months ago."

"Are you serious? Why didn't you tell me?"

"Because at the time you knew nothing about Molly. If you hadn't gone to Auntie Noreen's house that time there was no way you would have ever found out about her." She turned to face me again, her eyes brimming with tears. "Nobody knows I went over there. Not even your father. But I thought I needed closure just like you think you do now."

"But why didn't you tell anybody?"

"I wanted to do it by myself. Your father thought I was in town shopping but I went over to England for the day. And I found her. I found my real mother after all this time. Only on this occasion I wasn't banging on strangers' doors hoping for answers and having those same doors slammed in my face. I knew exactly where I was going. I had my mother's address."

I was so stunned I could barely speak. If only Mum had spoken to me sooner. She would have saved me going over there alone while I was heavily pregnant only to find out that my granny had passed away and bring on my baby prematurely.

"How did you get the address?" I asked.

"My mother had written me a letter a few weeks beforehand telling me she hadn't long to live."

"So you know that Granny is dead?" I said tearfully.

Mum bowed her head. "Yes, darling. I do know."

Diana x

71

3rd September

Dear Molly,

After five days I was finally able to bring my baby daughter home with me. I can't even tell you the joy I felt when I took her out of the Intensive Care Unit. I looked around at the other new mothers, exhausted from keeping vigil beside their babies' incubators and I gave them a little wave goodbye, feeling a bit guilty. I'd got to know them fairly well from going in and out of the hospital. Some of the babies in there were so tiny, like little dolls. It would break your heart just to look at them.

Molly is now here beside me, sleeping peacefully in her yellow Moses basket as I write. I'm availing of the time to write to you and catch up on normal day-to-day business which I can never do when she's awake. It's so true what they say about having a baby – no matter how much you prepare for it, the enormity of having a little person to look after is overwhelming.

I feel my life has been turned completely upside down and I'm trying to get into a steady routine, but the truth is that my days now consist of changing nappies, sterilising bottles, and washing baby clothes. I'm definitely suffering from baby-scramble brain at the moment. Sometimes baby Molly needs to be changed six times a day. I don't know how somebody so small can make such a dreadful mess all the time but she has a good bit of reflux, so it's not her fault. But when she's dirty I put her in the basin sink because she's too small for the bath and the warm water calms her down. She likes it. I think it's probably because it feels like being back in the womb.

At night I can spend forty minutes trying to get her wind up and I'm almost delusional with the sleep deprivation and could do with a pair of matchsticks to help keep my eyes open, but despite all this I'm very happy with my baby girl, and already she's brought me such joy. It's a feeling that's hard to describe to somebody who hasn't given birth themselves but I never thought I would feel a love as intense as this. Sometimes, of course, I still feel a bit lonely and wish I could share my thoughts with Roger, but so far I have got just two texts from him which I haven't replied to. What's wrong with him that he can't just ring me like a man?

However, the good thing is that over the last few days I've been able to get out and about a lot more, now that my scar is healing nicely. I do laugh, however, when people say that because my scar is so discreet I'll be able to wear a bikini again. To be honest I can never see myself wearing a bikini again but I suppose miracles sometimes do happen!

I bought a pram last week and took baby Molly for her first walk. Just around the block but it was a start. And another day I got a taxi to Peggy's house and she seemed thrilled to see my baby and hear all my news. She's even started knitting a cardigan for the baby, bless her. And Mum also drove us out to see Noreen who has now finally called a truce with her arch enemy Dorothy after the Agatha Christie book mysteriously turned up in the communal TV room one day.

The other really positive thing is that myself and my mother have become incredibly close, and she is far less anxious these days. I feel that for years she has bottled up all her emotions, thinking that if she didn't speak about them, they would somehow cease to exist.

We have spent quite a lot of time together in recent days. She sits at the end of my bed feeding the baby and lets me relax. We talk about my granny a lot. Dad is being a great support to both of us.

I still find the whole thing very surreal though. I mean, all the time that I fretted about my granny being in some institution with no family or friends, all that time I cried for her and pitied her, and worried that she had died in a doorway somewhere, with not a penny to her name, well, I couldn't have been more wrong.

When I got to Reading I was appalled to discover that it was huge, more like a city. Despairing, I asked to be directed to the nearest Catholic Church. Midday Mass was being said when I arrived. I sat down and prayed fervently for guidance, but drew a complete blank when I spoke to the priest afterwards. He explained that there were many parishes in the town and surrounding areas and it would be a huge task to unearth any trace of my grandmother. But he directed me to the nearby Parish Office – where I again drew a blank. Oh Molly, I'll never forget the despair that I felt!

Had I made a wasted trip? Had it all been for nothing? Should I have listened to my mother and not spent so much time and energy on somebody who was probably no longer alive? Everyone had warned me not to go looking for my granny but I couldn't let it rest. I had become completely and utterly obsessed. This wasn't just a mystery suspense film where I had fallen asleep and missed the ending. This was real life. My grandmother had left the country under a cloud of shame and everybody had seemed to think the best thing to do was forget about her. How could they? She was a human being, after all. None of us would even be here if she hadn't given birth to my mother.

I sat down on a nearby bench to gather my thoughts. I couldn't give up now. I'd come so far. This wasn't a rainbow I was chasing. No matter what anybody said, I couldn't just bury my desire to find out what had gone on. I kept thinking I had been given a sign. I was meant to go to Auntie Noreen's house that time. I was meant to have gone up to the attic and find the diary. And once I had read it I felt it was my absolute duty to do something about it. I identified with my granny's story because I was going through the same thing. Yes, I was older, yes, it wasn't as scandalous these days to be up the duff without a paddle, but I still had those feelings of absolute despair of going through a pregnancy all alone. My granny was my kindred spirit and I had to find her and let her know that I loved her.

So I went back to the Parish Office and I left my mobile-phone number with the administrator and also with the lady who worked in the nearby Parish Hall (just in case) and went for a walk. My head was swimming with disappointment. I'd honestly hoped by some great coincidence that somebody would know where she was and direct me to her house or nursing home. In my foolishness I imagined us having a hug and her telling me I looked just like she had imagined.

Instead I sat in a dark old man's pub beside a flashing slot machine and drank a pint of Fanta Orange. I felt like an idiot. Like I was losing my reason. Why, why, why had I come this far? Maybe Jayne was right and I was going mad in the head.

My flight home wasn't until the evening so I bought a

couple of magazines and went back to the pub where I ordered cheese sandwiches and crisps and drank more fizzy orange. So this was it, was it?

And then, just when I thought my day couldn't get any darker, it suddenly did. As I was sitting there with my huge belly in front of me reading the secret diets of the stars, my phone rang and it was a UK number and my heart gave a little leap. Who was that? Who even knew I was there?

I answered the phone with a trepid hello.

A friendly English accent came down the line and I recognised it as the lady in the Parish Hall. I felt my throat constrict. Oh God. Had they found my granny? Was she there right now waiting to speak with me?

But no. Angela (that was the woman's name) said she was calling because the cleaning lady had been in, and saw the name Molly Jones written on a piece of paper where Angela had jotted it down with a question mark. She happened to mention to Angela that her mother knew Molly Jones.

When she said this my heart gave a little leap. Seriously? God this was brilliant news. Maybe she still lived around here? I still had time to visit. I'd still be able to catch my train. All I needed was an hour or so.

But Angela then dealt me the devastating blow. Unfortunately Molly Jones had passed away three months ago. The cleaner's mother had been to the funeral and said that there were lots of lovely flowers and that there had been a great turnout. Apparently my grandmother had been a great employer and was very popular.

My head was then reeling. I could barely register what the chatty English lady was saying to me. Had Molly really died? It was too unbearable to take in. I couldn't believe it. She'd gone forever and taken my dream of ever meeting her away. I was too distraught to speak. I mumbled thanks to the lady, accepted her condolences, and turned off my phone with shaking fingers.

For ages I just sat there, staring numbly at a very old black-and-white poster ad for Guinness on the dull, nicotine-stained wall in front of me. So that was that then. I was enveloped in a cloud of despair. No happy ending for me, like the way things happened in films. My mission had failed. There was no mistake. The cleaner's mother had even been at the funeral, so it was true. She was gone.

But hang on, I thought, what had Angela meant about all those people being at her funeral? And her being a great employer? Surely that must have been a mistake? My granny had been a poor single mother who'd had a very hard life over in England. How could she have had anybody working for her? How could she have afforded to feed herself, never mind afforded to pay anybody else? My granny would certainly not have been in a position to give employment to lots of people in her lifetime. Maybe this Angela woman had got her mixed up with somebody else? Jones was a very common name. There must be millions of people with the name Jones out there. Could there have been a mistake?

I dialled Angela's number but there was no answer. The phone was switched off. Sugar, I thought, beginning to panic. I looked at my watch. Time was running out now. I gathered up my bits and bobs and walked as fast as I could back to the Parish Hall. The door was locked and nobody was about. Oh God, this was terrible. I knocked loudly on the front door but had no luck. Angela must have gone home.

"Can I help you?"

A voice behind me caused me to jump.

"Sorry, you gave me a fright, there," I said to the woman who was behind me slowly pushing an old-fashioned bike with a wicker basket on the front of it. She was a cheerful, hardy-looking woman in her fifties, I'd say, with rosy red cheeks, wearing a floral dress below the knee and flat brown shoes. "Actually, maybe you could help."

I was clutching at straws but I was confused and feeling like I was having an out-of-body experience. Maybe this woman, by some miracle, could make everything right again.

"I'm looking for a woman called Angela," I continued. "She is the administrator here and –"

"Oh, I'm afraid Angela clocks off at four every evening. You must have just missed her. Have you tried her mobile?"

"Yes," I sighed. "But it's switched off. I'm a bit desperate to talk to her. See, I came here looking for my grandmother who used to work here for one of the priests but I don't know where she went after that."

The woman brightened. "Are you the girl that came looking for Molly Jones?"

"Yes, but I think there's been a big mistake because Angela thinks that my granny had all these people working for her and –"

"She did," the woman insisted. "My mother worked for her for years. She was her personal housekeeper too. Molly was very kind to all her staff. Such a kind, lady. Very popular, she was."

"Are you the cleaner here?"

"I am."

"But Molly Jones couldn't have had lots of staff," I protested.

"How do you know?"

I was flummoxed. I didn't know. I suddenly realised that I knew hardly anything about Molly at all. I had read a few pages of a diary and thought I knew it all. God bless my imagination!

"Did you ever meet her?" I asked curiously.

The woman smiled. "Many times. When my mother was working for her, I used to go and play in the house. It was huge with a big garden. We didn't have our own garden so it was such a treat for me to go and play there with my sisters. Your granny used to give us sweets and all and her chauffeur used to bring us for spins in the car sometimes."

"No, no," I shook my head adamantly. "That wasn't my granny. My granny wasn't rich and didn't live in a mansion. She was poor."

The woman looked momentarily shocked. "Molly Jones?"

"Yes, but there must have been two Molly Joneses."

"I don't think so. There was never another Molly Jones that worked here."

I stared at her for what must have seemed like an age.

Then she coughed nervously. "Will I tell Angela you called back?"

I hesitated. "Wait. The Molly Jones you're thinking about – was she married?"

The cleaner shook her head. "No, she wasn't. Not that I remember. She had a son though. Same age as me. He was good fun. He used to let us play with his remote-control boat."

Remote-control boat?

"He actually had two of them. We'd play with them in the swimming pool."

Molly had a swimming pool?

"He went off to boarding school then and became all posh and stopped hanging around with us. He used to bring home his friends from school during the holiday. They were always posh."

"But what did Molly do?" I said. "What did she do to make all this money?"

"She ran laundries. Supplied half the hotels in London so

she did. Mostly the women who worked there were unmarried mothers, lots of them Irish, but not all of them, mind. My own mum was English and married, and she worked for Molly all her life. Molly did really good for herself. Especially for a woman, like. Even though she was a millionaire she was always very nice to everyone she met. She never looked down her nose at anyone."

I thought I was going to faint.

No wonder the shock of it all brought on early labour.

Diana xx

72

9th September

Dear Molly,
Baby Molly is sleeping a little better now I'm happy to say. We've got more into a routine now and I'm not as shell-shocked as I was when she first arrived. She slept six and a half hours last night and I just didn't know myself. I felt I'd won the lottery, haha!

Roger phoned me last night and accused me of shutting him out of his baby's life. I was stunned. I've never tried to push him away. He's done that all by himself. I said he could call over this afternoon and see her.

He said he wanted to take her over to his parents so that they could see her, but I put my foot down and said it was too soon. Baby Molly is only little and might be scared in a strange environment.

Then he called over with a little pink teddy and seemed very nervous. I made him a cup of tea and we chatted like we were two people waiting on a delayed flight, conversing with each other to pass the time. It was weird. I actually felt nothing for him. Nothing at all. And all the pain that I'd once felt whenever I heard his name mentioned had suddenly evaporated.

Don't get me wrong, I'm delighted that he's beginning to show an interest in Molly. I'd hate her to grow up not knowing who her father was, but that's where my personal feelings towards him begin and end. I'm really glad I've finally reached that point. I honestly thought the day would never come.

I kept the conversation light and breezy and I didn't tell him that I had a date lined up soon because I'd say he'd be shocked, and even annoyed, but frankly whatever I do now is none of his business anymore. That's just the way it's got to be from now on. He can lead his life and I'll lead mine. End of story.

Yes, I know I haven't told you about the date yet, and it does feel a bit weird going for a drink with a man just a few weeks after my baby has been born, but I'm looking forward to getting dolled up and going out. I'm not looking for anything heavy at the moment of course, but who knows what can happen?

Remember that guy John that I had lunch with in the Italian restaurant? Well, he sent me a congratulations email on Facebook when he saw me in the paper with my baby. I was surprised when I got it but immediately replied with a thank-you. Then he replied to that saying, if I was I was up for it, would I like to go to his brother's wedding in a few weeks' time? I said that would be very nice.

He told me in a later text that he'd stumbled across my column in his sister's magazine (well, he would say that, wouldn't he?) and found out that I was single and he was surprised because he didn't think somebody like me would be single.

Well, there's nothing like a bit of fresh male interest to

hurry along the healing process after a split, so now I'm very much looking forward to the day and looking forward to having a bit of fun too. Mum has even said she'll treat me to a new dress! When I asked her if I should meet John she didn't hesitate to tell me she thought it was a great idea.

I have to say, Molly, that even though finding out that my grandmother had passed away and that I had to grieve for my loss (and yes, I did go through a whole grieving process just as if I had known her), the experience has turned out to be a positive thing for our family. My parents are far less uptight, and I have finally got closure because I know what happened at long last.

Like me, Mum had got an awful shock when she realised her mother was not this pitiful downtrodden frail woman, but instead a very powerful businesswoman who had taken her experiences of working in a Dublin laundry to London and made an incredible success of her life in spite of everything that had happened to her as a teenager.

By the time Mum finally met her, Granny Molly had advanced breast cancer and had been told she had only weeks left to live. Mum immediately offered to bring her home and take care of her but Granny had been very firm and said that Dublin wasn't her home any more, that her home was now in England – that's where she had spent most of her life, that's where she was happiest and where she wanted to be buried. She said that Ireland had turned its back on her when she'd been at her most vulnerable and that was the reason she had no interest in returning.

Mum was genuinely upset because she felt Granny should have come home, and she felt her generous offer had been rebuffed. When Granny then passed away, my mother was overcome with guilt. Guilty that she'd been angry at her mother for not wanting to come home to Ireland.

I asked Mum how she found out that Granny had died.

"Through Ken," she said.

I raised an eyebrow. "Ken?" Who was he?

"My brother, well – half-brother. I found him on Facebook. That's how I got Molly's address – he got her to write to me."

"You're on Facebook, Mum?"

I was intrigued. I never knew my mum was visiting social-network sites in her spare time. Jesus, she was turning out to be quite the dark horse!

"How did you find him?" I asked.

"Well, I emailed or phoned nearly every Jones in London and the surrounding area, asking them their age and if their mother was Irish and if her name was Molly Jones."

"Christ, that must have taken months!" I exclaimed.

"You're right. It did. I'm sure some of the people thought I was a right weirdo but eventually I found a Kenneth Jones who was a couple of years younger than me and whose mother's name was Molly."

"Oh. My. God."

"And he flew over to Dublin for the day and we met in Bewley's for a coffee. And he was the right person – my half-brother. And he was the one who told me how our mother had become such a wealthy woman."

This was all amazing to hear. Mum had a half-brother. What was he like?

"Very nice, gentle, same eyes as my mother."

Wow! I wanted to meet him.

"He works as a doctor in London now. I think Molly was very proud of him."

"But where did she get all the money? To send him to boarding school, medical school," I trailed off. "I mean I know she set up the laundries but where did she get the capital in the first place? Granny wouldn't have had two shillings to rub together when she went to England."

And that's when Mum shifted uncomfortably in her kitchen chair and started fidgeting with her fingers. I hoped she wasn't going to back down. I was bursting to know the truth.

"You've got to tell me, Mum."

"My mother had two children by two different men. The first father, my father, went onto become a very successful judge here in Dublin."

"And the second?"

"He was the priest she went to work for in England."

"So it's true," I said resignedly.

"Who told you?"

"Auntie Noreen. But she told me not to tell anybody. She really didn't want to divulge that information but you know how persuasive I can be."

Mum took a deep breath. "I do know that. Anyway, basically your granny decided that she could either be a fallen woman and accept her fate, or instead go after the men who had made her pregnant. She saw an opening for laundries in London and she had the experience. All she needed was some capital to start her business."

"She went after them?"

"Yes. She knew well that neither the judge – he was a young barrister at the time and had just got married to a well-to-do solicitor – nor the priest for obvious reasons – would welcome any scandal in their lives and your granny basically told the pair of them that they'd better pay up or she'd speak up."

My eyes opened wide. This was incredible. What a brave, formidable girl! The image of my poor, innocent, desolate Molly was fast disappearing. To think she'd blackmailed not one but two powerful men!

"And so they paid handsomely to get her off their backs. And with the money she set up her business. When she began offering employment she gave preference to single mothers so that they could make a living and not have to give their children up for adoption. Deep down she had a very good heart."

But I still wanted to know why Mum had kept all this from me.

"She knew all about you, Jayne and Tony. And the last time I went over I brought a copy of the magazine you write for and she was so proud that you were her grand-daughter."

"But she never knew I was pregnant," I said, wiping away another tear. "She never knew I was trying to find her."

"Oh yes, she did know," Mum contradicted me sadly. "Ken told her. I told him that you had found her old diary and that you wanted to meet her but she said no. She was very ill by that stage and she said she would prefer you to remember her as the fifteen-year-old Molly that you read about in the diary. Young and innocent."

My hand flew to my mouth. I was shocked! Granny knew all along?

"And she wanted to help you because that's the sort of person she is. She gave us the money to pay for the deposit on Jayne's apartment and she also paid Noreen's nursing home fees so that she wouldn't ever have to sell her house in Spiddal. And now she has left you three hundred and fifty thousand euro in her will so you can buy a place for yourself and your baby girl and not have to ever rely financially on any man. I didn't know how to tell you. I couldn't find the courage to explain it all."

I couldn't believe my ears. I was still trying to absorb this as Mum went on.

"My mother died having made more money than she knew what to do with but she'd worked extremely hard all her life and deserved everything she achieved. She wanted to help her family out financially. She couldn't take it with her. That's what she told Ken. She said if she couldn't help her two children and their children, then what had been the point of it all?"

I tried desperately to fight back the tears but it was impossible. They were flowing incessantly now. My granny really had loved me after all.

"She truly was a wonderful woman," Mum said quietly. "As I said, she vowed never to come back to Ireland again because Ireland had rejected her and thousands of women like her when they were desperate. Your grandmother was stubborn to the end. A bit like yourself."

"And like you too," I added, wiping a tear from my cheek. "Stubbornness must run in the family."

Mum handed me a tissue. "It must. In the women anyway. What a great pity you never got to meet your grandmother."

I took the tissue gratefully and wiped my eyes. That was the thing though, wasn't it? I felt I HAD met her. Of course, I knew I had never actually met Granny Molly in the flesh but I had met her in my heart many, many times. And maybe, yes, I hadn't got to hug her in real life but she'd helped me after she'd passed on. Yes. Because when I was in that delivery room, at a time when I needed her most, when I was giving birth to my baby, and was completely terrified, she was there. She was right there in the room with me, holding my hand. Guiding me. And making sure everything was alright.

Diana xxx